THE NIGHTINGALE CHRISTMAS SHOW

Christmas 1945. The war is over, but its scars remain.

Matron Kathleen Fox has the job of putting the Nightingale Hospital back together. But memories and ghosts of those lost fill the bomb-damaged buildings, and she wonders if she is up to the task. In the name of festive cheer Kathleen decides to put on a Christmas Show for the patients. The idea is received with mixed feelings from the nurses, who are struggling with their own post-war problems. And the rivalry between newcomer Assistant Matron Charlotte Davis and ward sister Violet Tanner isn't helping matters. Could the Nightingale Christmas Show be just what the doctor ordered – not just for the patients, but for the nurses too?

THE NIGHTINGALE CHRISTMAS SHOW

The Nightingale Christmas Show

by

Donna Douglas

HIGHLAND
LIBRARIES

1800044343

Magna Large Print Books
Long Preston, North Yorkshire,
BD23 4ND, England.

British Library Cataloguing in Publication Data.

A catalogue record of this book is
available from the British Library

ISBN   978-0-7505-4715-4

First published in Great Britain by Arrow Books in 2017

Copyright © Donna Douglas 2017

Cover illustration © Colin Thomas

Magna Large Print is an imprint of Library Magna Books Ltd.

Printed and bound in Great Britain by
T.J. (International) Ltd., Cornwall, PL28 8RW

Acknowledgements

Like the Nightingale Christmas Show itself, this book could not happen without a diverse cast of characters. So my thanks go to the team at Random House, especially my editor Viola Hayden, Cassandra Di Bello, the designers for the great cover, my publicist Jasmine Rowe and the unsung heroes in the sales department who make sure the book gets on the shelves.

I would also like to thank my wonderful agent, Caroline Sheldon, and my family for their support. Especially my daughter Harriet, who is far more brutal than any editor I have ever worked with, and who made me change the ending. For the better, I have to say.

To Ken, with love as always

PART ONE

Kathleen

30th November 1945

A battered wooden sign hung over the crumbling remains of the old Casualty department. It swung lopsidedly from a single nail over what was left of the doorway, creaking in the cold wind.

The paint was peeling from the wood, but Matron Kathleen Fox could still read the words:

The Nightingale Hospital – more open for business than usual!

'I don't understand it, Matron.' Miss Davis, the Assistant Matron, looked perplexed. 'Why did it say the hospital was open for business? Surely that would have been obvious?'

'It was supposed to be a joke,' Kathleen said.

'A joke?' Miss Davis's small face puckered into a bewildered frown.

'I had it put up the day after the hospital took its first big hit during the Blitz. The bomb blast blew a hole in that wall over there.' Kathleen pointed to the other side of the courtyard. 'I thought it might be amusing to put up a sign, to remind people we were still here in spite of everything.'

Four years ago, she had stood in the same spot in the courtyard as she did now, smiling to herself as she watched the porters nailing the sign into place over the gaping hole where the doorway had been. She could remember the men laughing

13

as they put it up, and the grins on the patients' faces as they passed underneath it. God knows, they'd had precious little else to smile about back then, with the East End taking the worst of the bombing night after night.

She remembered that day as if it were yesterday, but somehow it also felt like a lifetime ago. Now she could barely recognise herself in that proud, defiant woman. The Luftwaffe's bombs had destroyed her fighting spirit, as surely as they had destroyed the old Casualty building.

'I see.' Miss Davis did not crack a smile. 'Well, it can't be left hanging like that. It might fall down and injure someone. I'll speak to the men in Maintenance and have it fixed right away.' She took out the notebook she always carried in her pocket and scribbled a reminder to herself.

Kathleen held herself rigid, trying not to give in to her irritation. Even the scratch of the Assistant Matron's pen on paper grated on her.

She didn't know why she disliked Charlotte Davis so much. It certainly wasn't like her to take against someone so fiercely. And Miss Davis had hardly given her any reason to resent her. The young woman was bright and keen, she worked hard and she was eager to please. Even her appearance was inoffensive, her slight figure always immaculate in her dark blue uniform, a perfectly starched headdress framing her unremarkable face.

And yet there was something about her that set Kathleen's teeth on edge.

'Don't bother,' she said. 'We might as well take it down. We don't need it now, anyway.'

14

'As you wish, Matron.' Miss Davis crossed out a few lines in her notebook and wrote in some more words in her tiny, spidery handwriting. 'They'll be pulling it all down soon, anyway, once they've finished building the new block.' She turned her gaze to where the work parties of German POWs were toiling under the wintry sky. 'Look, they've nearly finished the roof. It won't be long now, I'm sure. Then all this lot can be cleared away.'

Kathleen winced at her brisk tone. She couldn't blame Miss Davis. The Assistant Matron had only been at the Nightingale a few weeks; she had no fond memories of the hospital as it had once been. She had never witnessed the defiant spirit and the courage of the doctors and nurses who risked their lives day and night during the war. All she saw were the remains of bomb-ravaged buildings needing to be swept aside to make way for the new.

But Kathleen saw a different picture.

'I remember the night it got hit,' she said. 'It had just turned nine, and the night shift had come on duty. I was in my flat in the sisters' home when I heard the explosion, but I knew straight away what had happened. I came straight back, and–'

She paused for a moment, gathering herself at the memory of seeing those smouldering remains for the first time. Even now, when she thought about it, her heart started to hammer with panic, remembering how she had fought her way through the thick fog of smoke, choking on dust and the sickening stench of cordite, while all around her the air was filled with shouting and running footsteps and the screams of the dying.

15

'Were there many casualties?' Miss Davis's crisp voice broke into her thoughts, jarring her back to the present.

'Four patients were killed, as well as a young medical student and a second-year nurse. Devora Kowalski.'

'You remember her name?' Miss Davis sounded surprised.

'I'll never forget it.' It was imprinted on her mind as clearly as the devastated faces of Nurse Kowalski's parents when Kathleen had broken the news to them that their only daughter was dead. 'I remember them all. Everyone who died in the service of this hospital.'

'Of course,' Miss Davis said. 'Such a shame.'

Kathleen glanced sideways and saw the look of polite sympathy on the Assistant Matron's face. She didn't understand, Kathleen thought. She did her best to look as if she cared, but there was a kind of detachment about her that Kathleen found chilling.

Charlotte Davis had come to the Nightingale after resigning her commission with the Queen Alexandra Imperial Military Nursing Service. She must have witnessed some terrible tragedies of her own while serving in Europe. And yet she seemed curiously untouched by it all.

Kathleen wondered if that was what she didn't like about her. There was no warmth or empathy about Miss Davis. Even her pale blue eyes were like ice.

Even now, the Assistant Matron was consulting her watch, keen to move on, to push past their emotional conversation.

16

'It's past ten o'clock, Matron,' she said. 'They will be expecting us up on the wards.'

Kathleen bit back the retort that sprang to her lips. She wanted to remind Miss Davis that she had been Matron of the Nightingale for more than ten years, that she did not need anyone, least of all her new assistant, to tell her what she should be doing and when. But instead she managed an icily polite, 'Thank you for reminding me, Miss Davis. What would I do without you?'

The sarcasm was lost on her, as usual. Miss Davis straightened her shoulders and looked pleased with herself. 'Thank you, Matron.'

It had rained the night before, and the morning chill meant the broken cobbles of the courtyard were glazed with ice. The evidence of the war was still all around them, in the gaping holes in the brickwork and the roofs jagged against the dirty grey sky, with chimney pots missing, and sections of roof blown out.

As they passed the main building, Kathleen automatically averted her eyes. Four years on, she still couldn't look at it without remembering the night her former Assistant Matron Veronica Hanley died.

She had thought she would die that day, too. Those last hours, when she and Miss Hanley had been buried in a tomb of fallen rubble, masonry and twisted steelwork, would haunt her forever.

The outside of the hospital might still bear the scars, but from the inside no one would have ever known there had been a war at all. The staff who had been evacuated down to Kent when the war began had all returned now, and the wards that

17

had housed military patients were now filled with the usual winter bad chests, rheumatism and routine operations. The ceilings might have been cracked and the walls missing chunks of plaster here and there, but the floors shone, the windows gleamed and the air was filled with the scent of disinfectant and polish.

They visited each ward in turn, where the ward sister, her staff nurses and students were lined up at the double doors, like soldiers awaiting inspection. At every ward, Kathleen greeted the nurses and took report from the sister about any new cases that had come in, and those that were due for discharge. Then she went from bed to bed, speaking to the patients. As it was the last day of November and less than a month until Christmas, most of them were eager to know when they could go home. It had been seven years since the last peacetime Christmas, and everyone wanted to spend it with their families.

Miss Davis followed behind, but as usual she was more interested in the state of the ward than the people in it. She brandished a measuring stick, which she used to check the turned-down top sheets. She ran her finger along the bed rails and window sills, and sniffed the water in the flower vases on the bedside lockers to make sure it was fresh.

But never once did she pay any attention to the patients, Kathleen noticed.

Once again, she fought to keep her irritation in check. Inspecting the ward was supposed to be her job, but Miss Davis seemed to have taken it upon herself to do it. And from the hostile glances the ward sisters sent the Assistant Matron's way, it was dear they did not like her any more than Kathleen did.

They reached Jarvis, the male medical ward. Violet Tanner was waiting for them outside the double doors, tall and straight in her grey ward sister's dress, a sliver of raven black hair visible under her linen bonnet. She was flanked by two staff nurses and one shy-looking student, her eyes cast demurely down at the ground.

'Miss Tanner,' Kathleen greeted her.

'Matron.' Violet kept her expression formal, but the hint of a smile gleamed in her dark eyes. She and Kathleen had been friends ever since Violet joined the Nightingale as Night Sister ten years earlier. She had been evacuated down to the country with the rest of the Nightingale staff, but she had returned just before VE Day and taken over the running of the newly opened male medical ward.

If Kathleen had had her way, she might have been her new Assistant Matron. But the Board of Trustees had had other ideas.

Jarvis was identical to the other wards in the hospital, a long, high-ceilinged room with tall windows and two rows of twenty beds down its length. In the centre of the room stood a desk, and a table adorned with flowers where the patients who were well enough to get up took their meals. At the far end, beyond the tall, glass-fronted equipment cupboards, was a short stump of corridor that led to the private rooms, the kitchen and the sluice, and beyond that to Sister's office and her private sitting room.

They stood at Miss Tanner's desk while she gave her report. But all the while the ward sister was speaking, Kathleen was conscious that Miss Davis scarcely seemed to be listening. Instead her narrowed gaze roved around, up into the ceiling around the light fittings, over the windows and floors and along the lines of beds and lockers, looking for flaws.

Finally they began their inspection. As Kathleen would have expected from Sister Jarvis, the ward was spotless. But Miss Davis seemed to be on a mission to find fault. She strode off purposefully down the ward, brandishing her measuring stick.

'Aye aye,' one of the men laughed as she approached. 'Watch it, Percy mate. You know where she's going to put that stick, don't you?'

His friend in the next bed sighed. 'I've had that many enemas and Lord knows what else up there, I don't suppose it'd make much difference.' He grinned at Miss Davis, showing off an array of gaps where his teeth had been. 'I hope you've warmed it up first, Sister!'

Miss Davis pulled her slight figure up to her full height. 'It's Assistant Matron to you.'

'Ooh, I beg your pardon.' The man pulled a face and gave her a mock salute. 'I didn't know I was in the presence of royalty, I'm sure.'

'Take no notice of him, Miss, he ain't got no idea how to behave.' The man in the next bed shook his head at him. 'I wonder, do you think you could pick up my *Racing Post* for me? It's slipped on to the floor.'

Kathleen and Violet glanced at each other with amusement, both knowing what was coming

20

next. But Miss Davis seemed to have no idea as she sighed and bent down to pick up the newspaper. As she did, the man leaned over and slapped her smartly on the backside.

Miss Davis shot upright with a gasp of outrage. 'How dare you?'

'Sorry, Sister, I couldn't resist it.' The man grinned.

'Reg! It's Assistant Matron to you,' his companion in the next bed reminded him sternly.

They were still chuckling as Miss Davis stalked away, back up the ward. Her narrow shoulders were rigid under her grey dress, her face flaming.

'Oh dear, I am sorry, Assistant Matron.' Violet Tanner sounded sincere, but looking sideways at her, Kathleen could see her friend tucking in the corners of her mouth in a desperate attempt not to laugh. 'I should have warned you, Mr Donnegan and Mr Church do like their little jokes.'

'That man is a menace!' Miss Davis snapped.

'He's quite harmless, really. I suppose when you've been stuck in bed for six weeks you tend to find ways to amuse yourself. Most of the nurses have learned to take it in good part.' Violet smiled at her. 'I'm sure you got used to dealing with male patients when you were a military nurse?'

'I most certainly did not!' Charlotte retorted. 'I would never have tolerated such behaviour. The men would have been punished.'

'Yes, well, we can hardly make poor Mr Donnegan get up and run around the courtyard, can we?' Kathleen said, impatience getting the better of her.

'More's the pity!' Miss Davis snapped. She

21

straightened her shoulders, trying to hold on to what was left of her dignity, and headed off back down the ward, still clutching her stick. As she passed Mr Donnegan's bed, she made a point of looking the other way.

'Oh dear,' Violet whispered. 'I do hope she finds a cobweb or something, just to cheer her up.'

'If she doesn't, it won't be for the want of looking. Honestly, I don't think that young woman has any sense of humour at all.'

'She does seem rather a cold fish, I must admit. Perhaps she just needs time to come out of her shell?'

'I hope you're right.' Kathleen turned to Violet. 'Are you still free this evening?'

'For our night out? I'm looking forward to it.'

'So am I. Shall we take a taxi, or catch the bus?'

'Let's splash out and take a taxi, shall we? We can pretend we're wealthy ladies of leisure.'

'If only that were true!'

'Kathleen Fox! Are you telling me you'd like to be a kept woman?'

Before Kathleen had time to answer, Charlotte Davis was heading back towards them, her measuring stick tucked under her arm.

'The top sheet on bed ten is turned down twelve inches, not fourteen,' she announced with malicious satisfaction.

'Oh, I do apologise, Assistant Matron. I will have the bed remade at once.' Violet nodded to the student nurse, who jumped to attention immediately. Once again, her face gave nothing away, but Kathleen could see the gleam of mirth in her dark eyes.

22

Just at that moment, the double doors swung open and a second student nurse came in, staggering under the weight of a cardboard box full of Christmas decorations. She stopped dead when she saw Kathleen and Miss Davis standing there, her cap askew on her blonde head, knees buckling under the box's weight.

'Ah, there you are, Philips,' Violet said. 'Do put that down before you drop it. You found everything, then?'

'Yes, Sister.' The girl dropped the box and quickly straightened her cap and brushed the cobwebs off her apron, her fearful gaze still fixed on Kathleen.

'You see? There was nothing to be afraid of, was there?'

'No, Sister.'

'Then go and put the box in the cupboard. We'll start putting up the decorations later, when I can get a porter to bring a ladder.'

'Yes, Sister.' As the girl went off, still staggering under the weight of the box, Violet turned back to Kathleen. 'She was terrified of going down to the basement. The nurses all reckon it's haunted.'

'Ridiculous!' Miss Davis snorted. 'Everyone knows there are no such things as ghosts.'

'I agree with you, Assistant Matron. But I must admit when I was Night Sister here I did hear some strange things in the dead of night. Creaks and bumps and faint moaning sounds, and the like.'

'Probably the wind whistling through a loose roof tile,' Miss Davis dismissed. 'All old buildings make odd noises. Wouldn't you say so, Matron?'

23

'What?' Kathleen turned to see her assistant looking at her expectantly. 'Yes. Yes, I suppose so.'

But she was lying. She knew only too well that ghosts haunted the Nightingale. She had seen and heard them herself.

They finished their rounds with a visit to Wren, the gynae ward, and the maternity ward next door. Kathleen always left Maternity until last because she knew it would lift her spirits.

There were no sick people here, no tragedies waiting to unfold. It was full of new mothers, or women waiting to have their babies, which meant there was always an air of irrepressible antici-pation, despite the ward's tight regime.

Miriam Trott, the sister of Wren ward, was waiting with her nurses. She lived up to the name of her ward. She looked exactly like a bird, with her tiny frame, beaked nose and dark, inquisitive eyes. The hair under her cap was a thin, dusty brown colour, like a sparrow's wing.

'Good morning, Matron, Assistant Matron,' she greeted them. 'Everything is ready for you.'

Miriam Trott was even more of a stickler for order than the other ward sisters, and as Kathleen looked down the ward all she could see were two lines of freshly scrubbed faces, hands placed carefully on the top of their immaculate coverlets. Even the babies were silent in their nursery at the far end of the ward behind a firmly closed door.

The ward was spotless too, the polished floor gleaming, reflecting the wintry light from the windows.

Beside her, she heard Miss Davis's sigh of ap-proval. She and Sister Wren were much of the

24

same mind. Kathleen felt sure the Assistant Matron would find no badly turned-down beds or dusty corners here.

But nor would they find a great deal of laughter or fun. Miss Trott discouraged such things.

Before they could begin their inspection, Miss Trott gave her report.

'We have a new patient on the ward: Mrs Goodwood,' she said. 'She was admitted last night for observation due to high blood pressure and oedema.' She paused, then said, 'Perhaps you remember her, Matron? She was in charge of the local WVS during the war.'

Kathleen nodded. 'I do indeed.'

'Mrs Goodwood helped to organise a mobile canteen here when our dining room was bombed,' Miss Trott explained to Miss Davis. 'Such a wonderful woman. I don't know how we would have ever managed without her.'

'Indeed,' Kathleen said. But her memories of Mrs Goodwood were not as glowing as Miriam Trott's. She recalled a very bossy woman, bustling around giving orders in her green uniform, thoroughly enjoying every moment of her new-found power.

'We struck up quite a friendship during that time, actually,' Sister Wren continued. 'She's such a refined woman, not like some of the types we get in here.' Her thin mouth curled.

Mrs Goodwood was sitting up in bed waiting for them, the coverlet smoothed over her wide bump. She was a no-nonsense woman in her thirties, straight brown hair cut practically short to frame her square face. Even in a flannel night-

25

gown, she still gave off an air of self-importance. She was busy making notes in a book propped up in front of her, while her knitting lay half-finished on her bedside locker.

'Good morning, Mrs Goodwood,' Kathleen greeted her. 'You seem very busy?'

'Good morning, Matron. Yes, well, I have things to do.' Mrs Goodwood laid down her pen with the faint irritation of someone who resented the interruption. 'I must say it's rather a nuisance to find myself here when I have so much I could be getting on with.'

'Perhaps you're doing too much?' Kathleen suggested. 'Have you considered your raised blood pressure might be nature's way of telling you to slow down?'

'Well, it's most inconvenient,' Mrs Goodwood said briskly. 'We're supposed to be having a Christmas fête to raise funds for the church roof repair, and that won't organise itself.'

'I'm sure there are others who could help out,' Kathleen said.

'I hardly think so!' Mrs Goodwood looked put out at the suggestion. 'If you want something done properly, you should do it yourself, that's what I always say.'

'I'm sure you do.' Kathleen felt for the poor church roof committee. At least they might be able to breathe during Mrs Goodwood's absence.

'How long do you think I'll be here? No one seems to be able to tell me.'

'That's really up to the doctor,' Kathleen said. 'When is your baby due?' She went to pick up the notes hanging from the end of the bed.

26

'Not until the end of January,' Mrs Goodwood said.

'Another two months?' Kathleen consulted the notes.

'You seem rather big for your dates.' For once, Miss Davis said what Kathleen had been thinking.

Mrs Goodwood shot her a dark look. 'Yes, well, I can't help that, can I? Big babies run in my family, so my mother says.'

Miss Davis frowned. 'Nevertheless, you do seem very large. Are you sure you've got the dates right?'

Mrs Goodwood's face reddened. 'I should say I have! My husband didn't come home until May.' Two bright spots of colour stained her cheeks. 'I do hope you're not suggesting anything – improper?'

Kathleen looked away to conceal her smile. The idea of Mrs Goodwood doing anything improper was too amusing for words.

Miss Davis shook her head. 'No, no, of course not... I wouldn't suggest...' She looked helplessly from Sister Wren to Mrs Goodwood and back again. Both women glared back at her, tight-lipped. 'I was only saying–'

'Perhaps it might be best if you didn't, Miss Davis,' Kathleen said politely. 'Mrs Goodwood's blood pressure is already high. We don't want to push it up even further, do we?'

'I–' Miss Davis opened her mouth then closed it again.

But she'd not let the matter drop, even as they returned to Kathleen's office after the inspection.

27

'I still think that baby is too big for her dates,' she muttered under her breath as they made their way back down the winding corridors.

'I agree,' Kathleen said. 'But you heard what she said. The baby couldn't possibly be due before January. And Miss Trott doesn't seem to think that it's anything out of the ordinary.'

'Yes, but—'

Kathleen stopped, so abruptly that the Assistant Matron cannoned into the back of her. 'How many babies have you delivered, Miss Davis?' she asked.

Miss Davis blushed. 'A few, when I was training,' she mumbled.

'And how many since then?'

Miss Davis lowered her gaze. 'None.'

'Quite. Whereas Sister Wren has delivered more babies than you and I put together. So I think we should allow her to know best, don't you?'

Miss Davis's blush deepened. 'I'm sorry, Matron,' she said stiffly.

They walked back to Kathleen's office in silence. She was aware of Miss Davis quietly simmering beside her, but she ignored her.

Of course she knew that Mrs Goodwood was too big for her dates. She was also fairly certain that the baby would be born well before January, possibly even before Christmas. But she chose to accept Miss Trott's judgement, partly out of support for her ward sister, but mostly because it was another reason to disagree with her Assistant Matron.

When had she become so petty? she wondered. It really wasn't like her at all, but Miss Davis

28

seemed to bring out the worst in her.

But by the time they returned to Kathleen's office the Assistant Matron had started up again, this time on the subject of the new linen supplies.

'When will they arrive, Matron?' she wanted to know.

'I'm not sure. I ordered them last month.'

'Then surely they should be here by now?'

'I really couldn't say. The suppliers were making parachutes until six months ago. I daresay it will take a while for them to get back into the swing of things.'

'Yes, but the supplies we have are running low, and they're already in such bad condition. We need new linen urgently.'

'I am well aware of that, Miss Davis,' Kathleen replied tightly. 'But as I said, we must just be patient.'

Miss Davis paused for a moment, and Kathleen could almost see the words ticking around in her brain before they finally came out

'Perhaps I should telephone them and find out when–'

'You will do no such thing!' Kathleen cut her off. 'I told you I had placed the order, and the linen supplies will arrive when they arrive. Now, I'm sure you have other things you can be getting on with, besides chasing after me and making sure I'm doing my job properly!'

'I'm sure I didn't mean to suggest–'

Kathleen closed the door on the Assistant Matron before she could say another word.

She leaned against the door, breathing out a deep sigh. Just being with Miss Davis exhausted

29

her. It wasn't the young woman's energy that drained her, but the effort of controlling her temper.

How dare she question her? Did she really not think that Kathleen was well aware of the woeful state of the linen cupboards? She and her nurses had been struggling with the inadequate supplies for years, trying to make ends meet throughout the war, when everything was scarce.

And now Charlotte Davis had turned up, so fresh and smart and full of ideas, and acted as if she was the only one in the world who had ever noticed the problem.

You mustn't be too hard on the girl, you know, Matron. She is doing her best.

Kathleen looked up at the sound of the familiar voice. 'I might have known you'd be on her side!'

She turned to look into the shadows in the corner of her office, but there was nothing there.

I really don't understand why you've taken against her so much, Veronica Hanley's voice came into her head again, as clearly as if she had been standing at Kathleen's shoulder. *If you want to know what I think–*

'I don't,' Kathleen said out loud. 'But as usual, I'm sure you're going to tell me.'

I think you're resentful because you didn't choose her yourself.

'Perhaps,' Kathleen conceded. 'I certainly would have preferred to be consulted about it. We do have to work together, after all.' But as it was, the Board of Trustees had appointed Charlotte Davis without a by your leave to Kathleen about it. By all accounts Major Hugh McLaren, one of the six

30

board members, had pulled some strings to secure the position for Miss Davis.

'If it had been up to me I'd have chosen one of the senior nurses. Someone who knows the hospital well.' *Although there weren't many left to choose from.* Kathleen recalled all the senior nurses who had not returned to the Nightingale for one reason or another. Some, like Sister Blake, had got married when the war ended; others, like the Home Sister Agatha Sutton and Sister Tutor Miss Parker, had decided to retire.

And then there were the casualties of war, like Veronica Hanley herself. Kathleen had clashed so many times with the former Assistant Matron when they worked together, but she could never have imagined how much she would miss her.

But it would have taken more than death to keep the formidable Miss Hanley from her duties.

Kathleen couldn't remember when she had first become aware of her presence. Almost from the moment she died, Kathleen seemed to hear Miss Hanley's voice, see her shadow moving out of the corner of her eye. At first she thought she must be imagining it, but she knew the words that came into her head were not of her own making. Miss Hanley gave her advice freely, just as she had in life. And more often than not, they clashed with Kathleen's own opinions.

I suppose you would have chosen your friend, Miss Tanner?

'Yes, I think I would. She would have made an excellent Assistant Matron.'

She makes an even better ward sister. Such a waste to have her chasing linen orders and drawing up work

31

rosters when she should be nursing.

'Whereas Miss Davis is so good at that sort of thing,' Kathleen said, tight-lipped.

Miss Davis has many excellent qualities. She's hard-working, efficient, sensible–

'You're only saying that because she reminds you of yourself!'

No, indeed, Matron. She reminds me of you.

Kathleen swung round to look at the wall behind her. The curtain shivered in a draught from the window. 'Nonsense. She's full of rules and regulations. I was never like that.'

She's also full of energy and purpose, just like you were when you first arrived. Do you remember, Matron? You had no respect for traditions. You were never interested in the way things 'had always been done', only in how the hospital could do them better.

Kathleen smiled reluctantly. 'Goodness, I sound quite insufferable.' No wonder Veronica Hanley hadn't liked her very much to begin with!

Over time, however, they had adjusted to one another, and as the war went on Kathleen had come to appreciate her Assistant Matron's loyalty and courage. They might have made a good team, if only...

Now is not the time for self-pity, Matron. Miss Hanley's voice was brisk in her head. *Especially when there is so much work to be done. The Nightingale needs to be rebuilt, restored to its former glory.*

But am I the one to do it? Kathleen thought. Her gaze moved to the top drawer of her desk, where the letter she had received last week was concealed.

You're still thinking of taking the job, then?

32

'Why not?' It was perfect for her. A country hospital in Lancashire, close to where she had grown up. An idyllic little market town, largely untouched by the ravages of war. Not like the East End, which still bore its scars in every bombed-out building and empty space where a street had once been. 'I'd be closer to my sister and her family, too.'

And what about the Nightingale?

'What about it?' Kathleen said defensively. 'I've been here for nearly twelve years. I saw the hospital through the war, during the times when the building was falling down around our ears and no one else thought we could go on...' She stopped, pulling her emotions back together. 'I gave everything to this hospital, and now it's time I started thinking about myself.'

I seem to remember you saying those words before, and yet you stayed.

'Only because you talked me out of leaving!'

And do you regret your decision?

'Sometimes.' In fact, she often wondered what would have happened if she had followed her heart and run away with James Cooper. The war had thrown her together with the handsome consultant, and they had fallen in love. Their affair was as passionate as it was forbidden. They had made plans; he was going to leave his loveless marriage and they were going to start a new life together. But after Miss Hanley's death, Kathleen had decided the Nightingale needed her. The last thing the Assistant Matron ever did was to persuade her to stay. 'But it's different now. It's the right time to go.'

33

Then why haven't you written your letter of resignation yet?

'I – I haven't got round to it.' But that wasn't strictly true. She'd heard from the hospital over a week ago but had told them she needed time to think about the offer, and they'd given her until Christmas to decide. Now, even though she'd already made up her mind and was set on leaving the Nightingale behind, putting pen to paper was proving more challenging than she'd first thought.

Why don't you write the letter now, if you're so set on leaving?

'All right, then, I will!' She flung open her desk drawer and pulled out a sheet of notepaper, then picked up her fountain pen. Miss Hanley's voice fell silent, and Kathleen could almost sense the Assistant Matron holding her breath, waiting for her.

'You don't think I'm serious, do you?' Kathleen said, just as the door opened and Charlotte Davis walked in.

Kathleen looked up at her sharply. 'Don't you ever knock?' she snapped.

Miss Davis's pale blue eyes widened in shock. 'I did,' she said. 'Perhaps you didn't hear me? You seemed to be talking to someone?' Her eyes scanned the empty room.

'I was speaking on the telephone,' Kathleen said. 'Was there something you wanted?' she added, before the Assistant Matron could argue.

'Um, yes.' Miss Davis dragged her quizzical gaze away from the telephone and back to Kathleen's face. 'I wondered if you had managed to look at the duty rosters I wrote out yesterday?'

34

'Not yet.'

'Do you have any idea when they might be done?'

'I'll get to them as soon as I can.'

'It's just I promised to take them up to the wards this afternoon, and–'

'I said I'd do them as soon as I can!' Kathleen saw Miss Davis flinch. 'I'm not going to achieve anything with you bothering me every five minutes, am I?'

'No, Matron. I'm sorry.' Miss Davis retreated, subdued.

Seeing her face gave Kathleen a pang of guilt. 'Miss Davis, wait–' she started to say, but the Assistant Matron had already closed the door.

She laid down her fountain pen and sat back in her chair with a sigh. Poor Miss Davis. Irritating as she might be, it wasn't her fault that Kathleen was so weary.

Perhaps Miss Hanley had a point. Maybe the reason she found it so difficult to warm to the Assistant Matron was because she reminded her of how she had once been, before the war sapped her of her energy and her will.

'I suppose you think I was too hard on her?' she addressed the air of her book-lined office. But the leather-bound volumes on the shelves remained stubbornly silent. The only sound was the wind outside, shivering the branches of the plane trees in the courtyard.

Kathleen took the letter out of her top drawer to read through it again. The job offer could not have come at a better time. She was weary, and she had achieved as much as she was going to at

35

the Nightingale. Now it was time to hand it over to someone else. Someone who might be able to make a difference.

Why don't you write the letter now, if you're so set on leaving?

She put the letter away and closed the drawer. There would be time enough to write her resignation another day. For now, she had to get on with the duty rosters before Charlotte Davis arrived to nag her yet again.

After she had come off duty that evening, Kathleen met Violet and they took a taxi up west to Charing Cross. Kathleen could feel the tension leaving her as they left Bethnal Green, heading for the city of London.

'I'd forgotten how good it feels to get away from the hospital for a while,' she said, massaging the stiff muscles in the back of her neck.

'It sounds as if you've had a hard day?' Violet smiled sympathetically. She looked different out of her uniform, her make-up subtly enhancing her beautiful bone structure and the darkness of her eyes. Her stylish red coat contrasted with her sleek black hair. Violet had always dressed well, even when clothes were hard to come by, thanks to a wardrobe of elegant, expensive outfits from the life she had once had, but now never liked to talk about.

'Every day is hard at the moment.'

'Oh dear. Any particular reason?'

Kathleen caught her friend's look of concern and forced a smile. This was a rare night off for both of them; it would be wrong to burden her

36

with all her troubles.

'Take no notice of me. I'm just feeling a bit under the weather, that's all.'

'It sounds as if a night out might be just what you need,' Violet smiled.

'You may be right.' Kathleen looked out of the window at the buildings of the city rumbling past. She tried not to notice the ugly gaps where the Luftwaffe had left their mark, and instead concentrated on the great dome of St Paul's looming ahead of them. Despite the German air force's best efforts, it had remained miraculously intact. A sure sign that God was on their side, some said, even though it hadn't always felt like it when the bombs were raining down and half the city was ablaze.

'Isn't it lovely to see the streets all lit up again?' she said, changing the subject. 'It's so festive.'

'You wait until we get to the Strand,' Violet said. 'The shops and restaurants all look so lovely, I nearly cried when I first saw them.'

Kathleen saw what she meant when they got out of the taxi at Charing Cross. To see lights in shop windows and all the Christmas displays lifted her heart. They had lived in darkness for so long, stumbling along the streets in the blackout, with nothing but the dimmest of torchlight to show the way. But now the lights seemed dazzling in every window, more than making up for the lack of Christmas wares.

Violet crossed the road towards the station and led the way down a narrow little street that ran down to the Thames. Kathleen caught a whiff of dank river water and hesitated.

37

'Are you sure you know where we're going?'

'Of course.' Violet tucked her arm in Kathleen's. 'Come on, it's this way.'

They picked their way carefully down the cobbled street, following a throng of other well-dressed people all heading in the same direction. There certainly seemed to be quite a crowd there, pouring towards what seemed to be a domed railway arch set into the brick wall.

Kathleen and Violet had visited the Players Theatre Club several times during the war in their old premises in Mayfair, and some of the players had been kind enough to travel out to the East End to entertain the military patients at the Nightingale. Now the club had a new home, and Violet had managed to get tickets to the opening night.

'I didn't realise it was going to be such a grand affair,' Kathleen said, as they finally managed to squeeze inside and handed their coats to the cloakroom girl.

'Oh yes, it's quite an occasion. I've heard there's already a waiting list to become members here.' Violet looked around at the sea of bobbing heads. 'You never know, we might spot someone famous. Or someone we know, at any rate.'

As it turned out, they didn't see any famous faces. But Kathleen hardly cared because the show was so entertaining. Act after act took to the tiny stage, and she soon forgot her troubles as she laughed at the comedians' lively patter and sang along to the old Victorian music-hall songs, clutching the song sheets they had been given on the way in. Suddenly the Nightingale, Miss Davis and her future in Lancashire seemed a long way away.

But all too soon it was time to go home.

'Thank you for suggesting I come out with you tonight,' she said to Violet as they left the theatre and stepped into the freezing night.

'It was such fun, wasn't it? I loved that woman who led the singing, all dolled up in Victorian garb and a huge feathered hat.'

'Oh, that hat! I thought she was going to poke the conductor's eye out when she bent over! And the things she came out with!'

'She was a bit saucy, wasn't she? It was like watching Marie Lloyd herself.'

'I do love a bit of old-fashioned music hall,' Kathleen sighed. 'There's nothing quite like a good laugh and a sing-song to make you feel better.'

Violet smiled. 'Remember the Christmas shows we used to put on at the hospital for the patients before the war?'

'How could I forget? I think Mr Hopkins' endless monologues might stay with me forever.'

'Oh heavens, yes! The Head Porter and his recitations. But he wasn't the only one trying to hog the limelight, was he? Do you remember the ward sisters' choir, and how Miss Trott always insisted on having a solo?'

'"Lo, How a Rose E'er Blooming"?' Kathleen rolled her eyes at the memory. 'She sang it every year.'

'And it never got any better, did it? No one had the courage to tell her she couldn't sing, until Miss Hanley said she sounded like a cat sliding

39

down a blackboard by its claws!'

'Miss Hanley always was rather blunt!' Kathleen smiled.

'Perhaps we should do it again?' Violet said, as they stood shivering on the Strand, waiting for a taxi.

'Put on a Christmas show, you mean?'

'Why not? I'm sure we could get some of the staff to join in if we asked them. They always used to be keen, as I recall. In fact, I'm sure the performers enjoyed it more than the audience!' Violet grinned. 'Go on, it would be such a tonic.'

Kathleen considered it. 'Perhaps you're right,' she said. 'Heaven knows, I think we could all do with something to lift us out of the doldrums.' She smiled. 'As you say – why not?'

'That's the spirit,' Violet said. 'Although I would suggest we try to dissuade Mr Hopkins from yet another monologue...'

But Kathleen was no longer listening. She had caught sight of a face in the crowd spilling out of Villiers Street opposite. He was arm in arm with a woman in an extravagant fur coat.

For a moment Kathleen could only stand there, pinned to the spot by a lightning bolt of long-forgotten emotion. She wanted to look away but somehow she couldn't drag her eyes from his face.

And then, as if he knew he was being watched, he suddenly turned and looked at her, and she saw her own shock mirrored on his handsome face.

The woman noticed her, too. Her eyes narrowed, then the next moment she was making

40

her way determinedly across the road towards them, dragging her companion with her.

Kathleen was consumed with the sudden urge to run away. But it was too late; she could only stand there helplessly as James Cooper and his wife approached.

'Why, Mr and Mrs Cooper!' Violet greeted them with delight, unaware of the tension. 'Fancy meeting you here.'

'Good evening, Miss Tanner. Miss Fox.' James nodded, his eyes not meeting hers.

'Mr Cooper.' Kathleen's body was as stiff as a marionette's. 'Mrs Cooper.'

'How delightful to see you again.' Simone Cooper's voice was husky, with a hint of her native French accent. She was a brittle beauty, darkly exotic, with hooded eyes and jet-black hair caught up in a brocade turban. 'Have you been to the club, too?'

'Yes, we have.' Violet answered for her, as Kathleen's tongue seemed to stick to the roof of her mouth. 'Such fun, wasn't it?'

'It was amusing, I suppose. But a little too vulgar for our tastes, I am afraid,' Mrs Cooper simpered. 'We prefer opera, don't we, darling?'

Especially Puccini. Kathleen remembered a recital they had attended, sneaking away together one afternoon, creeping into the back of the concert hall after the music began so that no one would see them arriving together.

'I had no idea you were back in London?' Once again, it was Violet who spoke up.

'We returned last week.' James found his voice at last, his eyes still not meeting Kathleen's.

41

She had often wondered how she would feel when she saw him again. She had hoped that after all these years she would manage to be cool and civilised. But now she realised she was fooling herself. She only had to glance at him and all her feelings for him came rushing back in a wave that threatened to engulf her.

'But only for a few days. We have some matters to settle before we leave,' Simone said.

'Leave?' Kathleen blurted out the word before she could stop herself.

'That's right.' Simone turned to her, her eyes dark under finely arched brows. 'Didn't you know? We're moving to America.'

Kathleen held herself rigid. 'No,' she said quietly. 'No. I didn't know.'

'My husband has been offered a job as a senior consultant at a hospital in New York,' Simone went on. 'It couldn't have come at a better time. I'm so tired of this country, and all the dreadful shortages. Besides, James's talents are wasted here. It will be a new start for us, won't it, darling?' She clutched his arm tighter, gazing adoringly up at him.

A new start. That was what *they* were supposed to have. James had wanted them to run away together, and Kathleen had been writing her resignation letter when the bomb went off.

That bomb had changed everything. Kathleen had decided to stay in London and help put the Nightingale back together, and James had gone down to the sector hospital in Kent. That had been four years earlier, and their paths had not crossed since.

42

What would her life have been like if that explosion hadn't happened? she wondered. Perhaps she might be the one clutching James Cooper's arm, planning her new life in America.

'We'll miss you, won't we, Miss Fox?' Violet's voice interrupted her thoughts.

'Yes,' Kathleen managed to reply. 'Yes, we will.'

'I daresay you will.' Simone sent her a considering look, her long, thin fingers still curled possessively around her husband's arm. Did she know about their affair? There was something, almost pitying, in her expression.

You tried, her look seemed to say. *But you were a fool, and now he's mine again.*

At that moment a taxi approached. Desperate to escape, Kathleen stepped into the road to flag it down, just as a car went through a puddle, sending an icy arc of slush over her.

'Oh no!' Violet cried. 'You're soaked.'

'Here, let me–' James moved towards her but Kathleen jerked away from him.

'No! It's only water, I'm sure it will come off.' As she brushed herself down, Kathleen looked up and caught the look in Simone Cooper's eyes.

Oh yes, she knew.

'Bad luck, Miss Fox,' she said softly.

First thing the following morning, Kathleen sent for Miss Davis. While she was waiting for her, she went through the duty rosters the Assistant Matron had left on her desk. She knew Miss Davis would be bound to ask for them the moment she walked in.

She had just finished going through them when

43

there was a knock on the door.

'Come in.' Kathleen heard the door open, and without looking up, she said, 'You'll be pleased to know I've looked at the rosters, and—' She glanced up and found herself staring into the piercing blue eyes of James Cooper.

'Hello, Kath.' It was so long since she had heard him say her name. His deep voice always made it sound like a caress.

Her breath stopped in her chest. 'What are you doing here?'

'I had to come and see you. I wanted to apologise for what happened last night.'

'Apologise?'

'You shouldn't have found out that way.' He paused. 'I swear I was going to come and see you before I left. To explain—'

She looked down, straightening the rosters with shaking hands. 'You don't owe me an explanation.'

'I owe you that and a damn sight more!'

Kathleen looked up at him as he stood over her. His dark hair was threaded with grey, but he was still as handsome as a film star. The nurses always used to swoon over him when he did his rounds.

But it wasn't just his good looks she had fallen in love with. Behind that handsome face was a sensitive, intelligent and fiercely passionate man.

The thought of the passion they had shared brought an uncomfortable heat to her face and she looked away sharply.

'You don't owe me anything,' she said. 'It's all in the past. It's over. We said all we had to say to each other four years ago.'

44

'Did we?' Kathleen shrank back in her seat as James leaned forward, planting his hands on the desk. He was so close she could feel the warmth of his body, the male scent of him. 'Did we really, Kath? Did it really end there?'

'I – I don't know what you mean–'

'I think you do. Last night, when I saw you again, I felt something between us. And you felt it too, didn't you?'

'You're wrong–'

'Look at me now and tell me that you feel nothing for me.' His blue eyes burned into hers. 'Look at me, Kath! Tell me you don't still love me.'

Her gaze slid away to her fingers, still clutching the rosters as if her life depended on it. 'Stop it,' she begged. 'You mustn't talk like that.'

'Why not? I've spent four years pretending it never happened, trying to forget you. But I can't, and I never will. Those few weeks we spent together were the happiest I've ever been. You don't know how often I've thought about you, wished we could have run away together when we had the chance.'

'So have I.' There was no point in denying it, Kathleen knew. James could see into her soul.

'So why can't we? When I saw you last night, I realised you felt the same, that there might still be a chance for us.'

'How can there be? You're leaving.'

He sighed impatiently. 'Why do you think I'm going to America, if not to get away from you?'

'I – I don't understand–'

'I've been dreading seeing you again, Kath. I wasn't sure I could cope with coming back to the

45

Nightingale, knowing I would have to see you every day. Knowing I still loved you. But now I know you feel the same–' He paused. 'I don't have to go. I'd stay, if you wanted me to.'

She stared at him, shocked. 'You'd do that?'

'I'd do anything for you, Kath. You must know that?'

'But your wife–'

'Simone and I stopped loving each other a long time ago. I'm useful to her, that's all. If I wasn't here I know it wouldn't take her long to find someone else to take my place. God knows, she's tried hard enough during our marriage!' He reached across the desk and seized her hand. 'What do you say? Can we start again? We've tried to do the right thing, now surely it's time for us to be happy.'

His words were like darts, piercing her skin. The intensity in his eyes frightened her, and Kathleen had to fight for composure. 'I – I don't know what to say–'

'Then say yes!' His fingers tightened around hers. 'I asked you once before and you turned me down. Now I'm asking you again. One last chance for us. What do you say?'

Kathleen felt her mouth go dry, her strength of will ebbing away from her. 'I–'

Suddenly the door burst open, breaking the spell.

'I'm sorry I didn't come straight away, Matron, I was – oh!' Charlotte Davis stopped dead on the threshold and looked from Kathleen to James and back again. 'I beg your pardon. I didn't know you had company–'

46

'For heaven's sake, what have I told you about knocking?' Guilt and tension made Kathleen snap.

'I'm sorry, Matron.' Miss Davis started to retreat.

'No, it's quite all right,' James said. 'I'm leaving now, anyway.' He glanced at Kathleen. 'I'll be leaving on Christmas Day. If you need to speak to me before then, just send word. You know where to find me—'

'Thank you, Mr Cooper, I'll remember that.' Kathleen stared down at the desk, fighting for composure. She did not dare look up again until she heard the door close. Then, when she finally dragged her gaze from her blotter, it was to see Miss Davis standing over her, prim as ever.

'I beg your pardon, Matron,' she said quietly. 'I didn't realise you were busy...'

Kathleen studied the Assistant Matron's face, but her expression was carefully neutral, giving nothing away.

She glanced at the door, still trying to work out what had happened. Had James Cooper really just come in and turned her carefully ordered world upside down all over again?

'You asked to see me?' Miss Davis prompted her, her voice clear in the silence.

'Yes.' Kathleen pulled herself together with effort. 'There's something I want you to do.'

'Yes, Matron?'

'I have decided we should have a Christmas show, and I want you to organise it.'

The Assistant Matron's expression fell slightly. 'A Christmas show, Matron?'

47

'Yes, Miss Davis.' Kathleen felt her impatience rise. Her encounter with James Cooper had left her emotions in a turmoil. 'Surely you know what I'm talking about?'

'Well yes, Matron.' She looked perplexed. 'But I'm not sure I'm the right person to organise such an event. I don't think I'd know where to start...'

'Well, you'll have to work it out, won't you?' Kathleen saw the young woman's face fall and felt a pang of guilt. 'I'm sure the other nurses will help you,' she said, more kindly. 'Perhaps you could ask Miss Tanner for advice, if you get stuck–'

Miss Davis stiffened instantly, drawing herself upright. 'It's quite all right, Matron, I'm sure I'll be able to manage.'

'I'm sure you will,' Kathleen said, her moment of sympathy disappearing. Miss Davis had seemed almost human for a moment, but now she was back to her chilly self. 'You'd best get on with it,' she said, handing her the duty rosters.

Miss Davis left, closing the door softly behind her. Kathleen looked out of the window over the broken rooftops, and thought about James Cooper.

We've tried to do the right thing, now surely it's time for us to be happy.

If she was really honest with herself, James Cooper had been the only thing keeping her at the Nightingale. Much as she didn't want to admit it, she had clung to the thought that one day they would be working together again. She knew they couldn't be together, but it might be enough for her starved heart to see him from afar.

48

I asked you once before and you turned me down. Now I'm asking you again. One last chance for us. What do you say?

She caught sight of her reflection in the glass and was startled at the old woman who stared back at her. The war had aged her. Every time she looked in the mirror she was dismayed by the lines she saw fanning out from her grey eyes, and the sad droop of her mouth. She looked every one of her fifty years.

She felt them, too. Deep inside, she was too weary to carry on. All the energy and fight had drained out of her, sapped by the war. She no longer cared about the Nightingale, or if and when the building work would be completed. The thought of another ten years sitting behind this desk no longer filled her with excitement.

Why shouldn't she follow her heart while she still had time? She had spent years doing the right thing, devoting her life to the Nightingale. Now fate had given her a second chance.

She went back to her desk and pulled a sheet of notepaper from the drawer. As she did, she paused, waiting for Miss Hanley's voice. But for once the Assistant Matron was silent, and no shadows hovered over her as she picked up her pen.

One way or another, come Christmas Day she would have made her decision to leave the Nightingale.

49

Charlotte

1st December 1945

Charlotte Davis sat at her desk in the outer office, utterly perplexed and not a little troubled. It was not like her to be out of her depth and she didn't like it.

She stared down at the blank sheet of paper on which she had written just two words: *Christmas Show*. Not a single idea had sprung into her head in the half-hour she had been looking at it. For once, her mind seemed to have gone blank with panic.

She raised her gaze to Matron's office door. Why would Miss Fox even think to give her such a responsibility? She usually relished a challenge, but even she had to admit she was entirely unsuited for this particular task.

She had done her best to convey her dismay, but Miss Fox had either not noticed or she had chosen to ignore her. And Charlotte couldn't refuse outright because she was desperate to make a good impression on her new matron. She was already aware that Miss Fox didn't much care for her.

She tasted blood and realised she was biting her nails. They had grown back since she returned to England but now her cuticles were raw and ragged where she had started worrying at them again.

Come on, Charlotte, you're just being silly. She picked up her fountain pen and forced herself to think. Surely it could not be that hard? After all, she had tackled much more difficult tasks over the past few years.

At the age of twenty-one, she had evacuated a hospital under German fire, escaping in an ambulance with wounded patients. Within a year, she was back behind enemy lines, treating injured soldiers in a Casualty Clearing Station. Later, she had nursed four hundred men in a field hospital with space for half that number, begging and cajoling food and supplies from locals when their own rations ran out. And later...

Her mind shied away. What had happened later was something she could never allow herself to think about.

At any rate, after everything she had been through, surely getting a few doctors and nurses to perform a simple show for the patients couldn't be too difficult. All she had to do was make a start.

But how?

Christmas Show. She looked down at the words, neatly written at the top of the page.

She knew what was expected, of course. The hospital where she trained in Surrey had put on a show for the patients every Christmas. And when she was stationed abroad, the QAs would try to organise some kind of festive entertainment to cheer themselves up and raise the spirits of the wounded men.

Charlotte tried to cast her mind back to her student days, ten years earlier. Goodness, it seemed like a lifetime ago now. She could remember the

51

dining hall filled with patients, rows of them in their dressing gowns, some in wheelchairs, singing and laughing and clapping their hands in time to the out-of-tune piano played enthusiastically by the Home Sister, Miss Clegg.

Charlotte had been such a giddy young girl then, painting her face and dressing up with the other nurses. She remembered standing on the makeshift stage, shaking maracas made from bedpan bottles while one of the medical students gave a spirited rendition of 'The Peanut Vendor'. She remembered the black wig she wore, and how it kept slipping over her eyes as she jiggled about...

She caught herself smiling at the memory, and stopped abruptly. That girl was long gone, and the less she thought about her, the better.

She shook herself mentally. This was not like her. She had a job to do, and she was never one to shirk her responsibilities. It was only a silly Christmas show, after all. She didn't know why she was making so much fuss about it.

So what to do first? Muster the troops, she decided. Then she could get everyone organised and give them their orders.

She put aside the piece of paper and instead drew up some notices, summoning the staff to a meeting in the dining hall the following evening. Then she took them round to each ward.

She went first to Parry, the children's ward. As she approached the double doors, she could hear the sound of childish laughter drifting up the corridor. Curious, she swung them open, only to be greeted by complete disarray.

52

The long table in the centre of the ward was strewn with pots of glue, scissors and piles of paper scraps. Half a dozen children sat around the table, a couple busily cutting the paper into strips which the others glued together. They were supervised – if that was indeed the word – by Atkins, a middle-aged woman who volunteered on the ward.

They were so occupied with their various tasks, no one noticed Charlotte until she cleared her throat and said, 'What is going on here?'

The children fell silent, all eyes swivelling in her direction. Atkins jumped up, smoothing her apron down. Paper fluttered around her in a snowfall.

'Assistant Matron!' she stuttered, a blush rising in her face. There was a scrap of wallpaper stuck to her sleeve, Charlotte noticed. 'I'm sorry, I didn't hear you come in. I was just making paper chains with the kids.'

Charlotte stared at the woman with dislike. She never knew quite what to make of Peggy Atkins. From what she understood, she had arrived as a part of the Voluntary Aid Detachment when women were first conscripted three years earlier. But six months after the war ended she was still there, turning up every day for duty. She still wore the blue dress of a VAD, but her plain white apron no longer bore the Red Cross.

The sight of her irritated Charlotte's sense of order. Peggy Atkins was neither fish nor fowl, as far as she was concerned. She had no official nursing qualifications, apart from her basic VAD training, and she was far too old to be considered

53

a student. But for some reason the ward sister of Parry seemed to think she was indispensable.

'Making a mess, more like,' she snapped. She looked around the ward. 'Where is Sister Parry?'

'Bed eight, Miss, helping Nurse Tovey give an injection.'

'Is Nurse Tovey not capable of giving an injection by herself?'

'Oh yes, Miss, but the little boy gets a bit upset so Sister likes to be there to help calm him down, if she can.'

'I see.' Charlotte looked with distaste at the child closest to her, a small girl in a patched dressing gown. Thick rivulets of mucus ran from her nose, pooling on her top lip.

At that moment Sister Parry herself appeared from behind the screen around bed eight, rolling down her sleeves.

'Hello, Assistant Matron. I thought I heard your voice.' She took the starched cuffs from her apron pocket and fastened them in place. A stray curl of red hair escaped from beneath her linen bonnet.

Dora Riley was another one Charlotte could not understand. Whoever heard of a married nurse? She appreciated that they had needed women with Riley's experience and training at one time, but as far as the Assistant Matron was concerned, these messy remnants of the war should have been tidied away a long time ago. They certainly should not be acting as ward sisters. Women like Riley and Atkins made a mockery of her profession.

And the shambles on the ward proved it.

54

'Sister.' Charlotte looked back at the scene in front of her. 'I was just commenting on the mess I see before me.'

'Oh, it's only a bit of glue and paper. It can easily be cleared up,' Sister Parry said cheerfully. Even her ghastly cockney accent grated on Charlotte. 'It's better that the children are busy and enjoying themselves, don't you think? It's no fun being in hospital when you're a kid, especially at this time of year.'

'The children should not be out of bed,' Charlotte snapped. 'This is a hospital, Sister. They are here to recover.'

'They'll recover quicker if they've got something to keep them occupied, surely?'

She was smiling as she said it, but there was a hint of insolence in her muddy green eyes. Charlotte would have liked to put her in her place, but Matron in her infinite wisdom had made her a ward sister so Charlotte had no choice but to respect her rank.

'Get it cleaned up, if you please,' she said shortly. 'And have this put up where the nurses can see it.' She thrust the piece of paper at her. 'Tell everyone I expect to see them at the meeting tomorrow evening.'

'Yes, Assistant Matron.'

As Charlotte walked away, she heard Atkins' muffled snort of laughter, but she didn't turn round. She had a nasty feeling Dora Riley would be making a face behind her back.

On Jarvis, she hoped to catch Miss Tanner in a similar state of disarray, but to her frustration the ward was immaculate.

55

Violet Tanner greeted her with a smile. 'Two visits in one day, Assistant Matron? We are honoured.'

Charlotte stared up into the woman's dark eyes. As with Matron, she never quite knew whether the ward sister was making fun of her or not.

'This is not a social call, Sister,' she said.

'I never imagined it would be. So what can I do for you?'

Her smug smile disappeared when she saw the notice Charlotte handed her.

'Miss Fox never told me you were organising the Christmas show?' She sounded stunned.

'Perhaps she didn't realise she had to ask your permission,' Charlotte replied sweetly.

Miss Tanner ignored the barb, still staring at the piece of paper in her hand. 'Actually, I thought she might – but it doesn't matter.'

You thought she might ask you to do it? Charlotte finished for her silently. She smiled to herself, feeling a brief flare of satisfaction.

The friendship between Matron and Miss Tanner had always rankled with her. They were forever having whispered conversations together and sharing little private jokes.

The next moment Violet's frown had disappeared and she was smiling again. 'I'll certainly be at the meeting,' she said. 'And if you need any help with organising the show, I'd be happy to help.'

I'm sure you would, Charlotte thought sourly. And wouldn't Miss Tanner just love that? She would be very quick to tell her friend Miss Fox all about it, too. And she would make sure she took

56

all the credit.

The ward sister's so-called kindness might fool everyone else, but not Charlotte. She knew exactly what Violet Tanner was up to.

It was plain to her that Miss Tanner thought she should be in Charlotte's place. And Miss Fox felt the same. Together, they seemed to go out of their way to make her feel left out.

But not any more.

'I'm sure I can manage by myself,' she said.

'Well, you know where I am if you change your mind. I'd hate to think of you struggling.'

Charlotte almost laughed at that. She made up her mind there and then that whatever happened she would manage this show all by herself. And she would make a big success of it.

This was her chance to prove herself to Miss Fox once and for all, and she meant to take it.

Miss Fox was already at her desk the following morning. Charlotte glimpsed her through the half-open door to her office as she hung up her cloak on the stand. The matron looked tired, and Charlotte wondered if it had anything at all to do with the handsome man who had come to her office the previous day. Miss Fox had been very subdued since his visit.

'Good morning, Matron,' she greeted her. She took off her gloves and warmed her hands briefly before the crackling fire. It was another freezing day, and even the short walk from the sisters' home had been enough to chill her to the bone. 'The fog is settling in. I could barely find my way in this morning.'

57

She glanced back through the half-open door. Matron was in the middle of composing a letter, from what she could see. A difficult letter, by the look of it. She was lost in her own world, the pen still in her hand.

Charlotte took her seat behind her desk, carefully smoothing her thick cotton dress under her to stop it from creasing. But no sooner had she picked up her own pen than Miss Fox appeared in the doorway.

'You will have to do the morning rounds on your own this morning, Miss Davis. I have a meeting with the Board of Trustees.'

Charlotte glanced up. 'The Trustees are coming here? Today?'

'Yes. They're due in at ten o'clock.' She gave Charlotte a quizzical frown. 'You seem dismayed, Miss Davis. Is something wrong?'

'No. No, nothing's wrong, Matron.' Charlotte glanced away quickly. 'Of course I will carry out the ward rounds by myself.'

'I'm sure you'll rather enjoy it,' Matron said.

Charlotte watched the door to her office closing firmly, shutting her out. She wasn't sure why she annoyed Matron so much. All she ever wanted was to do her best.

And Miss Fox was right, she did enjoy doing the ward rounds by herself. She managed to get through them far more efficiently than she ever did with Matron, who would insist on stopping to chat to everyone, not just the new admissions and the patients due for discharge that day.

Miss Tanner was waiting for her outside the doors to Jarvis ward, lined up with the other

58

nurses. When Charlotte started to explain why Miss Fox would not be joining them, Miss Tanner said, 'Oh yes, she did mention she had a meeting with the Board of Trustees this morning.'

There was no mistaking the glint in her dark eyes. *You see,* her look said. *She does tell me everything.*

Charlotte gritted her teeth. 'Shall we get on?'

To her annoyance, the ward was once again in perfect order, with nothing for her to pick on. Charlotte ran her finger along the bed rails and carefully measured each turned-down sheet, but try as she might she could not find a single fault.

'I hope everything was to your satisfaction, Assistant Matron?' Miss Tanner said, when they had finished.

'It's quite acceptable,' she replied, tight-lipped.

'High praise indeed.'

Charlotte opened her mouth to reply, then decided against it. She might be senior in rank, but she knew she was no match for Miss Tanner's quick tongue.

As she turned, to go, Miss Tanner called after her, 'I'll see you this evening.'

Charlotte looked back at her blankly. 'I beg your pardon?'

'The meeting. About the Christmas show?'

'Oh, yes. You're coming, then?'

'I wouldn't miss it for the world, Assistant Matron.' Was that a smirk on her face? Whatever it was, Charlotte didn't trust it.

She returned to Matron's office just as the Trustees' meeting was coming to an end. As Charlotte rounded the corner, they were walking

59

up the passage towards her with Miss Fox. Charlotte had no choice but to stand where she was and wait to greet them.

There were six trustees, but Charlotte only noticed him. She picked him out immediately, standing head and shoulders above the others. Even in civvies, he still had the tall, straight, military bearing of an officer.

Major Hugh McLaren, late of the Royal Artillery Regiment.

She took a deep breath, and fought down the treacherous flutter in her stomach.

He looked up, saw her and smiled. 'Miss Davis.'

'Hello, Major.'

As he walked towards her, her hand automatically went up in salute, only to falter halfway and fall back to her side. He noticed the gesture, his green eyes twinkling.

'How are you enjoying your new posting?'

Charlotte was aware of Miss Fox watching them. She was saying goodbye to the other Trustees, but Charlotte could tell she was listening to their conversation.

'I like it very much. Thank you, Sir.'

'Good, good. Settling in all right?'

'Yes, I think so.'

'Splendid.' He lowered his voice. 'I'm glad I caught you. When Miss Fox said you were doing the ward rounds, I feared I might not get the chance to see you.'

Charlotte caught the searching look in his eyes and glanced away. The other trustees had gone, leaving just the three of them in the passageway.

'Well, if you'll excuse me–' she started to say,

60

but Major McLaren cut her off.

'I wonder, Miss Davis, would you care to walk with me to my car? There's something I wish to discuss with you.'

'I–' Charlotte glanced at Miss Fox. 'I'm not sure...'

'I'm sure Matron can spare you for a few minutes?' He turned to Miss Fox. 'That would be all right, wouldn't it?'

Charlotte willed her to say no, but of course Miss Fox nodded and said, 'Of course, Major.'

'Thank you.' He turned back to Charlotte. 'Shall we go?'

Charlotte took her time fetching her cloak and fastening it around her shoulders. 'He's just a friend,' she told herself, murmuring the words under her breath. Just an old comrade from the war, taking a kindly interest in her. There was no need to feel flustered, or to think there was any more to it than that.

They walked downstairs in silence. Charlotte was careful to keep the width of the staircase between them, not wanting to betray the feelings that refused to go away.

Major Hugh, as they always called him, was fair-haired and good-looking in an aristocratic way, with sharp cheekbones, a firm jaw and a long, aquiline nose. But it was the kindness in his green eyes and the warmth in his smile that Charlotte had first noticed.

Finally, he turned to her and said, 'How are you? Really, I mean?'

'I'm very well, Major.' She kept her gaze fixed ahead.

61

'And you really are settling in all right?' He sounded anxious.

'Yes, thank you. I'm very grateful to you for finding me this post.'

'Nonsense, they're lucky to have you. A nurse of your abilities is hard to come by.'

Charlotte allowed herself a smile. *I'm not sure Miss Fox would agree with you,* she thought, but said nothing.

'Bit different from the military life though, eh?' he said wryly.

'Yes, Sir.' Charlotte didn't want to tell him how much she missed the QAs. It was a hard life, but there was order and routine, and everyone knew where they stood. It didn't matter whether you liked someone or not; you respected their rank and carried out your orders and that was that.

She had hoped that she might find a similar kind of life at the Nightingale, but she was surprised to find how difficult it was to fit in. There was still the same order and routine and respect that one might expect in any well-functioning hospital. But Charlotte had forgotten how personal hospital life could be. There were all kinds of friendships and grievances and alliances to be taken into account. One needed to tread more carefully, and that simply wasn't Charlotte's way. Not any more, at any rate. Somewhere, out there in the dirty business of war, she had forgotten how to deal with people.

But she could hardly tell that to Major Hugh. He had pulled so many strings to get this position for her, she didn't wish to seem ungrateful.

They left the hospital building and stepped out

62

into the cold, foggy air. Charlotte pulled her cloak more tightly around her. She could see the Major's car waiting at the end of the long drive beyond the gates, his driver behind the wheel. Another fifty yards, and he would be gone.

'Miss Fox tells me you're organising the Christmas show?' Major McLaren said.

'That's right.'

'That sounds like a first-rate idea. It will help you make friends.'

Charlotte sent him a sharp glance. What had Miss Fox been telling him? But his face gave nothing away. 'I don't need friends,' she said.

He smiled ruefully. 'Everyone needs a friend, Charlotte.'

'I don't.'

'Typical Nurse Davis! You always did like to keep yourself to yourself.'

'You make it sound like a bad thing?'

'There's no harm in leaning on others, occasionally. You don't have to be strong all the time.'

That's where you're wrong, Charlotte thought. It was only by being strong that she had managed to survive.

She remembered the first time a soldier had died, a young artillery boy with pneumonia. He was just turned eighteen, the same age as her own brother. Charlotte had cried over him, but the matron at the field hospital had dragged her outside and shaken her by her shoulders.

'You must not cry,' she had ordered. 'It's silly and self-indulgent. Do you think it will do the rest of the men any good to see you weeping and wailing? You must be strong, or you'll be no use

63

to anyone.'

She had taken those words to heart, and they had stood her in good stead, especially in her last posting. While the other QAs had sobbed on each other's shoulders, Charlotte had ploughed on, doing what needed to be done.

She had despised them for their weakness. Matron was right, they were silly and self-indulgent, and no use to anyone.

'I don't need to lean on anyone,' she said.

'No. Of course you don't.' There was an edge to his voice. 'You've made that clear enough.'

Charlotte looked sideways at him. She knew Major Hugh would have liked her to lean on him. There was a time when she had wished she could, a time when she had longed to give in to the feelings she had for him. But that wasn't her. She had grown so used to being strong, she had forgotten how to be anything else.

They reached the gates. The Major's driver was out of the car, opening the door for him. Charlotte started to turn away from him, wanting to avoid the awkwardness of a long drawn-out goodbye, but he put out his hand, gently touching her arm, holding her back.

'You know where I am, if you ever need me,' he said softly.

She looked down at his gloved hand. She could feel its warmth through her woollen cloak.

'Thank you, Major. You've been very kind.'

He sighed impatiently. 'Kindness has nothing to do with it.'

'I should be getting back,' she said, shifting herself from his grasp.

64

'Of course.' His hand dropped back to his side. 'I won't keep you,' he said shortly.

Charlotte walked away, not looking back at him. It was only when she heard his car drive off that she allowed herself to glance over her shoulder.

Dear Major Hugh. If she could ever have allowed anyone past her defences, it would have been him.

She returned to the office, where Matron was waiting for her, standing at her desk.

'Has Major McLaren gone?' she asked.

'Yes, Matron.'

'What did he want to speak to you about?'

Panic flared inside her. She glanced out of the window and said the first thing that came into her head. 'The rebuilding work.'

Miss Fox's mouth tightened. 'He could have asked me about that. I am Matron, after all.' She paused. 'Did he ask about anything else?'

Charlotte read the look in her eyes. Did she suspect Charlotte was a spy, placed there by the Trustees to report on her? 'No, Matron.'

Miss Fox picked up some papers from Charlotte's desk, read through them, then put them down again. 'You two seem very friendly?' she remarked.

'We were stationed together in Europe for a time,' Charlotte said quietly.

'Well, you must have made quite an impression on him,' Miss Fox said. 'He worked very hard to have you appointed to this hospital.'

Charlotte lowered her gaze. 'He's been very kind to me.'

Kindness has nothing to do with it.

65

'It must be nice to have friends in high places.'

Her comment stung. 'I'm sure he wouldn't have recommended me for the post if he didn't think I was fit for it,' Charlotte said, then regretted it when she saw the chilly look in Miss Fox's eyes.

It wasn't my idea to come here, she wanted to tell her. All she wanted was to prove she was worthy of the position, but Matron never seemed willing to give her a chance.

Perhaps the Christmas show would finally give her the opportunity to prove she could fit in.

With that in mind, Charlotte arrived early to the meeting that evening. She pushed back the long tables and set out the dining-room chairs in neat rows. Then she arranged a table and chair for herself at the front. She had just sat down when the double doors opened.

Charlotte looked up expectantly, only for her heart to sink again at the sight of Violet Tanner.

'Oh, am I the first?' She looked around the empty dining room.

'Yes, but it isn't six o'clock yet,' Charlotte said defensively. 'The others will be here soon.'

'I'm sure they will.'

The ward sister took a seat in the middle of the front row, right in front of Charlotte. 'You've certainly put out enough chairs,' she said, smiling. 'Are you expecting an army?'

Charlotte was saved from answering by the arrival of Miss Trott from Wren ward. Charlotte smiled with relief. At last, a friendly face. She liked Miriam Trott. They were of a similar mind,

66

she decided. Like her, Miss Trott had no time for nonsense.

But the ward sister had been in rather a sulk when she had visited the ward that morning. Charlotte wasn't sure why, but she suspected it had something to do with her questioning that pregnant patient's due date. Miss Trott did not like her authority challenged.

Now the ward sister barely glanced her way as she looked around the room, her mouth down-turned. 'Are we the only ones here?'

'So it seems,' Miss Tanner replied. 'But it isn't six o'clock yet,' she added, with a quick sideways glance at Charlotte.

'Hmm.'

As Miss Trott plonked herself down in the middle row, Charlotte cleared her throat. 'Miss Trott, would you mind moving down to the front?' she asked.

Miss Trott looked at her for the first time. 'May I ask why?'

'I want to keep all the ranks separate from each other.'

Now it was Miss Tanner's turn to frown at her. 'Is that necessary, Assistant Matron?'

'I wouldn't have asked if I didn't think so,' Charlotte replied, irritated.

'Yes, but surely–'

'Oh, don't argue with her, Violet!' Miss Trott said irritably as she shifted along the row to sit beside Miss Tanner. 'You should know by now that Miss Davis always knows best.' She glared at her as she said it.

Charlotte stifled a sigh. It was only a simple

67

request yet somehow she had already managed to upset the only two people in the room. She only hoped the rest of the meeting would go more smoothly.

Over the next few minutes, more people started to arrive. They came in dribs and drabs, a few with confidence, others giggling and looking embarrassed. There were nurses, ward sisters and orderlies, plus a few medical students and junior doctors. They stood at the back in their white coats, laughing and joking among themselves.

Charlotte busily arranged the other nurses into their rows, sisters at the front, then staff nurses, students and probationers, and finally the porters at the back. All the while she was conscious of Miss Tanner watching her from the front row, silently passing judgement.

Finally, when she was satisfied by the neat rows of grey dresses, then blue, then striped, she called the meeting to order.

'Can we all pay attention, please?' she called out, sternly eyeing the two third-year students from Wren ward who were giggling together on the end of the row. They fell silent, their heads down, shoulders still shaking with mirth. 'Now, as you know, Matron has given me the task of organising this year's Christmas show—'

'God help us!' someone muttered from the back of the room. Charlotte looked up sharply, but rows of blank faces stared back at her, giving nothing away.

'I have come up with a list of suggestions for songs and recitations that I feel would be suitable for inclusion—' She produced the piece of paper

68

she had been working on late into the previous night. 'I suggest that over the next day or two you all take the chance to look at the list and put your names beside the piece you would like to perform.'

'Pardon me, Assistant Matron, but that is not how we have done things before,' Miss Trott piped up from the front row.

'No, indeed,' Sister Theatre agreed beside her. 'In the past we always came up with our own suggestions and gave them to Miss Wallace, Sister Blake as was, and she made the list from there.'

'Yes, well, I believe this is a more efficient way of getting things done,' Charlotte said.

'Yes, but Miss Wallace—'

'Miss Wallace is no longer here, is she?' Charlotte snapped.

'More's the pity,' a voice muttered in the front row.

Charlotte straightened her shoulders, taking control. 'I am in charge of this event, and this is the way I have decided I want to do things,' she announced. 'Things will go much more smoothly if we do it my way.'

She looked along the rows of faces. A few murmurs of discontent rippled around the room, while others simply glared at her in silence.

'May I see this list of yours?' Miss Trott held out her hand imperiously from the front row. Charlotte was about to refuse, but then she saw the ward sister's mutinous expression and handed it over.

Miss Trott perused the list, with Sister Holmes and Sister Hyde looking over her shoulder on

69

either side.

'I don't see Mr Hopkins' usual monologue on here?' Sister Hyde remarked.

'That's one blessing, I suppose,' one of the junior doctors said, and everyone laughed.

'I don't see my solo, either.' Miss Trott looked up at Charlotte accusingly.

'Your solo, Miss Trott?'

'I always perform "Lo, How a Rose E'er Blooming". Everyone expects it.'

'I'm sure no one will mind if you sing something else this year,' Charlotte said politely.

Miss Trott blinked at her. 'But I don't know any of these songs.'

'Then you'll have to learn, won't you?' Suddenly the room seemed very hot, in spite of the cold outside. Charlotte could feel perspiration building up under her linen headdress. 'It will make a nice change for you, I'm sure.'

'We've all had a bit too much change around here, if you ask me,' Miss Trott muttered.

More grumbling went around the room. In the back row, Atkins laughed out loud at something the man beside her had said.

'Will you be quiet back there?' Charlotte turned on her furiously. 'If you don't want to listen to what I have to say then you can leave now.'

Atkins' face flooded red with mortification. Beside her, the man shot Charlotte a dirty look.

'The list will be on the wall next to Matron's office,' Charlotte went on. 'I expect the names to be filled in by the end of this week, and we will be starting rehearsals next Monday. That will be all, thank you.'

70

Everyone shuffled out, their heads down, muttering among themselves. Charlotte watched them go, miserably aware that the meeting hadn't quite gone as she had hoped.

As if to make matters even worse, Miss Tanner had witnessed every painful minute of it. No doubt she would be scurrying straight off to Matron with all the details.

Charlotte refused to meet the ward sister's eye as she gathered up her papers. But a moment later she was aware of Miss Tanner approaching the table.

'May I offer you some advice, Miss Davis?' she said.

No, Charlotte thought, *but I'm sure you will anyway.* 'Of course.' She managed a brittle smile.

'Try to remember that everyone is here out of goodwill, and because they think it might be fun. If you start ordering them about, you may not have a show on your hands.'

'So you think I should turn it into some kind of free-for-all?' Charlotte said bitterly. 'That sounds like a recipe for chaos.'

'I'm only saying you should try to stay on the right side of them, if you can,' Miss Tanner replied. 'Honestly, Miss Davis, what does it matter if Miss Trott performs her blessed solo, or Mr Hopkins does yet another of his endless monologues, as long as the show goes on and everyone enjoys themselves?'

Charlotte stared at her. That was so typical of Miss Tanner's easy-going, lackadaisical attitude. She had no idea about the importance of following orders.

71

'Thank you for your advice,' she managed stiffly. 'I'll certainly bear it in mind.'

Charlotte half expected Miss Tanner to raise the matter in front of Matron the following morning when they did their ward round. She certainly wouldn't have put it past her to try to stir up trouble.

But Miss Tanner seemed rather preoccupied when they arrived, and not at all her usual smiling self. She trailed round behind them, offering only the barest details about the patients as they went. Even when the repulsive Mr Donnegan made one of his off-colour remarks at Charlotte's expense, Miss Tanner didn't crack a smile.

It was a relief not to have to listen to her chattering away to Matron. Better still, Charlotte was able to point out a thin film of dust on one of the bedside lockers, and a water jug that had not been refilled. But best of all was when she spotted a patient's temperature chart had been filled in with the wrong time beside it.

Miss Tanner frowned. 'Are you sure? I'm certain I checked it.'

'See for yourself.' Charlotte thrust the chart under her nose. She glanced sideways at Miss Fox as she did it, and was gratified to see a look of concern on the matron's face.

Miss Tanner stared at the figures. 'I don't understand,' she murmured.

'I do,' Charlotte said. 'Someone made a mistake, and you didn't notice it. It's as simple as that.'

'I suppose you're right.' Miss Tanner looked dazed.

72

They finished the round quickly after that, and Charlotte was quietly satisfied when she heard Miss Fox say, 'Would you come to my office and see me later, Sister?'

'Yes, Matron. Of course.'

Now she's for it, Charlotte thought. Miss Tanner might be a good friend, but Matron would not tolerate mistakes with patients. She risked a glance back at the ward sister's anxious face. It served her right

Charlotte could hardly look at Miss Tanner when she arrived half an hour later for her meeting with Matron. She tried to concentrate on the new student applications she was supposed to be working on, but she couldn't stop herself straining to listen to the voices coming from the other side of the door.

They were in there for a long time. Charlotte had almost started to feel sorry for the ward sister when the door suddenly opened and the pair of them emerged.

'Now, remember what I said, won't you?' Miss Fox was saying. 'I'm always here if you need to speak to me.'

'Thank you, Matron.'

Charlotte stared at them, bemused. Why was Matron patting her arm like that? And why was Miss Tanner smiling? She had almost been expecting tears.

She watched Matron ushering the ward sister out quietly furious. She was still frowning when Miss Fox closed the door and turned back to her.

'Miss Davis, what's all this I've been hearing about the Christmas show?' she asked.

73

Charlotte looked up at her sharply. 'I don't know, Matron. What have you been hearing?'

'Someone told me you had a near rebellion on your hands at the first meeting?'

Charlotte felt the heat rising in her face. 'I really don't know–' she started to say, but Miss Fox cut her off.

'This show is supposed to be an entertainment, not a punishment,' she said. 'I know it's difficult for you, but please try not to antagonise people.'

Charlotte puffed out her cheeks. 'I'm sure I haven't deliberately set out to–'

But Miss Fox had already closed her office door behind her.

Charlotte glowered at the list on the wall. No prizes for guessing who had been telling tales, she thought bitterly.

She pulled the list from the wall, ripped it up and tossed the pieces of paper into the waste-paper basket. Very well, if Matron wanted chaos, then that was what she would get.

Of course, everyone else was delighted when they found out they could come up with their own acts, and soon they were lining up in the office to add their names to Charlotte's new blank list. But far from being relieved about it, all Charlotte could feel was despair. There was no order or shape to it at all, and there were far more performers than they had time to include. At this rate, the Christmas show would still be going on by Boxing Day, she decided.

She gazed over the assembled muddle at the first rehearsal and wished Miss Tanner was there to see the chaos she had helped to create. But typically, when she really wanted the ward sister there, she was nowhere to be found.

'We had a late admission on the ward, Assistant Matron,' Philips, a student nurse, explained. 'Sister sends her apologies and says she'll be here as soon as she can.'

'Well, this is most inconvenient,' Charlotte said. 'Who is going to play the piano for us?'

'I can do it, if you wish.' Miss Trott stepped forward.

'You?' Charlotte stared at her.

'Why not, if it will help? I have nothing better to do while I'm waiting to perform my song. But I'm warning you, I'm rather rusty.' The ward sister propped her music up on the stand and seated herself at the piano, smiling round at everyone.

They all stared back at her, and for once Charlotte could tell what they were all thinking. Miriam Trott seldom put herself out to help anyone.

Her piano playing *was* rusty, to put it kindly, but it was by no means the worst part of the rehearsal. After twenty minutes Charlotte began to grow tired of the endless parade of stuttering medical students and giggling nurses who fell to pieces the moment they stepped on to the stage. She sat behind her desk, making crosses on the piece of paper in front of her. She had intended to whittle down the list of performers, but at this rate she would have no one left.

And then one of the porters took to the stage, moments after a junior doctor's woeful magic performance, which had ended with the idiotic young man tying himself in a knot of coloured handkerchiefs. Charlotte would have felt sorry

75

for him if she had had any patience left.

The porter was a big, burly man, still dressed in his brown overalls. Peggy Atkins was with him, looking nervous.

Charlotte frowned at them. 'Name?'

'Brigham, Miss. Bill Brigham.'

Charlotte consulted the paper in front of her. 'Your name doesn't appear to be on my list.'

'No, Miss, it won't be.' He sent Atkins a sideways glance. 'It was a bit of a last-minute decision, you might say.' He looked as shocked as anyone to be standing there in front of her.

Charlotte sighed and put down her pen. She would have dismissed him, had it not been for the fact that she was rapidly running out of people with any talent.

'And what do you do?' she asked.

'Magic tricks, Miss.'

'Not again!' Charlotte glanced sideways at the young doctor, who was standing in the wings still trying to disentangle himself from his handkerchief string. 'Well, I do hope you're better than the last one.'

He was. Charlotte found herself staring, the pen forgotten in her hand, transfixed by his lightning-fast card tricks. Even Miss Trott was watching him avidly from her place at the piano. Atkins did her best to help him, ending each trick with a little flourish and a curtsey, the perfect magician's assistant, even though it was plain she was as amazed as the rest of them.

Finally, the act was over. Bill Brigham and his assistant stood side by side on the stage, looking down at their shoes.

76

'Thank you,' Charlotte said. 'That was quite – acceptable.'

'Thank you, Miss.'

As they hurried from the stage, Charlotte put a tick beside Bill Brigham's name. The porter didn't realise it, but he might have saved the show.

Things took a dive again after that. As Charlotte listened to a succession of tedious monologues, tone-deaf singers and dismal comedy routines, she began to despair. The only one who didn't seem to mind was Miss Trott. She thumped away on the piano, smiling encouragingly at everyone, and behaving most unlike herself. Charlotte wondered if perhaps she had been on the medicinal brandy.

At last it was over. As she tidied away her papers, Charlotte's only satisfaction was that Miss Tanner was not there to tell her what a mess she was making of it all.

Much to her annoyance, Charlotte didn't even have the chance to admonish Miss Tanner for her absence the following morning. When she and Miss Fox arrived for their rounds, Miss Tanner said, 'Oh, Miss Davis, I'm so sorry I wasn't able to come to last night's rehearsal. As Philips probably told you, we had a late admission to the ward last night. Acute phlebitis. He was rather difficult to settle and I didn't want to leave him.'

'Really, Miss Tanner, I can hardly imagine how a case of phlebitis, acute or not, would have needed your full attention!' Charlotte retorted.

'Perhaps you'll understand when you meet him,' Miss Tanner said. 'Isaak Gruber is a German Jew. Until a few months ago, he was a

77

captive in a concentration camp. His family in England had all but given up on him until the camp was liberated and they received word that he was alive. They managed to get him out and bring him here.'

'How dreadful,' Miss Fox said. 'When you see the Pathé newsreels about those places, it hardly seems possible, does it? So much cruelty...' She shook her head. 'The poor man must be in a terrible state.'

'Actually, Matron, he may surprise you,' Miss Tanner said. 'You'd best come and see him for yourself.'

Isaak Gruber was lying flat on his back, holding a book above him so he could read. He was a small, elderly man, with thinning white hair and a gaunt, sallow face. He lay in the bed, his inflamed legs supported in a cradle for comfort.

'Dr Gruber, this is our matron, Miss Fox, and our assistant matron, Miss Davis,' Miss Tanner introduced them.

'Good morning.' He looked up at them over his spectacles, his eyes brown and inquisitive in a nest of wrinkles. He spoke in a heavy accent Charlotte knew well.

'Good morning, Dr Gruber,' Miss Fox smiled. 'How are you feeling today?'

'Very well, *danke*. Everyone is taking good care of me.'

'I'm very glad to hear it.' Miss Fox picked up his chart and studied it. 'May I say your English is very good.'

'I spent a great deal of time in London as a student.'

78

'And you're a doctor?'

'A psychiatrist. Or I was, until the Nazis took my patients away, and me with them.' He spoke calmly, his words carefully measured.

Charlotte looked down at the string of numbers etched into the delicate blueish skin inside his left forearm. They mesmerised her, holding her attention so she couldn't drag her eyes away.

She didn't realise she was staring until Dr Gruber tugged down his sleeve to cover them. Charlotte looked up sharply to meet his eye. He was regarding her curiously, his brows drawn in a frown.

It was a relief when they left his bedside and made their way around the rest of the ward. But as she followed Matron, Charlotte was aware of Dr Gruber's gaze tracking her down the ward.

Just as they were about to leave, Miss Tanner asked if she could speak to Matron in private.

'Certainly, Sister.' Miss Fox turned to Charlotte. 'Wait for me by the doors, Miss Davis. I shan't be a moment.'

'Perhaps I could go to the next ward, Matron, and make a start–'

'I asked you to wait for me, Miss Davis.' Miss Fox's voice was sharp.

Charlotte watched in annoyance as they retreated to Miss Tanner's office at the far end of the ward. What a complete waste of everyone's time for her to be left standing here like a child, she thought. They were probably only gossiping, anyway.

'Pardon me, *Schwester?*' She looked around. Dr Gruber was calling out to her, his hand raised. 'I

79

wonder – could you fetch my other book from my locker? I can't reach it myself.'

Charlotte looked around for one of the other nurses, but there was no one in sight. Reluctantly, she went over to his bedside and found the book. As she handed it back to him, she read the title.

Geisteskrankheit.

'Diseases of the mind,' she translated automatically.

'You speak German.' He didn't sound surprised.

Charlotte looked away. 'A few words,' she muttered.

'More than a few words, I think, if you can translate a medical textbook.' He ran his hand over the book cover. 'I thought perhaps you must have spent time in my country – when you recognised my number for what it was...'

'I didn't recognise anything,' Charlotte said, a little too quickly. 'I – I've read the newspapers, that's all.'

'Ah.' He rolled up his sleeve and studied the figures etched on his skin. 'It is the number they gave me in Buchenwald,' he said. 'That's where they sent us all. My wife, my children, my sisters... But I am the only one left now.' His voice was heavy with sadness.

'I'm sorry,' Charlotte said.

'I am one of the lucky ones,' he said. 'My family found out I was alive, and brought me here to live with them. Now every morning I wake up in a clean bed and I know I am safe and I thank God for his mercy. But there were so many months

80

when I didn't think I would see another day. The things they did to us there, the way we were forced to live, worse than animals–'

Bile rose in Charlotte's throat, making her cough.

'I am sorry,' Dr Gruber said. 'I did not wish to upset you. It is hard for some people to talk about, I know.'

She didn't like the way he was looking at her, those bright brown eyes so searching, as if they could see into her soul.

Much to Charlotte's relief, at that moment Miss Tanner and Matron emerged from her office. At least they could leave, and she could forget about Dr Gruber.

But that night she had another nightmare, as she feared she would. She tried to put off going to sleep for as long as she could, sitting up in bed reading until her eyes stung. Finally she had no choice but to put her book to one side and surrender to sleep.

That was when they came to her. The army of the dead. Picking through piles of bodies, finding the ones that were still breathing among the rotting corpses. The sickening stench of them, crammed in their huts, diseased, filthy with excrement and crawling with lice. They were pitiful, grotesque, their bodies so shockingly emaciated they barely looked human.

Charlotte woke up trembling, her face wet with tears, still trying to fight off the hands that grasped at her, eyes staring from gaunt faces, mouths open, pleading for help.

Schwester, schwester. Hilf mir. Help me.

81

She groped for the alarm clock. It was barely four, and still pitch dark outside. She rose and pulled on her dressing gown. She knew she would not sleep again. She did not dare.

She felt disappointed in herself. It had been so long since she'd had a nightmare, she had almost dared to hope that they had finally stopped. But last night's had been more vivid than ever.

During the following week, the night sister succumbed to a bad winter cold, and Miss Fox asked Charlotte to cover the night shifts for a few days.

'But there is another rehearsal tomorrow evening, Matron,' Charlotte said.

'Oh, I'm sure they can manage without you,' Miss Fox replied. 'Perhaps Miss Tanner could step into the breach, just this once?'

'I don't see how, when she wasn't at the last rehearsal–' Charlotte tried to protest, but Miss Fox wasn't listening to her as usual.

Very well, she thought. *Let her try to organise the rehearsal.* She would like to see even the perfect Miss Tanner coax a decent performance out of that raggle-taggle bunch of performers.

In a way, it was a relief to be on night duty. She had not been sleeping well, and it was good to have a reason to be awake. Charlotte enjoyed the peace and quiet as she toured the wards by torchlight, her soft shoes barely making a sound on the polished floors. In each ward, she would pause to speak to the night nurse and make sure all was well, their voices whispering in the dim light.

Nurse Wesley was on duty on Jarvis. She was a

young girl, still a year away from her Finals. But she was competent enough.

She had little to report about her patients, apart from Isaak Gruber, who was awake and restless.

'Why hasn't the doctor prescribed a sleeping draught for him?' Charlotte wanted to know.

'He has, but Dr Gruber refuses to take it,' Nurse Wesley said. 'Sister says not to force him, she reckons he's been through enough. And to be honest, he's quieter when he's awake than when he's asleep and screaming the place down.' She looked rueful. 'Sister's had him moved to one of the private rooms, so at least he won't disturb the other patients any more.' She looked at Charlotte. 'I don't know whether you'd have more luck persuading him, Assistant Matron?'

Charlotte had no desire to see Isaak Gruber. But the idea of being able to succeed where Miss Tanner hadn't was too tempting for her.

Dr Gruber was flat on his back, reading as usual. He looked up with a smile at Charlotte.

'*Schwester.*'

Charlotte lingered in the doorway, reluctant to step into the room. 'Nurse Wesley tells me you're not sleeping well?' she said.

He shook his head sadly. '*Nein.* Not for many months.'

'And yet you've refused to take the medicine the doctor prescribed for you?'

'I don't care to sleep, *Schwester.* It's too difficult for me. That's when they come, you see. When I see their faces.'

'Your family?'

'Sometimes. But to see them again is a com-

83

fort.' He smiled sadly. 'It is the others I fear. The dead, and the dying. So many of them, burying me so I can hardly claw my way out.' He shuddered. 'Night time is a dangerous time, *Schwester.*'

You don't have to tell me that, Charlotte thought. She was haunted by their faces too.

'*Schwester?*'

Charlotte looked up sharply. Isaak Gruber was staring straight at her. 'You have nightmares too, perhaps?' he ventured.

Charlotte pulled herself together, forcing a brisk smile. 'Goodness, what would I have nightmares about?'

'I don't know, *Schwester.*' He went on looking at her, his expression thoughtful, unnerving. 'But you seem like a sensitive soul. Someone who understands.'

Charlotte managed a smile. 'I've never been called sensitive before.'

'That is because you take great pains to hide it from others.'

Charlotte looked away, brushing down her apron. 'You should sleep,' she said. 'I can fetch you something else, if you won't take the sleeping draught. A warm drink, perhaps?'

'I would be happier with my book, if you don't mind?'

Charlotte glanced down at the weighty volume in his hands. 'More psychiatry?'

He nodded. 'I find it comforting.'

'Does it help you – to cope?'

'Sometimes. It is a comfort indeed to know that the mind can be healed.'

'Can it?' Charlotte spoke without thinking.

84

'If the body can be healed, why not the mind?'

'But how?' she asked. 'You can hardly put a splint or a dressing on it, can you?'

'*Nein, Schwester.* But like any injury, the mind needs time to heal. And you need to be able to clean out the infection, by opening up the wound.'

'Talking about it, you mean?' Dr Gruber nodded. 'And what good would that do, except to bring back all the pain?' She heard the bitterness in her voice.

'Sometimes the pain needs to be exposed, in order to get rid of it.'

'And sometimes it's better left where it is. In the past.'

'If only that were possible, *Schwester.* But in my experience infection only gets worse if you try to ignore it.' He smiled at her. 'Look at me. If I can learn to heal my wounds, then anyone can. You just have to ask for help.'

Charlotte caught his eye and looked away, sharply. 'You may read your book for another half an hour, but no-more,' she said, trying to recover her authority. 'I hope you manage to get some sleep, Mr Gruber.'

'You too, *Schwester,*' she heard him say softly as she closed the door.

As she made her way down to the maternity block to continue her round, she passed the doors to the dining room. From beyond them came the sound of a piano playing and voices singing.

Charlotte looked at her watch. It was past ten o'clock. If the rehearsals were still going on, then it could only mean Miss Tanner was struggling as badly as she had.

85

She couldn't resist sneaking a quick look. She pushed the door open a fraction, and peered through the crack.

Everyone was gathered around the piano, their voices all joined in a rousing rendition of 'We Wish You a Merry Christmas'. From the look of them, they were all enjoying themselves immensely.

And there, in the middle of it, was Miss Tanner, looking enormously pleased with herself as she played the piano.

Jealousy curdled in her stomach. Charlotte let the door shut, but the sound of the ward sister's easy laughter seemed to follow her, taunting her as she hurried away.

After a week, the night sister had recovered sufficiently to resume her duties, just in time for that week's rehearsal.

Everyone seemed rather disappointed to see Charlotte when she arrived in the dining hall.

'I thought Miss Tanner had taken over?' Miss Trott said, looking put out.

'Only last week,' Charlotte snapped. 'I am still in charge.'

She had hoped that after last week everyone might have improved. But if anything, it was an even bigger shambles than the first week. No one seemed to have prepared at all. Cues were missed, lines fluffed and words forgotten. Two student nurses who had always seemed so friendly were suddenly bickering between themselves, while the young doctor they were with was caught help-lessly in the middle.

'Really, I can't think what you did last week,'

86

Charlotte said, glaring at Miss Tanner. But the ward sister hardly seemed to hear her as she sat at the piano, staring vacantly into space. She looked as if she were a million miles away.

Charlotte was so exhausted from a week of night duties that her nerves and her patience were worn thin.

Even Bill Brigham, her star act, seemed to let her down. Or rather, his assistant did. When Peggy Atkins dropped a pack of cards for the third time, scattering them over the stage, Charlotte felt herself snap.

'Good lord, can't you do anything right?' she cried, as the woman scrambled about on the floor, trying to gather them up.

'It doesn't matter, Peg,' Bill Brigham jumped in loyally to defend her. Charlotte turned on him.

'Of course it matters! It needs to be perfect. If you can't understand that then you shouldn't be here!'

A stunned silence followed her words. All around her, she could feel the other performers exchanging uncomfortable looks.

Bill Brigham took Peggy Atkins' arm. 'Come on,' he said. 'We don't have to stand here just to be shouted at by the likes of her. This is supposed to be a daft show, not a Royal Command Performance!' He stomped off the stage, Peggy Atkins following behind.

Charlotte watched them go, consumed by white-hot rage.

They didn't understand, none of them did. This show had to be perfect, it had to be. It was her one chance to prove herself to Matron, and

87

no one was going to ruin it for her.

'Miss Davis–' Miss Tanner's voice broke the silence.

Charlotte whirled round to face her. 'Oh, I might have known you'd have something to say about it!' she snapped. 'Well, if you don't like the way I do things, you can go too!'

For a moment no one moved. Then, slowly, Miss Tanner lowered the lid over the piano keyboard, gathered up her music and stood up.

Charlotte watched her walk out of the room, her tall figure stiff with injured dignity. A moment later, Miss Trott followed her, sending Charlotte an accusing look over her shoulder.

Gradually, one by one, the others left, their heads down, shuffling out of the door. Charlotte watched them go, her spine straight, head held high. Now her white-hot rage had cooled, she suddenly felt very foolish.

Afterwards, she sat alone in the dining room and stared at the empty stage.

She blamed Miss Tanner. She must have turned their minds against her last week. She could just imagine her winning them all over to her side with her smiles and her charm.

Charlotte had no charm to fight back with, she knew that. She didn't know the right words to say, or how to smile her way out of trouble. All she had done was to try to get the job done as efficiently as she could.

It was all she had ever done.

That night they came to her again. This time she was trying to count the bodies, writing the num-

88

ber on the blackboard outside the tent for the artillery boys to collect them. But she kept getting it wrong, over and over again. And then the lorries came to take them away and dump them in the mass grave, and as they rumbled off Charlotte heard the groans of pain coming from the back, and knew she had got it wrong, that people would be dumped in the pit, buried alive among the diseased corpses, and it would all be her fault...

The following night she was in the human laundry, as they had called it. The vast tents, with their lines of trestle tables. The lines of emaciated naked bodies, some of them barely more than bags of bones, diseased and rotting and crawling with lice.

It was for their own good, she told herself as she shaved and scrubbed and sprayed them with DDT as if they were little better than animals. But still she couldn't look in their eyes.

She was just trying to get the job done, as efficiently as she could.

She had the same nightmare the next night, and the one after that. Every night she would wake herself up, sobbing and terrified. One night she cried out so loud that Sister Hyde knocked on her door to see if she was all right.

After that, Charlotte gave up sleeping. Instead she would sit up in the hard armchair in her room, staring out of the window into the wintry darkness to stop herself thinking.

All too soon, the week went by and the next rehearsal approached. Charlotte hoped that after her outburst the previous week people might have

89

decided to take the show more seriously. After all, there was only the dress rehearsal before their Christmas Day performance.

She was the first to arrive in the dining room as usual. She set out the chairs, laid out her papers, sat down and waited.

And waited.

Charlotte glanced at her watch. A quarter past six. Really, this was unacceptable. She would have to talk to them all again, she decided. Everyone needed to buckle down, start taking this show seriously.

By the time she heard the double doors creak behind her, she was too angry to turn around and face the latecomers.

'There you are!' she snapped. 'Really, if you can't be bothered to attend rehearsals on time–'

'No one is coming.'

Charlotte swung round in her seat at the sound of Miss Tanner's voice. 'I beg your pardon?' she said.

'No one is coming.' Miss Tanner stood in the doorway. 'They've all decided they don't want to take part in the show. And after the way you've treated them, I'm not surprised.'

Charlotte stared at her, nonplussed. 'But they can't do that! They have to take part–'

'You still don't understand, do you?' Miss Tanner sounded almost pitying, if Charlotte hadn't known better. 'They don't have to do anything, Miss Davis. You're not in the army now. You can't just give orders and expect people to obey them.'

Charlotte stared at Miss Tanner. There was something about the ward sister's calm face that

90

made her throat burn with rage.

'You're enjoying this, aren't you?' she accused.

Miss Tanner's brows rose. 'I beg your pardon?'

'It's what you wanted, isn't it? To ruin everything?'

'Why on earth would I want to ruin the Christmas show?'

'So you could make a fool of me, and prove to Matron that you're better than I am.'

Miss Tanner shook her head. 'You're being ridiculous. I came here to let you know what was happening because I didn't want you to sit here looking foolish. Now I wish I hadn't bothered!'

'I suppose it was your idea for them to walk out?'

Miss Tanner narrowed her eyes. 'You're not seriously suggesting I had anything to do with this?'

'Why not? You've been trying to undermine me ever since I came here! You think I haven't seen you cosying up to Matron, whispering together?'

'Miss Fox and I are friends—'

'Don't I know it!' Charlotte snapped. 'You want my job, don't you? You think you should have been made Assistant Matron. And because you weren't, you want to make a fool of me—'

'You're doing a very good job of making a fool of yourself!' Miss Tanner shot back. 'I tried to warn you, but as usual you wouldn't listen. You always think you know best.'

'You sabotaged me—'

'Oh, for goodness' sake! Do you really think all I have to think about is getting one over on you?' Miss Tanner's voice was full of exasperation. 'Believe me, some of us have more important things

91

to worry about than you and your wretched show!'

For the first time, Charlotte caught a glimpse of real pain in the other woman's eyes. She looked tired, she noticed. Her smile was gone, and there were lines of tension around her mouth.

She opened her mouth to speak, then closed it again.

'If you must know, I wanted to help you,' Miss Tanner said, more quietly. 'I felt sorry for you. I thought you could do with a friend–'

'I don't need a friend!' Charlotte spat back. 'And I don't need anyone's help, either.'

'That's where you're wrong, Miss Davis.'

Charlotte kept her back obstinately turned as she heard Miss Tanner leave, the door closing behind her.

She sank her head into her hands in despair. She didn't need help. She was strong, she was capable. She could deal with anything. She had proved that, hadn't she? Time and time again, going where the others didn't dare, doing all the jobs that no one else could. She was invincible. All she had to do was keep her head up, refuse to show weakness.

That's where you're wrong, Miss Davis.

She had another nightmare that night. This time she was alone, in the middle of a field. The lorry was there, stacked up with dead bodies, and she was trying to dig a mass grave, all alone with her bare hands. She woke to the sound of Major Hugh's voice.

Everyone needs a friend, Charlotte.

And then another voice, heavy with a German

accent. *You have to ask for help.*

She sat bolt upright in the darkness. Was it really that simple?

The hospital was in silence, slumbering in the middle of the night. The Night Sister had done her rounds and there was not a soul in the empty passageways as Charlotte made her way up to Jarvis ward.

Isaak Gruber was awake as usual. He looked up from the book he was reading by the dim light of the green shaded lamp. He didn't seem too surprised to see her.

'*Schwester,*' he said.

'I was there.' The words came out in a rush, terrified that if she stopped she might never say them. 'The day they liberated Bergen-Belsen.' She looked up at him. 'I need help,' she whispered.

Isaak Gruber nodded, as if this was something he had been expecting, and laid aside his book.

'I think you had better sit down and tell me everything, don't you?' he said kindly.

Violet

2nd December 1945

Violet came away from the first meeting with a sinking heart. It was just as she'd feared; Charlotte Davis was hopelessly out of her depth with this Christmas show. She might be able to make lists and organise rosters, but she didn't know the first thing about dealing with people.

Look at the way she'd spoken to her. All Violet had done was try to offer the girl some friendly advice, but Miss Davis had thrown it back in her face.

Well, if that was the way she wanted to behave, she couldn't expect any more help from her.

But irritated as she was, Violet still couldn't help feeling a twinge of compassion at the thought of Miss Davis standing there, so helpless and uncomprehending in the face of everything, clutching that wretched piece of paper like it was a lifeline.

Violet was on her way back up the stairs to Jarvis ward when Miss Trott caught up with her.

'Well?' she said. 'What did you think?'

'About what?' Violet replied, although she knew very well what the ward sister was talking about.

'The meeting, of course.' Then, before Violet had a chance to answer, she went on, 'She's going to make a terrible mess of it, don't you think? Anyone can see she's completely out of her depth. I must say, I'm surprised at Matron for giving her the job in the first place.'

So am I, Violet thought. 'I daresay she had her reasons,' she replied carefully.

Miriam shot her a scornful look. 'Trust you to be tactful, just because you and Miss Fox are such good friends. But I'm telling you, it will be a miracle if we even have a Christmas show, the way things are going.'

'It was only the first meeting,' Violet said. 'We shouldn't rush to judge anything.'

'Hmm.' Miriam Trott pursed her lips. 'Well,

I'm telling you now, I for one certainly won't be taking part if she continues to take that attitude. Did you see those dreadful songs on that list? As if anyone wants to hear that nonsense. What's wrong with "Lo, How a Rose E'er Blooming", that's what I want to know?'

'Well–'

'The Assistant Matron has no idea about the way we do things here,' Miriam continued. 'But that's hardly surprising, I suppose. I mean, it's not as if she's one of us, is she?'

Violet's skin prickled. 'One of us?' she said coldly.

'You know what I mean. She's barely been here a few months. She doesn't fit in.'

Violet stared at Miriam's prim little face, so full of spite. She knew only too well what it was like not to fit in. Ten years ago, when she had first arrived at the Nightingale, she was the one Miriam Trott regarded as an outsider. For months, the ward sister had made it her business to poke and pry about in her personal life.

'Perhaps we should wait and see what she comes up with?' she said. 'You never know, she might surprise us all.'

'I very much doubt it,' Miriam sniffed. 'You mark my words, this will all end in disaster.'

And no doubt you'll be there to clap your hands in glee when it does, Violet thought as she watched the ward sister's diminutive figure strutting off down the corridor. There was nothing Miriam Trott enjoyed more than watching someone else come a cropper.

But then, Miriam wasn't the only one who

95

wanted to see Charlotte Davis get her come-uppance. The girl didn't go out of her way to make friends, that was for sure.

She put Miss Davis from her mind as she changed out of her uniform and headed home. Unlike the other ward sisters, who mainly lived in, Violet rented a house in one of the few remaining terraces that looked over Victoria Park.

It was a cold, foggy night, and the street lamps barely pierced the gloom as Violet picked her way carefully along the wintry streets. It was a relief to reach Cheshire Street at last, and to see the welcoming light that blazed in the window of number three.

She paused for a moment, looking up at the house. She was lucky to have found such a nice place, especially when so many poor East Enders were having to make do in hastily constructed prefabs. Violet had thought they would have to do the same when they first returned from the sector hospital in Kent.

But then fate had brought her to Mrs Morgan's door.

Violet let herself into the narrow hallway, and was met by the warm, fragrant aroma of baking. She sniffed appreciatively, smelling cinnamon and spices.

'Is that you, Oliver?' Mrs Morgan emerged from the kitchen at the end of the passageway, wiping her hands on her pinny.

'No, Mrs M, it's me.' Violet unpinned her hat and set it on the hallstand. 'Terrible night, isn't it?'

'I'll say. I went down to Atkins' to buy some

96

ham earlier, and I'll be blowed if it didn't take me half an hour to get there and back. Could hardly see me hand in front of me face, the fog was that bad. Here, let me help you.' She took Violet's coat for her as she shrugged it off, and hung it up on the hallstand.

'You say Oliver isn't home yet?' Violet fought down a twinge of anxiety.

'Not yet. But the buses back from the city have been shocking. They've barely been crawling along in this fog. He'll find his way home soon, I'm sure.'

'You're right.' Violet forced herself to relax. She had spent so many years watching out for her son, keeping him safe, sometimes she forgot he was nearly a grown man, and no longer in need of her protection.

She sniffed the air appreciatively. 'Have you been baking, Mrs M?'

'I've made a start on the Christmas cake.'

'It smells delicious.'

'It will be.' Mrs Morgan looked proud. 'Atkins have managed to hold some stock in reserve for their most valued customers, so I'll be able to make something decent for once, instead of making do with grated carrots and prunes, and pretending it tastes the same. This will be the best Christmas we've had in years,' she beamed.

'I should think it will,' Violet agreed. 'Heavens knows, we've waited for it long enough.'

'You're right there, ducks. Now, you go in and warm yourself by the fire, and I'll bring you a nice cup of tea. How does that sound?'

'Bliss. You're a gem, Mrs M.'

A blush rose in Mrs Morgan's cheeks. 'Oh, get

97

on with you! I'm just happy to make myself useful.'

Mrs Morgan had proved herself more than useful. She was a widow whose two sons had been killed during the war, one in North Africa and one in the D-Day landings. The house was too big for her on her own, so she rented half of it to Violet and Oliver.

'I'd only rattle around in it by myself!' she had told her cheerfully, as she had shown her round. 'It'll be lovely to have some company.'

Over the months Mrs Morgan had become more than just Violet's landlady. She cooked for them, and kept house while Violet went to work. Violet knew that Mrs Morgan appreciated having them around, especially Oliver, who had become almost a replacement for her own son.

They had become a little family, the three of them in their warm, cosy house. For the first time in a long while, Violet was beginning to feel as if she had found a real home at last.

'Oh, I nearly forgot. Another one of them solicitor's letters came for you,' Mrs Morgan called out from the kitchen. 'I put it on the mantelpiece.'

'So I see,' Violet sighed. She didn't need to open it to know what it would say. She had not been in touch with Victor's solicitors since his death ten years earlier. But with Oliver about to turn eighteen, they had taken to writing to her every month, reminding her about his inheritance and urging her to get in touch.

So far Violet had ignored them. She knew she would have to address the matter soon, but she

98

could not bring herself to do it. It would mean unearthing all kinds of memories she did not want to think about.

She plucked it from the mantelpiece and turned it over in her hands. The letter seemed fatter than usual. What else had they found to say? she wondered.

She tore it open and pulled out the letter, hardly bothering to read the neatly typed words. But this time there was something else tucked inside. Another letter, smaller and handwritten.

Apprehension crawled up Violet's spine as she unfolded it and saw the familiar flowing writing on the envelope. Even after nearly fourteen years, she would know her mother's hand anywhere.

She hesitated, wondering whether to open it, but then she noticed the name on the front of the letter.

It was addressed to Oliver.

'I'm home!'

Just at that moment the front door banged, startling her. Violet hastily stuffed the letter into her pocket and turned to greet her son as he came in, bringing a gust of cold air from the street with him.

She could never look at Oliver without feeling a huge swell of pride. It hardly seemed like a couple of years since he was a little boy, and now he was a young man. A handsome one too, with her height and dark colouring.

Or so it seemed to anyone else. Only Violet noticed the way his black hair grew in a widow's peak like Victor's, and how his intense dark eyes resembled his father's.

99

She pushed away the thought. Oliver might look like his father, and he had the same quick mind and fierce intelligence. But that was where the similarity ended. Violet had made sure of that. She had worked hard to bring him up as a kind, caring young man, to give him the compassion his father had lacked.

But it was still hard to look into those eyes and not feel a shiver sometimes.

'Hello, Ma.' Oliver leaned forward and planted a noisy kiss on her cheek. Violet pushed him away, laughing.

'Get off, you're freezing!'

'I'm not surprised. The bus gave up halfway up the Mile End Road and we had to walk the rest of the way.'

'Never mind, you're home now. Sit down by the fire and get warm. Mrs Morgan's just brewing up a pot of tea.'

'Sorry, I can't stop. I'm supposed to be meeting some friends, and I'm late as it is.' He hurried into the hall, shedding his coat, hat and scarf as he went.

Violet followed him. 'Where are you going?'

'To the dance hall.' He blushed as he said it. His new-found interest in girls was something he found hard to admit. 'I need to get changed and then I'm off.'

'What time will you be home?'

'Not late, I promise.'

'Oliver, wait. A letter came–' Violet started to say, but he was already thudding up the stairs.

Mrs Morgan emerged from the kitchen with a tea tray. 'Someone's in a hurry,' she commented.

'He's going out.'

Mrs Morgan smiled affectionately. 'I wish I had half his energy. He don't stop still for more than a minute, does he?'

'No, he doesn't.' Violet managed to smile back. But all she could think about was the letter still burning a hole in her pocket.

It would have to wait until the morning, she decided.

But the following morning came, and Oliver was still asleep when Violet left for the hospital, so the letter remained locked away in the bureau drawer.

It stayed on her mind all morning, occupying her thoughts. And when Matron and Miss Davis arrived for their ward round, for once Violet was too preoccupied to notice the Assistant Matron's carping, or her endless fault-finding.

Until they reached the bedside of a bronchitis patient, and Miss Davis took great delight in pointing out that his temperature had not been filled in on the hour as it should have been.

'See for yourself.' Violet could only stare at the chart Miss Davis thrust under her nose.

'I don't understand,' she murmured.

'I do,' Miss Davis said. 'Someone made a mistake, and you didn't notice it. It's as simple as that.'

Out of the corner of her eye she could see the distraught face of student nurse Philips, chewing her lip.

'I suppose I must have done,' she said quietly.

She saw Miss Fox's reproachful look and shame washed over her. How could she be so careless? It

101

wasn't even Miss Davis's smug expression that bothered her; it was the fact that she had been so absorbed in her own problems she had neglected her duties.

She wasn't surprised when, after the round, Miss Fox said quietly, 'Would you come to my office and see me later, Sister?'

'Yes, Matron. Of course.' Violet could hardly meet Kathleen's eye. They might be friends outside the hospital, but as Matron she would not tolerate mistakes. Friends or not, she would not hesitate to tear Violet off a strip if she thought she had let down a patient.

Nurse Philips approached her after they had gone. 'I'm sorry, Sister,' she said. 'I was the one who made the mistake. Should I go to Matron and tell her it was my fault?'

Violet shook her head. The poor girl looked near to tears. 'It was my responsibility to make sure it was done correctly,' she said. 'I'll take the consequences. But you must make sure it never happens again,' she warned.

'Yes, Sister. I swear I'll check it properly next time.'

Violet was heavy-hearted when she stood outside Miss Fox's office half an hour later. She felt like a silly probationer, on report for breaking a thermometer. And just to make it worse, Miss Davis seemed to be enjoying every minute. She pretended to be absorbed in some paperwork or other, but Violet could feel the Assistant Matron watching her avidly from behind her desk.'

By the time Miss Fox called out, 'Enter,' Violet's hand was so clammy with nerves she could barely grip the doorknob to let herself in.

Kathleen looked up, smiling. 'Ah, Sister, do sit down–'

'I'm sorry,' Violet blurted out. 'I made a mistake and I only have myself to blame for it. I wasn't concentrating on what I was doing, and there is no excuse for that. All I can do is promise it won't happen again–'

'I'm sure it won't.' Kathleen's voice was gentle. 'You're an excellent nurse, Violet, and it's not like you to make a mistake like that. Which is why I called you here.' She steepled her fingers and looked at Violet consideringly over the top of them. 'What's going on?' she asked

Violet blinked. 'I'm sorry, Matron, I don't understand–'

'There's clearly something troubling you, and it's affecting your work. I would like to know what it is.' She smiled. 'I'm asking you as your friend, not as your matron,' she said.

Violet was about to deny everything but then she looked into Kathleen's warm grey eyes and realised how much she needed her friend's good advice.

'I've had a letter from my mother,' she said. 'Or rather, Oliver has.'

'I see.' Kathleen sat back in her seat. She was one of the first people Violet had dared to share her story with when she came to the Nightingale, so she understood what the letter meant. 'What does she say?'

'I don't know, I haven't given it to him yet.'

Kathleen's face was calm and composed, framed by her starched white headdress. But Violet could

103

see the deep thought in her eyes. 'How long is it since you've been in contact with her?'

'Nearly fourteen years.'

'It must be strange to hear from her again after so long.'

Strange was one way of putting it, Violet thought. She had lain awake all night, going over what had happened between her and her mother, reliving their argument and the rift that had grown between them.

'Why has she written now, I wonder?' Kathleen mused.

'I don't know.' She had been asking herself the same question, and she still hadn't come up with an answer.

'Perhaps she wants to build some bridges between you?'

'After fourteen years?' Violet couldn't stop her bitterness spilling out. 'Anyway,' she said, 'she wrote to Oliver, not me. I'm not the one she wants to build bridges with.'

She knew that after all these years she shouldn't be hurt by it, but it still felt as if her mother was rejecting her all over again.

'What are you going to tell Oliver?' Kathleen asked.

'I don't know.' That was something else that preoccupied her. 'He knows we had a disagreement years ago, and we haven't spoken to each other since. That's the truth, after all.'

'But you haven't told him why it happened?'

'How could I?' If she tried to explain then she would have to tell him the truth about his father. And she couldn't do that. Whatever happened,

104

Oliver must never know the kind of man Victor really was.

'So are you going to give the letter to him?'

Violet sighed. 'I suppose I'll have to. It is addressed to him, after all.' But even as she said it, she felt a pang of anxiety. Why had her mother decided to appear now, just as she had found some kind of peace in her life at last?

As if she could read her thoughts, Kathleen said, 'I'm sure you don't need to worry, Violet.'

Violet forced a smile. Kathleen might be a very wise woman and a kind friend, but she would never understand how deeply Dorothy Tanner had hurt her.

'I know,' she said. 'I'm worrying over nothing, I'm sure. I'll give Oliver the letter and see what happens.'

As they left the office, Miss Fox asked, 'How did the first Christmas show meeting go?'

Violet hesitated. 'Why do you ask?'

'Sister Wren came to see me first thing this morning.'

'And?'

'She was rather more forthcoming than you,' Kathleen said ruefully.

'I daresay she would be,' Violet said. Trust Miriam Trott to go rushing to Matron, trying to make trouble.

'Was it as bad as she makes out?' Kathleen asked.

Once again, Violet paused, trying to choose her words carefully. 'Miss Davis has a – different way of doing things. It's bound to upset a few people.'

'It's upset Miss Trott, that's for sure.' Kathleen

105

shook her head. 'I can see I shall have to keep a close eye on our Assistant Matron. I notice she's put a rather odd list up on the wall this morning. I wonder what that's all about?'

'You'd better ask Miss Davis that.'

'Oh, I will. Don't you worry.' Violet spotted the light of battle in Kathleen Fox's eyes.

'Why did you give her the job?' The question had been troubling Violet ever since Miss Davis had waved the piece of paper under her nose so triumphantly the previous day.

'I thought it would be interesting for her,' Kathleen replied. 'She strikes me as the kind of young woman who likes a challenge.'

'And is that the only reason?'

'What other reason would there be?'

Violet looked into her friend's blandly smiling face and realised she had been mistaken to suspect her. Kathleen Fox would never be cruel or devious enough to set someone up to fail. Or would she?

As Kathleen followed her from the office, she said, 'Now, remember what I said, won't you? I'm always here, if you need to speak to me.'

'Thank you, Matron.' Violet caught Miss Davis's eye, and saw her coldly furious expression. If it wasn't such an absurd notion, she could have sworn the Assistant Matron was jealous.

As she walked away and closed the door behind her, she could already hear Miss Fox bringing up the subject of the Christmas show. Poor Miss Davis, she thought. She hoped for her own sake she managed to get a grip on the matter before too long.

106

Her earlier mistake with the patient's notes forced her to focus her mind on her work for the rest of the day. But try as she might to ignore them, Violet could feel her anxieties about her mother's letter encroaching on her thoughts. In spite of what she had said to Kathleen, she was worried. She had worked so hard to make a good life for herself and Oliver. All the hardships they had faced over the past years had forged a close bond between them.

And now she was afraid her mother would come along and ruin everything.

When Oliver came home that evening, Violet was waiting with the letter.

'This came for you yesterday.' She handed it to him, trying hard to sound casual. 'It's from your grandmother.'

'My grandmother?' His gaze flew to hers, full of concern. 'Why is she writing to me?'

Why indeed, Violet thought. She forced a smile. 'You'd better read it and find out, hadn't you?'

She watched as he tore the envelope open. Her mouth was as dry as sand as he read through it, his dark eyes moving swiftly over the lines. She watched him closely, trying to guess what thoughts were going through his mind.

Finally he stopped reading. 'Well?' Violet said.

He held it out to her. 'You can read it yourself, if you like.'

It was all she could do to stop herself shrinking back from the piece of paper in his hand. 'She wrote to you, not me.'

Oliver scanned through the letter again. 'She

107

says she misses me, and thinks about me all the time,' he said. 'She says she's never forgotten me.'

Does she mention me? Violet pressed her lips together to stop herself speaking out loud. She hated herself for even thinking the question. What did it matter to her whether her mother ever thought of her? Besides, Dorothy Tanner had made her contempt for her very clear the last time they had come face-to-face.

'Is that all she says?' she asked.

Oliver hesitated. 'She says she'd like to see me.'

Violet felt a lurch in her chest. 'And is that what you want?'

'I don't know. What do you think?'

She wanted to snatch the letter from his hands, throw it on the fire and never have to think about her mother again. But somehow she managed to hold back her feelings. 'You're a man now,' she said. 'It's your decision, not mine.'

'But I don't want to do anything to upset you.' Suddenly he looked like a little boy again, his dark eyes vulnerable. He glanced down at the letter. 'Besides, I hardly remember her.'

'You don't have to make up your mind now,' Violet said. 'Why don't you think about it?'

'I will.'

A week went by, and Oliver said no more about his grandmother's letter. He might have forgotten about it, but Violet was still troubled. It took all her will to concentrate on her work, and the forthcoming Christmas show.

But she missed the first of the rehearsals, thanks to the arrival of a new admission on Jarvis

108

ward, just as they were due to begin.

Isaak Gruber arrived with a bossy little woman, who introduced herself as his cousin. She instantly tried to take charge, and no amount of gentle but firm persuasion from Violet could budge her from Dr Gruber's side.

'Gerte, the nurse is too polite to tell you she wants you to leave, so I will have to do it for her,' Isaak Gruber said. 'You will have to excuse Gerte, she does like to think she knows best,' he added with a sigh to Violet.

'You need someone to take care of you, Isaak,' Gerte insisted. 'After everything you've been through—'

'After everything I've been through, you think I'm going to be upset by a hospital like this?' Isaak Gruber peered at her over his spectacles. 'Look around you, Gerte. Look at the *schwester* here. I will be quite safe here, I assure you. So go back to fussing over your husband and your children, and allow these people to look after me for once.'

Gerte still looked fretful. But at least Violet managed to convince her to go off and have a cup of tea, with the promise that she could return and check on her cousin later.

Dr Gruber sighed with relief when she had gone. 'Dear Gerte,' he said. 'I am a lucky man to have such family as hers, but sometimes...' He shook his head in regret.

Violet had just finished supervising the other nurses in setting up the cradle for Isaak Gruber's leg when Tom Armstrong, the junior registrar, arrived to examine him.

109

He confirmed the man's swollen limb was a result of phlebitis, an inflammation of the vein.

'Ah yes,' Dr Gruber nodded wisely. 'I have had this before. A result of typhoid fever, I believe.'

'Good lord!' Tom Armstrong said. 'We haven't had a case of typhoid in the hospital for years. Have we, Sister?'

'No, Sir.'

'Then you are fortunate indeed,' Isaak Gruber said. 'There was barely a soul in Buchenwald who did not suffer from it. Of course, we had no medical care then. We survived, or we died.' He gave them a weary smile. 'My wife and my children died.'

Violet looked at Dr Armstrong's stunned face and realised they were thinking the same thing.

Buchenwald. Violet had seen the Pathé newsreels and read the newspapers, but no matter how much evidence she'd encountered, she could not imagine the horror she had seen was real, that there were people who were capable of committing such cruelty to their fellow human beings.

The young doctor pulled himself together. 'Give him fomentations for the pain. Glycerin of belladonna. And of course, plenty of rest, no sitting up and no excitement.'

'Yes, Doctor.'

'Do you have trouble sleeping?' Dr Armstrong asked the man.

Isaak Gruber shook his head. 'I do not sleep,' he said.

'Then I'll prescribe a sleeping draught–'

'*Nein, Herr Doktor*, I would rather not, if you

110

don't mind?' His voice was polite but firm. 'I prefer not to sleep, as I suffer from nightmares. I am worried I may disturb the other patients.'

Dr Armstrong looked at Violet. 'What do you think, Sister?'

Violet read the silent plea in the young man's eyes. Junior doctors often looked to the ward sisters for help and advice. It wasn't until they had reached the lofty heights of senior consultant that they decided they knew everything.

She glanced at Isaak Gruber's worried face. 'I believe it might cause Dr Gruber unnecessary agitation if we try to give him something he doesn't want to take,' she said. 'Perhaps you could prescribe a sleeping draught just in case, on the understanding that we only administer it if it's strictly necessary?'

'Good idea.' Dr Armstrong looked relieved. 'I'll write out a prescription, and you inform the night staff.'

'Yes, Sir.'

As they walked away from the bed, Dr Armstrong said, 'Well, Sister, what do you think of him? I bet the old man has quite a story to tell, don't you?'

'Indeed, Doctor. But he really isn't that old. Just turned fifty according to his notes.'

'Really? I could have sworn he was much older than that.' Dr Armstrong let out a low whistle. 'I suppose that's what being locked up in one of those filthy places does to you.'

'Yes, Sir.'

They stopped at the ward desk so Dr Armstrong could write a prescription. As he pulled out his pen, a tangled knot of coloured silk handkerchiefs fell from his pocket and rolled across the floor.

'Oh, leave them,' Dr Armstrong said carelessly, as Violet went to retrieve them. 'I won't be needing them any more, anyway.' He looked rueful. 'They were for my magic act, for the Christmas show,' he explained. 'But I made rather a mess of it.'

'Oh dear.'

'I fell to pieces under the Assistant Matron's steely gaze,' he sighed.

'I understand she has that effect on some people,' Violet said.

'Anyway, it looks as if my performing days are over. I don't suppose Miss Davis will give me another chance.'

'Perhaps you should consider a new act?' Violet suggested.

His handsome face, lit up. 'Perhaps I could. It's worth thinking about, at any rate.' He grinned at her. 'Thank you, Sister. Perhaps my stage career might not be over after all?'

He went off, humming to himself, considerably cheered up. Violet smiled after him. He was a brave man if he was willing to step into the lion's den and put himself in front of Miss Davis a second time.

She waited until Nurse Wesley took over the night shift, so she could instruct her properly on Dr Gruber's case. Then she stayed a while longer to make sure he was as settled as he could be, before finally making her way home.

Oliver was waiting for her.

112

'Mrs Morgan's gone to bed, but she left you some supper on the stove,' he said. 'I'll fetch it for you, shall I?'

'Bless you, that's very kind. But I'll eat it in the kitchen, it'll be warmer in there. I thought you were going out dancing again tonight?' She carried her plate carefully over from the stove to the table.

'I changed my mind. I wanted to speak to you.'

'Oh yes? That sounds rather ominous!' She smiled across the table at him.

Oliver didn't return her smile. He said nothing for a moment, staring down at his fingers as they tangled and untangled themselves in front of him. Then he said, 'I've decided to meet her.'

Violet stopped, her fork halfway to her mouth. Her heart plunged in despair, but she forced herself to stay calm. 'I see.'

He looked up at her. 'You don't mind, do you?'

'It's your decision, my love.'

'I know, but – I don't want to upset you,' he said.

Then don't go, Violet wanted to say.

She looked at his earnest face. He was such a wonderful, good-hearted young man. She had brought him up that way, to care deeply about other people's feelings.

She forced her fork to her mouth, even though her appetite had quite gone. 'You must do as you think best,' she said.

'You could come with me?'

'No!' The word came out too quickly.

'Why not?'

Violet took a calming breath. 'It's you she wants

113

to see, not me.'

He paused. 'Why did you stop speaking to her?' he asked. 'I keep wondering about it.'

Violet opened her mouth, then closed it again. 'I told you, it was something and nothing,' she said finally. 'A stupid disagreement that got out of hand.'

'Was it about my father?'

Violet stared at him. 'Why do you ask that? Has she said anything to you?'

He shrugged. 'I thought there must be a reason why you two stopped speaking. I wondered if she disapproved of you marrying him?'

Violet nearly laughed. *If only you knew,* she thought. But she would never tell him. 'No,' she said. 'Your grandmother liked your father very much.'

'Then why–'

'Oliver, I'm too tired to talk about this,' Violet cut him off. 'Do you think we could discuss it another time?'

'Of course.' Oliver stood up, pushing his chair back with a clatter. 'I'll go upstairs and leave you to your supper. Goodnight, Mother.'

He never called her mother, except when he was in a bad mood. He didn't kiss her either, something he had done every night since he was a baby.

'Oliver?'

He turned back to face her. 'Yes?'

'You mustn't – expect too much of your grandmother.'

He frowned. 'What do you mean?'

Violet paused, trying to choose her words carefully. 'I mean she can be a rather selfish woman. If she's got in touch with you, then it's probably because she wants something from you.'

'Like what?'

'I don't know.' Violet had her suspicions, but she didn't want to share them with her son. 'Just be careful, that's all.'

Oliver's frown deepened, his dark brows lowering. 'Perhaps she's changed?'

Violet shook her head. 'She'll never do that. Believe me, my mother always thinks she is right.'

'Perhaps you're more alike than you think,' Oliver said.

'Oliver!' She tried to call him back as he left the room, but either he couldn't hear her or he chose not to.

She stared down at her plate of food, all her hunger gone. Tension knotted her stomach, making it impossible to eat.

She could already feel her son slipping away from her. The close bond between them was coming loose, and it was all her mother's fault. How long before she managed to drive a wedge between them, just as Victor had tried to do?

The following day, Violet waited until Kathleen had finished her rounds, then asked to speak to her in private. Miss Davis didn't look too happy about it, but Violet was too anxious to care about the Assistant Matron's petty jealousies.

Once they were in her office, Kathleen said, 'What is it? Is it one of the patients?'

Violet shook her head. 'I'm sorry to trouble you with my personal problems, but it's this business

115

with my mother. Oliver's decided he wants to meet her.'

'I see. And what did you say?' Kathleen asked.

'What could I say? I can't very well stop him, can I?' Violet muttered.

'And would you want to?'

'I'm sure I don't care either way.'

Kathleen gave her a wise smile. 'Are you certain about that?'

'What do you mean?'

'I mean, if you're that indifferent about it, why are you so worried?'

Violet frowned. She had expected Kathleen to be as shocked and outraged as she felt. Her friend knew everything Dorothy Tanner had done to her, after all.

But all she said was, 'Perhaps it would be for the best if you both met her?'

Violet fought hard to control her anger. 'And how do you work that out?'

'You've been angry with her for a long time, and I'm sure it can't be good for you. If you saw her again, perhaps—'

'I don't want to see her again!' Violet snapped. 'And you're right, I really don't want Oliver to see her, either.'

Kathleen nodded, as if that was the answer she had been expecting. 'And why is that?'

'Because I don't trust her. I'm worried she'll hurt him.'

'Or are you worried she'll hurt you again?'

Violet lifted her chin. 'She can't hurt me any more. She can't,' she insisted, seeing the sceptical look on her friend's face. 'I don't care enough to

116

let her affect me any more. I just don't want Oliver to feel let down, that's all.'

Kathleen just gave another of her infuriatingly wise smiles. 'If you say so,' she said.

But as the days went by, it seemed as if she might be worrying over nothing. Oliver didn't mention visiting his grandmother again, and Violet began to relax.

In the meantime, Kathleen asked her to take over the Christmas show rehearsal while Miss Davis was covering the night sister's duties.

'What does Miss Davis say about that?' Violet asked.

'Miss Davis doesn't have much say in the matter,' Kathleen replied, with a hint of a smile. 'Do see if you can knock them into some kind of shape, Violet. I must say, I'm getting rather worried about this show.'

But Violet could see no reason for Matron to fear. Without Miss Davis's endless criticism and sour looks, everyone seemed to relax and enjoy themselves. Violet was able to enjoy herself too as she played the piano, laughed at the skits and tapped her feet to the songs. Even Mr Hopkins' chosen recitation didn't seem too dreary for once. And they finished the evening with a rousing chorus of 'We Wish You a Merry Christmas'.

Violet was still humming to herself when she returned home, tired but happy.

'Cooee,' she called out as she shrugged off her coat. 'I'm home, Mrs Morgan. Put the kettle on, would you, I'm parched–' She stopped as Mrs Morgan herself appeared in the kitchen doorway,

117

wringing her hands. Even in the gloom of the hallway, Violet could see the strained look on her face. 'Why, Mrs M, whatever is the matter?' she asked.

Mrs Morgan nodded towards the living-room door. 'You've got a visitor, ducks,' she said in a low voice.

Violet frowned. 'Who? It's a bit late for visitors, surely–'

She walked in and stopped dead when she saw the woman sitting in the armchair beside the fire.

'Hello, Violet,' said Dorothy Tanner.

Violet was shocked at how much her mother had aged in the last fourteen years. She was still as elegant as ever, done up to the nines in a smart green coat with a fox-fur collar. But the hair under her neat hat was quite white, and the powder on her carefully made-up face had settled into a network of lines around her eyes and mouth.

Even so, there was still a self-possessed air about her that made Violet's hackles rise.

'What are you doing here?' she demanded.

Oliver stood up. 'I asked her to come,' he said with a touch of defiance. 'I thought it would be a good idea for you two to meet after all this time.'

'Oh, you did, did you?' Violet stared at her son. Blood surged, ringing in her ears. Between him and her mother, she felt cornered, like an animal.

Her mother rose to her feet. 'I'm sorry,' she said. 'I didn't realise... Oliver told me you were expecting me...'

'No,' Violet said. 'No, I wasn't expecting you.'

'I suppose I'd better go–'

'I think that would be best.'

118

'No! You don't have to leave, Grandmother.' Oliver faced Violet. 'I want her to stay.'

Violet recognised his father in his blazing eyes. Oliver had never spoken to her in that tone before. Fear clenched her stomach. Her mother had come, and she had brought Victor Dangerfield's spirit with her.

'If your mother doesn't want me here–' Dorothy Tanner started to say. Violet turned on her.

'Oh no, of course you must stay, if that's what Oliver wants!' She spat out the words.

Just at that moment Mrs Morgan came in with a tea tray, breaking the tension.

'Here you are, ducks,' she said. Violet noticed the wary look she gave Dorothy Tanner as she set the tray down.

'Thank you, Mrs M.' Mrs Morgan turned back towards the door, but Violet called her back. 'Won't you join us?'

'Well, I–' Mrs Morgan shot a quick look at Dorothy. 'I wouldn't want to intrude if you've got company?'

'Nonsense, I insist.' Violet pleaded with her silently. She badly needed an ally. Left alone with Oliver and her mother, she wasn't sure what she would do.

Fortunately, Mrs Morgan seemed to understand her unspoken terror. She seated herself with an uneasy smile at Dorothy Tanner.

Violet's mother said nothing, but her mouth was pressed into a tight line of disapproval.

The atmosphere was tense around the tea table. Oliver and his grandmother made stilted conversation. Mrs Morgan did her best to join in

119

where she could, while Violet stared into the flames of the fire and remained obstinately silent. She knew she was acting like a sulky child but she couldn't help herself. It was late, she was tired and she wanted to go to bed. Besides, she hadn't asked Dorothy Tanner to come here, and she had no intention of making her welcome. The sooner she left, the better.

But all the while, the sound of her mother's voice unnerved her, bringing back memories. Her laughter made Violet think of happier times, before Victor came into her life, when she had been secure in her mother's love. She had to keep reminding herself over and over what Dorothy had done, how she had treated her. Anything to keep up the barrier between them.

'You have a lovely house, Violet,' her mother made another attempt at conversation, looking round her. 'Really quite charming.'

'It belongs to Mrs Morgan,' Violet replied sullenly, not looking at her. 'We needed somewhere to live when we came back to London, and she was kind enough to take us in,' she added, hoping the point was not lost on her mother.

Mrs Morgan waved away the compliment. 'I like having the company,' she said.

'You should have seen some of the places we've had to live in over the years,' Violet went on. She saw her mother wince but she wanted to hurt her. 'Filthy hovels, some of them, with bugs crawling up the walls and neighbours stealing from us. Oliver used to suffer terribly with bronchitis every winter because of the damp. One year he even ended up in hospital. We weren't sure if he would

120

even survive, his chest was so bad.'

'I'm sorry to hear that,' her mother said stiffly, not meeting her eye.

'Are you?' Violet said. 'Are you really?'

'Mother!' Oliver protested.

'Where do you live, Mrs Tanner?' Mrs Morgan interrupted them.

'Over the river in Camberwell.'

'Camberwell, eh? Very nice,' Mrs Morgan commented approvingly. 'You've got lodgings there, have you?'

'Actually, I'm a live-in housekeeper for a well-to-do family.'

'Fancy that. Did you hear that, Violet?'

'Only the best for my mother,' Violet murmured.

Her mother turned to her. 'Like you, I was lucky to find somewhere,' she said. 'My house was bombed during the Blitz.'

'Bombed out, eh? That was bad luck,' Mrs Morgan said.

'I was out shopping at the time. Queuing up to buy fish, would you believe? If there hadn't been such a long wait I might have been in the house when it happened.'

'Well, bless me! So shortages had their good side, after all!' Mrs Morgan chuckled. 'Did you hear that, Violet? Lucky thing, wasn't it?'

Violet stared back at her. What was wrong with them all? Even Mrs Morgan seemed to have fallen under her mother's spell.

'My mother always falls on her feet,' she muttered.

Mrs Morgan picked up the teapot. 'This is

121

empty,' she said. 'I'll make us a fresh pot, shall I? Oliver, love, help me with the tray, will you? Give your mum and your gran a chance to have a talk properly.'

Violet watched them go, seized with panic. She caught Mrs Morgan's eye as she closed the door behind them. *Talk to her,* her look said.

But that was easier said than done. Fourteen years and a chasm of bitterness lay between them.

Violet went on staring at the door long after it had closed, unable to bring herself to look at her mother.

Dorothy cleared her throat. 'Oliver is a fine young man,' she said quietly.

'Yes,' Violet said. 'Yes, he is.'

'He was telling me he has a place at Oxford next year, to study medicine? He must take after his father–'

'No!' Violet turned on her, angrily. 'No, he doesn't take after his father. I've made sure of that.'

Her mother looked taken aback. 'I'm sorry, I didn't mean–'

'I don't care what you meant. Don't even speak that man's name in this house.'

'I – I beg your pardon.' Dorothy retreated into hurt silence.

Violet turned to her, her tension spilling over. 'Why have you come, Mother?' She voiced the question that had been preying on her mind night after night.

Her mother blinked at her. 'I wanted to see you,' she said, her voice faltering. 'It's been such a long time...'

122

'Nearly fourteen years,' Violet said. 'All that time without a single word from you, and now suddenly you're interested in us. Why is that, I wonder? It wouldn't be anything to do with Oliver's inheritance, would it?'

Her mother's face was blank. 'What inheritance?'

'Don't pretend you don't know! Oliver stands to inherit Victor's estate once he turns eighteen, in two months' time.'

Dorothy shook her head. 'I didn't know ... supposed you must have inherited it, as his widow?'

'He tried to leave it to me, but I didn't want it. I told the solicitor to give it all to Oliver, that I didn't want anything to do with him or his wretched estate.' Violet curled her lip. 'Unlike you, I've never been interested in Victor's money.'

Dorothy frowned. 'You really think that's why I'm here? Because I'm after Oliver's inheritance?'

'Why not? You've always been obsessed with Victor's wealth. That's why you pushed me into marrying him in the first place!'

Her mother stared at her. 'I didn't push you. You were in love–'

'I was young and naïve. But foolish as I was, even I soon realised what kind of man he was. I wanted to call off the wedding, but you wouldn't let me.'

'I thought you were just being silly,' Dorothy said. 'I know Victor could be – difficult – sometimes, but he was a good man. I knew he would look after you–'

'Look after me? Do you want to know how well he looked after me?' Violet rolled up her sleeve.

123

'Look,' she said, proffering her arm. 'This is what he did to me. This is how good a man he was!'

The scar had faded over the years, the once livid flesh now pale and puckered. But there was no mistaking what it was.

Dorothy stared at it. 'Victor did that?'

'He held my arm to the fire when I dared to answer him back,' Violet said matter-of-factly, ignoring her mother's appalled expression. 'But that wasn't the worst thing he ever did to me. Oh no, he did much worse than that. He broke my bones, dragged me downstairs by my hair, smashed my head against the wall until I passed out. And he raped me. Night after night, he pinned me down and forced me to–'

'Don't!' Dorothy begged her. 'Please ... I don't want to hear it.'

'Of course you don't,' Violet said derisively. 'You didn't want to hear it then, either. When I came to you and begged you for help, when I told you I wanted to leave him, you closed the door on me. You told me to go back to him!'

'I didn't know!' Her mother's voice was raw with pain. 'You only said you wanted to leave. You didn't tell me he – he–'

'How could I? I could barely admit if to myself that the man I loved was a violent monster. But you should have trusted me, you should have listened...'

That was what hurt, more than anything Victor had ever inflicted on her. That her mother had taken his word over hers, that she had not believed her own daughter.

'I know.' The words came out as barely a

124

whisper. At first Violet wondered if she had heard them.

But then her mother turned to her, and Violet saw her eyes were shimmering with tears.

'I let you down,' she said quietly. 'You're right, I should have trusted you. I should have listened, protected you. But I didn't. I thought you were being foolish. I didn't know what was going on in your marriage, truly I didn't. All I knew was you telling me you wanted to leave your husband and go off on your own. It made no sense to me why you should want to do such a thing, especially with a baby...' A tear spilled down her cheek, making a track in her heavily powdered face. 'I know what it's like to be on your own with a child,' she said quietly. 'After your father died, it was difficult for me. I'm not as strong or as resourceful as you, Violet. Surely you must remember what a struggle it was for us just to get by when you were young?' She sounded weary, defeated. 'All I wanted was for you to have a good life, the kind of life I could never give you. So when Victor came along – well, I was just so glad that at last you'd have someone to take care of you. I thought if you married him you'd never have to struggle again...'

Violet watched her in silence. She had never heard her mother admit she was wrong before, and hearing those words was like a huge weight rising from her shoulders.

She couldn't blame Dorothy Tanner for being so captivated by Victor Dangerfield. Violet herself had been so dazzled she had fallen in love with him.

125

To the outside world, Victor seemed like a charismatic, sophisticated man, a skilled surgeon who saved lives every day. It was only behind closed doors that the veneer of charm disappeared, revealing the ugly monster underneath.

She had run away from him to save her son from ever turning into him. But Victor had hunted her, haunted her every move until the day he died. Only then had Violet been free of him.

She looked down at the scar on her arm. 'I lived in fear for years,' she said. 'Running from place to place, never settling long enough for him to find me.'

'Oh, Violet–'

'I could have escaped him,' she cut her mother off bluntly, not wanting to hear the gentle sympathy in her voice. It was too late for pity now, far too late. 'I could have stopped running, if only you'd been on my side...'

'I know that now. But it isn't too late to make amends, surely?'

Violet looked away so she wouldn't have to see the desperate plea in her mother's eyes. She wasn't sure she would be strong enough to resist it.

'You didn't answer my question,' she said. 'Why did you decide to come back now, after all this time?'

'Do you think I wanted to wait this long?' Her mother shook her head. 'After you'd gone, I tried so hard to find you. I put advertisements in the newspapers, wrote to everyone I knew in case you'd been in touch with them. But Victor told me you'd run off with another man and wanted

126

nothing more to do with any of us.'

Violet gasped. 'Victor told you that?' She shouldn't have been surprised. She was beyond being shocked by her husband's cruelty. 'And you believed him?'

'Why shouldn't I have? It made sense of everything that had happened. Besides, I didn't think to question your husband. I had no idea what kind of man he was–' Her gaze strayed to Violet's scar, now hidden under her sleeve again. 'After he died, I asked his solicitor for your address, but he wouldn't give it to me. He also refused to pass on any letters. I assumed it was you who had given the instruction.'

Violet shook her head. 'I knew nothing about it. I suppose it must have been Victor's orders.'

Her mother looked confused. 'But why would he do such a thing?'

'Because he took pleasure in hurting people.' Violet could see the dawning realisation on her mother's face. She had felt the same bewilderment as a young bride, the first time Victor had driven his fist into her face.

'Anyway, I asked the solicitor if he could pass on a letter to Oliver, and he said no, not until he came of age. So I decided to wait.'

Violet had a sudden picture of her mother, steadfastly marking off the days on a calendar, ticking off the months and years until she could speak to her grandson again.

She felt tears pricking her eyes and looked away, driving the picture from her mind.

'But perhaps I have left it too late?' Dorothy sighed. 'I know I should have tried harder,

127

refused to take no for an answer. That's what you would have done, isn't it? But I know you're a far better mother than I could ever be.' There was a touch of pride in her voice. 'Seeing what a fine young man Oliver is, and hearing all the terrible things you had to go through – well, it makes me feel very humble. I'm proud of both of you, even though you probably don't want to hear that. I just wish I could have done something to make you proud of me, too–'

Just then the door opened and Mrs Morgan came in, Oliver following behind her with the tea tray.

'Here we are, a nice fresh pot,' she said. 'And I've managed to find a bit of cake in the tin, too – oh! Are you leaving, Mrs Tanner?'

Violet glanced over her shoulder. Her mother was pulling on her gloves.

'Yes,' she said. 'I'm sorry Mrs Morgan, I didn't realise how late it was. I really should be getting home...' Her voice trailed off.

'Must you go?' Oliver's voice was pleading.

'I'm afraid so, my dear.' Dorothy sounded regretful.

'It's late, and the buses have stopped running,' Mrs Morgan said. 'How will you get home?'

'Oh, I'm sure I can get a taxi.'

'Shall I walk with you up to the taxi rank?' Oliver offered.

'No, I shall be quite all right. Night time holds no fears for me, since the blackout.' Dorothy smiled bracingly.

'Will you come and visit again?' Oliver asked anxiously.

128

There was a slight pause, and Violet could feel her mother's eyes on her. 'We'll see.'

'When?'

'Soon, I promise.' Violet held herself rigid, not turning round. In the mirror's reflection she could see her mother planting a kiss on Oliver's cheek. 'Goodbye, my dear. You're a wonderful young man, and a credit to your mother.' She met Violet's gaze in the mirror. 'Goodbye, Violet.'

'Goodbye,' Violet replied stiffly, looking away. She longed to say more, but pride stopped her.

'Your mum seems like a very nice woman,' Mrs Morgan commented, as Oliver showed Dorothy Tanner out. 'Brave, too. I daresay it can't have been easy for her after all these years. She must have really wanted to see you.'

'It was Oliver she came to see,' Violet said stiffly.

'Is that what you think?' Mrs Morgan said. 'I was watching her, Violet. She could hardly take her eyes off you the whole time she was here.' She paused. 'You know, it ain't like you to be so uncharitable, ducks. Everyone deserves a second chance, don't you think?'

'Do they?'

'Well, it's up to you, I suppose,' Mrs Morgan said. 'But all I'll say is this. I would give anything to have my husband and sons back. There are so many things I wish I'd said to them when they were alive, and now I know I'll never get the chance.' She paused. 'You make sure you don't leave it too late, Violet.'

Mrs Morgan's words stayed with her for the next

129

few days. No matter how much Violet tried to push them aside, they kept coming back to her.

Everyone deserves a second chance.

She should have said something to her mother, she knew that now. She was wrong to let her walk away without making some kind of amends with her.

She was still feeling troubled as she joined the other nurses for the next rehearsal.

'Oh, Miss Tanner, it's such a pity you're not still in charge,' Miriam Trott said in a stage whisper as Violet took her place at the piano. 'We had such fun last week, didn't we? Such a change from the week before.'

Violet looked at Miss Davis. The Assistant Matron's shoulders stiffened, but she said nothing. Violet prayed that Miriam's remark wouldn't set her off. The last thing she needed was an argument with Miss Davis.

But half an hour later, when Miss Davis lost her temper with a hapless orderly and his assistant for messing up their magic act and ended up ordering them out, Violet couldn't help but speak up.

'Miss Davis–' she started to try to reason with her, but Charlotte turned on her.

'Oh, I might have known you'd have something to say about it!' she snapped. 'If you don't like the way I do things, you can go too!'

For a moment no one moved. Violet could feel all eyes on her, everyone waiting to see how she reacted. At any other time, she might have laughed off the Assistant Matron's petulant remark, absurd as it was. But today she was on

130

edge, and she'd had enough of Miss Davis and her pettiness.

She lowered the lid over the piano keyboard, gathered up her music and stood up.

She only meant to go outside long enough to calm down. But a moment later the doors opened and a gaggle of ward sisters walked out, followed by a group of medical students. Soon there was no one left in the dining hall except for Charlotte Davis, still sitting at her table alone.

'Well, that's showed her!' Miriam Trott declared triumphantly. 'She can't speak to us like that and get away with it. Let's see how she manages to produce a Christmas show with no performers!'

Violet returned home wearily to Cheshire Street. As usual when she turned the corner she could see light blazing in the living-room window. The curtains were open and through them she could see Oliver and Mrs Morgan decorating the Christmas tree.

Violet watched them through the window for a moment. Oliver was grinning as Mrs Morgan struggled to hang a bauble from one of the topmost branches.

Her family. Not the family she had been born into, but one that had come together out of friendship and necessity.

Until recently they had been all she needed, but now it troubled her that someone was missing.

There were so many people who had lost loved ones during the war. Poor Mrs Morgan, left alone without her two sons. Dr Gruber, who had watched his whole family perish in the concentration camp. There was scarcely a nurse or

131

doctor at the Nightingale who had not lost a husband, wife, a mother, father, brother or sister or a child in the war.

She could have easily lost her mother. Dorothy had said herself she was lucky to escape the bomb that fell on her house. But instead of being grateful, Violet had chosen to turn her back on her.

Perhaps Mrs Morgan was right: everyone deserved a second chance. But not everyone was lucky enough to get one.

'Have you heard from your grandmother lately?' Violet asked Oliver later, as she helped them finish off decorating the tree.

He shook his head. 'I've written to her, but I haven't had a reply yet.'

'Perhaps you should drop her a line yourself?' Mrs Morgan suggested.

Oliver nodded. 'You're right, Mrs M. She might not say yes if she doesn't think it's what Ma wants. Will you write to her, Ma?'

'Or you could go round and speak to her in person?' Mrs Morgan said.

Violet snapped a look at her, but the other woman's face was the picture of innocence as she draped tinsel on the tree.

'What a good idea, Mrs M,' she said tightly. 'Very well, I'll go and see her. Give me the address, Oliver.'

As luck would have it, the following day was her afternoon off. Violet caught the bus up west, then another over London Bridge to Camberwell.

It took her a while to find the address her mother had given. Dorothy had told them she

132

was a housekeeper, but none of the run-down Victorian villas in Church Terrace looked particularly well kept.

Violet went back and forth down the street several times, counting the numbers to make sure she had the right place. Yes, number eighteen was definitely this one. Violet stood for a moment, staring up at the dilapidated house, with its cracked windows, lopsided gate and overgrown front garden. She had lived in enough grim lodging houses for it all to be depressingly familiar to her.

A thin woman answered the door, drying her hands on a grubby apron.

'Yes?' she said, looking her up and down.

'Is Mrs Tanner at home?'

The woman frowned. 'Mrs Tanner? I'm sorry, I don't – oh, hang on a minute. You're Dot's girl, ain't you? I recognise you from the pictures.'

Violet frowned. 'Pictures–' she started to say, but the woman cut her off.

'Wait there a minute,' she said, and closed the door in Violet's face.

Violet stared at the peeling paintwork, taken aback. Just as she was about to knock again, the door opened once more and another woman stood there, broad with a flat, broken nose and fleshy lips.

'You're Dot Tanner's girl?' she said, glaring at Violet. 'You'd best come in. I'll be wanting a word with you.'

Her sour expression puzzled Violet. 'I'm sorry. I don't understand – my mother does live here, doesn't she?'

133

'She did,' the woman said. 'She walked out on us last week.'

'Walked out?'

'Did a flit,' the woman sniffed. 'Left owing me five bob rent, too.'

Violet was confused. 'Rent? But I thought she was the housekeeper here?'

'Housekeeper?' The woman roared with laughter, opening her mouth wide to reveal rotting teeth. 'That's a good 'un! Do we look like we have a bleedin' housekeeper?' She shook her head. 'She did a spot of cleaning here and there, but she rented a room, same as everyone else. And she told you she was a housekeeper, did she?' The woman sneered. 'That sounds like Dot Tanner. Always did have ideas above herself.'

'You mean she had a bit of pride,' Violet said.

'Not too proud to slink off owing me rent!' the woman retorted. 'And she left a load of her stuff behind. I can't rent out the room with all that rubbish in there. I was going to sell it off to the rag and bone man to get some of the money I was owed.'

'I'll pay your rent for you.' Violet took out her purse. 'How much did she owe, did you say? Five shillings, wasn't it?'

'Ten. I haven't been able to rent out her room because she left her stuff behind.'

Violet handed over the ten-shilling note. 'And I'll take her belongings with me. Everything you haven't nicked, anyway.'

The woman did her best to look outraged. 'Nicked? I'll have you know, I run a respectable establishment here. Besides,' she sniffed, 'there

134

weren't anything worth nicking anyhow.'

She directed Violet to a room at the top of the house, a draughty attic with threadbare curtains and a stained horsehair mattress. Like the rest of the house, it reeked of damp and stale cooking. Mould blossomed in the corners.

But Violet could see her mother had done her best to make it homely. There was a vase of faded chrysanthemums on the window sill, and cross-stitched cushions on the chair. Violet recognised her mother's careful hand in embroidering them. She was always sewing when Violet was growing up. And the pictures. An array of photographs on the dresser, all of Violet and Oliver as a baby.

There was a box on the bed.

'Not much in there,' the woman remarked. 'Just some old photograph albums.'

'You've already been through it, then,' Violet said.

The woman had the grace to look embarrassed. 'I was looking for a forwarding address,' she mumbled.

Looking for something valuable, you mean, Violet thought. She had been robbed enough times by light-fingered landladies to know her type.

The pages of the albums were rimmed with damp and mould. When Violet opened them, several loose pages fell out.

As she bent to pick them up, she saw her own image staring back at her. She was a young woman, nursing a baby on her lap. Turning to the next page, she saw herself as a baby, then as a child collecting a Sunday School prize, well turned out in her best dress and white socks.

135

'They're all of you, every single one,' the woman said. 'That's how we knew who you were.' She paused. 'I s'pose she must have thought a lot about you.'

'Yes,' Violet replied quietly. 'Yes, I suppose she did.'

Peggy

1st December 1945

'I hope I ain't got you into trouble, Sister,' Peggy Atkins said worriedly as she tidied up the mess of leftover paper chains from the table.

'Oh, I wouldn't fret about it, Peggy.' Sister Parry shook her head. 'Our assistant matron always has a bee in her bonnet about something. Anyway, the kids enjoyed themselves, and that's the main thing.' She looked at the notice Miss Davis had handed her. 'So what's all this? A Christmas show, eh? That'll be a right old laugh, if she's got anything to do with it!'

'What's a Christmas show, Sister?' Peggy asked, scooping an armful of wallpaper scraps into an old cardboard box.

'Of course, you won't have seen one before, will you? We used to have them every year when I was training. The staff get together and put on a show for the patients on Christmas Day. We used to have a right laugh doing it, too.'

'Sounds like a hoot, Sister. It's such a shame I

136

won't be here to see it,' Peggy said sadly.

Sister Parry looked at her sympathetically. 'That is a shame. I reckon you would have loved it. Couldn't you stay on a bit longer? Just till after Christmas?'

Peggy shook her head. 'I don't think my Eric would like it. He's been patient enough as it is.'

Her husband had wanted her to give up working at the hospital as soon as VE Day was over, but Peggy had persuaded him to let her stay on until the end of the year.

'Well, I'll be sorry to see you go,' Sister Parry sighed. 'I don't know how we'll manage without you, I really don't.'

Peggy laughed off the compliment. 'All I do is make beds and scrub bedpans!'

'You do much more than that and you know it,' Sister said. 'You're like a breath of fresh air, Peggy. You're a natural with the kids, and you cheer us all up.' She looked at her consideringly. 'I wish you'd think about what I said, about getting some proper training.'

'What, me? Train to be a nurse?'

'Why not? Like I said, you're a natural.'

Peggy shook her head. 'I'm not much for book learning, Sister. Besides, they'd never want me. I'm nearly forty, and my daughter's older than most of the students here. Matron would have a fit if I applied.'

'Matron would welcome a good nurse at this hospital, whatever her age. And as for book learning – well, I never had much of an education either. I used to sew shirts in a garment factory, remember?'

137

Peggy did remember. She recalled Sister Parry when she was plain old Dora Doyle, a red-haired kid running errands for her mum and her gran in Griffin Street. She remembered her coming into the shop, ushering all her younger brothers and sisters like a little mother hen.

And now look at her, a ward sister no less, in her starched grey dress and white bonnet covering her ginger curls. She had done well for herself, there was no doubt about that. But she was still the lovely, down-to-earth girl Peggy remembered.

Peggy admired her, but she had no illusions about joining her. 'It's not for me, Sister. Besides, my Eric needs me to help him in the shop.'

Dora smiled. 'Of course, Peggy. But I do wish you could stay on till after Christmas, in any case. It would be a great help to me if you could.'

Peggy looked around at the rows of beds. She would miss the children, more than she wanted to admit to herself. She loved seeing them every morning, and helping to bring a smile to their little faces.

'I'll see what my Eric says,' she said. 'I must admit, I'd like to see this Christmas show.'

But Eric wasn't too impressed by the idea when Peggy mentioned it over tea that night. And neither was his mother.

'You mean to tell us you'd rather spend Christmas in a hospital with strangers than with your own family?' Nellie Atkins said through a mouthful of food. 'Well, that's nice, that is.'

'I wouldn't be spending all day there,' Peggy protested as she handed round the vegetables. 'Besides, it'd only be for an extra week or two. I

138

don't see as it would make much difference.' She turned her pleading gaze to her husband.

Eric ruminated on it for a moment, his face thoughtful. 'Mum's right,' he said at last. 'Christmas is our busiest time in the shop.' He shook his head. 'Your place is here, Peg. With me and the kids.'

'The kids have grown up and flown the nest, in case you hadn't noticed,' Peggy's sister Pearl spoke up. Peggy's heart sank. She knew Pearl was only sticking up for her, but she wished she wouldn't. She antagonised Eric every time she opened her mouth. 'Your Alan's still out in India, and now your Amy's engaged I daresay once she's demobbed she'll be setting up home on her own.'

'It's a pity you don't do the same,' Nellie muttered.

Peggy shot a tense look at her sister, willing her not to answer back. It was a vain hope.

Pearl stuck out her chin. 'And what's that supposed to mean?'

'I mean how long are you going to carry on living here? You're a grown woman and a mother and it's high time you started fending for yourself.'

'This is my home for as long as I need it. Peggy said so. Ain't that right, Peg?'

'I–'

'Peggy had no business telling you that. This is my son's house, and he says what goes. You've imposed on our goodwill for too long.'

'Goodwill! I ain't seen much goodwill from you, you old bag!'

'Pearl!' Peggy gasped, but with her sister and

139

her mother-in-law both spoiling for a fight, there wasn't much she could do to stop it.

'Did you hear what she said to me?' Nellie turned on Peggy, her eyes bulging with outrage. 'You ain't going to stand for that, are you?'

'Pearl, please–'

'She sits there like Lady Muck, eating our food and not lifting a finger,' Nellie went on, her flabby jowls wobbling with anger. 'And then she goes out and leaves you to look after her boy–'

'I don't mind. I like looking after Charlie.' Peggy flashed a quick smile at Pearl's ten-year-old son, who sat beside his mother, steadily eating and watching the conversation bat back and forth with nervous, squinting eyes.

'Just as well, since he sees more of you than he does his own mother!' Nellie muttered.

'You don't mind him being here when he's running errands and fetching and carrying deliveries for you,' Pearl retorted. 'And all for free, too. Where are his wages, that's what I'd like to know?'

'You're eating 'em,' Eric said, gesturing for Peggy to serve him more carrots. Peggy jumped to her feet, the spoon in her hand.

'Anyway, you'll be glad to know I won't be imposing on your charity much longer,' Pearl said haughtily. 'Once Ralph and I get married–'

Nellie cackled with laughter. 'You reckon he's going to marry you? The Thames will freeze over before that day happens!'

Pearl ignored her. 'Once Ralph and I are married, we'll have our own place. Somewhere smart, out in Essex.'

'I'll believe it when I see it,' Nellie muttered.

140

'More pie?' Peggy jumped in, desperate to keep the peace.

'I won't say no.' Nellie held up her plate.

'You never do,' Pearl said. 'Honestly, you complain I'm a sponger, but you take the cake.'

'What are you talking about? This was my house, and my shop before it passed to my son. I have every right to be here, unlike you! Not too much pastry.' She held up her hand as Peggy dolloped pie on her plate. 'It's too dry. You're a bit too heavy-handed with it, if you ask me.'

'Sorry,' Peggy mumbled, shaking her head at her sister as Pearl opened her mouth to speak.

After tea, Eric said to Peggy, 'You're going to have to have a word with that sister of yours. I won't have her upsetting my mother.'

'She can't help herself,' Peggy sighed. 'She don't mean any harm by it, she's just got a quick tongue, that's all.'

'Well, I won't have her spouting off in my house. Mum's right, it's time she started looking for a place of her own.'

'Give her another chance, please?' Peggy begged. 'She'll be moving out soon, I promise.'

Eric sighed. 'All right,' he agreed. 'But have a word with her, will you? Tell her to keep her trap shut.'

It was easier said than done, Peggy thought.

Pearl was in Amy's old room, getting ready to go out, when Peggy went to talk to her.

'I do wish you could make more of an effort to get on with Eric and his mum,' she sighed, as she watched her sister powdering her face, sitting at her daughter's old dressing table mirror. She had

141

her own room in the attic, but she had commandeered the bigger room when Amy joined the ATS. She reckoned the light was better for putting on her make-up.

'Tell that to the old battleaxe, not me. She's the one who starts all the trouble. I don't say a word unless she starts on me.'

'I know she can be a bit difficult,' Peggy conceded. 'But she's still Eric's mother, and he doesn't like her being upset.'

'Oh, and we mustn't upset the Lord and Master, must we?' Pearl said sarcastically.

'He's been very good to us,' Peggy said.

'Oh yes, he's a proper knight in shining armour.'

Peggy stared at the back of her sister's blonde head, stung. 'He was to me,' she said. 'Don't you remember the desperate state we were in? I dunno where you and I would have ended up, if Eric hadn't come along.'

'So you're always telling me.' Pearl made a face in the mirror. She spat on her mascara and stroked the brush along her lashes.

'I suppose you're too young to remember it.' But Peggy knew she would never forget.

'Anyway, I'll be gone soon,' Pearl said. 'Once Ralph's latest deal comes off, he's going to pop the question, I know he is.'

Peggy looked away so Pearl wouldn't see the doubt in her eyes. Her sister was touchy when it came to her boyfriends.

'Are you seeing him tonight?' she asked.

'Of course. You don't think I'm painting my face for your Eric's benefit, do you?' Pearl laughed over her shoulder at Peggy. She was five years

142

younger, but she could have passed for late twenties easily. Pearl took care of herself, bleaching her already fair hair to a silvery platinum shade. Any money she had went on clothes and make-up. She knew how to make the best of herself, a skill Peggy had never learned. She always felt dowdy in comparison, in her faded pinny and slippers, her blonde curls hacked short with the kitchen scissors.

'We're off up west,' Pearl went on, turning back to the mirror to apply her lipstick. 'Ralph's taking me to some posh new club. He's even bought me a new dress for the occasion, look.' She nodded to the silk gown hanging up on the wardrobe.

Peggy looked at it. She could just imagine how it would look, flowing over her sister's slender curves. 'It's lovely.'

'Yes, well, Ralph likes me to dress up for him. He says he likes to show me off!' she giggled.

'And I suppose you'll be wanting me to look after Charlie while you're gone?'

Pearl turned pleading eyes to hers. 'You don't mind, do you? You know how much he loves his Auntie Peg.'

Peggy smiled reluctantly. 'Of course not. He's always welcome here.' Although even as she said it, she could see Eric rolling his gaze heavenwards in her mind's eye.

'Thanks, Peggy. You're a diamond.' Pearl blew her a kiss from scarlet-painted lips. 'I won't forget you when I'm all set up.'

'I should blooming well hope not!' Peggy laughed, relieved to see her sister happy.

But for how long? she wondered apprehens-

143

ively. Ralph was just the latest in a long line of chancers that Pearl had got involved with. She went for that type, unfortunately. She was attracted to them like a moth to a flame, no matter how many times she got burned.

And sometimes she ended up with more than a broken heart. Charlie was the result of another engagement to a man who promised her the world and then did a runner, leaving her high and dry.

Peggy tried to talk to Eric about it that night as they got ready for bed.

'I hope our Pearl's all right,' she said, looking out of the window into the dark, frosty night. The streets of Bethnal Green were deserted, but she knew that up west it would be a different story. That was the world Pearl inhabited, a world of lights and parties and jazz music and dancing till dawn.

'Of course she will be. You know what Pearl's like. She'll be having the time of her life. And I daresay she'll come home with the milkman, crawling in with her shoes in her hand. Then she'll sleep till noon and won't be fit for anything, least of all helping me in the shop.'

Peggy looked at her husband, sitting up in bed, self-righteous in his striped flannel pyjamas. As a mother, Pearl was not conscripted as Peggy was. The plan was that she should take Peggy's place helping out in the shop while Peggy worked at the Nightingale. But Pearl wasn't cut out for shop work. She hated early mornings and being on her feet all day behind the counter. She was surly to the customers, and complained that the

144

work made her hands rough and her hair stink of mouldy cheese.

Peggy wished her sister would try a bit harder, for her sake. Perhaps if Pearl was slightly more amenable, Eric wouldn't mind her staying on at the hospital a while longer.

'I know she's a devil, but I can't help worrying about her. She is my little sister, after all.'

'She's a grown woman!'

'Yes, but you know how daft she can be, especially when there's a man involved. And Ralph doesn't strike me as the reliable type.'

Eric sighed. 'She's old enough and ugly enough to take care of herself. And with any luck this one will take her off our hands.'

'Eric!'

'I'm only speaking the truth. I know she's your sister, but I'll be glad when she's finally married and you can start looking after us again. It's me you should be worrying about, Peg. Not your wretched sister and her son.'

'You're right,' Peggy sighed. But it was a hard habit to break. She had been looking out for Pearl for as long as she could remember.

Their father had upped and left when Pearl was a baby, and their mother had been too drunk to care for her daughters. When she was five, Peggy was changing Pearl's nappies. By the time she was ten she was getting her up for school. When she wasn't keeping house or taking care of her sister, Peggy helped her mother with her piecework at the box factory, finishing off the boxes herself by the gas light when her mother fell asleep, drunk.

Even then, it was a constant struggle to stop her mother drinking away everything she earned. Small as she was, Peggy would join the queue at the factory gates to collect the earnings, then go straight to buy food. More often than not she got beaten soundly for not handing the money over, but at least it meant they could eat.

By the time Peggy reached twelve, her mother had drunk herself to death. For a while, the workhouse had beckoned for the two girls, but Peggy took matters into her own hands. She gave up school and kept up the piecework at the box factory to keep a roof over their heads. Once she turned fifteen, she started work in the factory itself to earn more money.

But the foreman turned amorous and started trying to have his way with her. When Peggy turned him down, he trumped up an excuse to sack her. At the age of seventeen, she found herself out on her ear with no references and no idea what to do next. She was crying on a bench in Victoria Park in the rain when Eric Atkins came along.

Pearl was right, the gawky young man with his long face, sparse light brown hair and ill-fitting suit wasn't anyone's idea of a knight in shining armour. But he was kind and polite, he offered her a corned beef sandwich and a very clean, neatly pressed handkerchief, and he listened as Peggy poured out her woes to him. Then, when she had finished, he offered her a job behind the counter at the grocer's shop on Valiance Street he had just inherited from his father.

It was a dream come true for Peggy, even if she

146

did have to put up with Eric's spiteful mother Nellie. Nellie Atkins quickly spotted a potential rival for her son's affections and disliked her on sight. But Peggy gradually won her over with her cheerful manner and hard work. And as long as she was willing to tolerate Nellie, then at least it meant that Eric had to do the same with Pearl, who came to live with them shortly after their marriage.

Peggy had been looking after all of them and her own two children ever since, and she did not mind a bit. After living in the shadow of the workhouse for so long, it was a relief to have a home and a family she could call her own at last.

Even though she knew she would not be there to see the final result, Peggy decided to go along to the first meeting of the Christmas show, just out of curiosity.

On the way down to the dining hall she met Bill Brigham, a porter on Parry ward. It was hard to miss him, he was such a tall, imposing figure, with his shock of sandy hair and booming voice. It would have been easy to be afraid of Bill, but he was a real gentle giant, and so full of fun all the children loved him.

Bill had only been working at the Nightingale for a few months, since he came out of the merchant navy. But Peggy knew him of old. She used to chat with his wife Alice when she came into the shop with their little girl.

'Going my way?' he said.

'Looks like it. I thought I'd be nosey.'

'Me too. Mr Hopkins asked a few of us to make ourselves useful, putting out chairs and the like.'

147

But the chairs were already in place by the time they reached the dining room. And they were nearly all occupied, too.

'Looks like we ain't needed after all,' Bill said.

'We could still stay for a bit, just to see what's going on. Look, there are a couple of seats in the middle there...'

They shuffled their way through the throng and had almost reached the row when Miss Davis suddenly turned round and called out, 'I say, you two. You can't sit there, the front row is for staff nurses only. Go to the back!'

'That's us told!' Peggy grinned. 'No one can say we don't know our place.'

But Bill stood his ground. 'Who does she think she is? You're a nurse, same as them.'

'I ain't, Bill.' Peggy shot a quick, embarrassed glance at the nurses who were all looking their way. 'Come on, let's get to the back.'

A couple of the orderlies budged up to make space for them, just as Miss Davis called the meeting to order. She waved a sheet of paper and announced that she expected everyone to put their names down next to their chosen act.

'Are you putting your name down, Bill?' Peggy asked him.

He roared with laughter. 'Me? What could I do?'

'What about your magic tricks?'

He was famous for them on the ward. He could always coax a smile from a crying child by showing them a card trick, or producing a paper flower out of his pocket.

'You mean like this one?' Bill reached behind

148

Peggy's ear and produced a gleaming halfpenny.

Peggy clapped her hands, earning herself a quick glare from Miss Davis at the front of the hall. 'You see? You'd be a marvel on that stage.'

Bill shook his head and looked embarrassed. 'I'm not one for performing in public.'

'What are you talking about? You're always doing tricks for the kids.'

'All right, then. I'll put my name down if you will.'

'You're having a laugh, ain't you? Who'd want to see me cavorting about on a stage? I leave that to the likes of Sister Wren.'

'Talk of the devil...' Bill craned his neck to see what was going on at the front. 'I think that's Miss Trott speaking now.'

'It sounds like they're having a row,' Peggy said.

'Already? That didn't take long, did it?'

Peggy laughed, and Miss Davis promptly turned on her.

'Will you be quiet back there?' she snapped. 'If you don't want to listen to what I have to say then you can leave now.'

All heads turned in Peggy's direction and she felt herself flushing with mortification. It was a relief when the meeting broke up shortly afterwards, and she could leave.

'Take no notice of her, Peggy,' Bill said, as they shuffled out with the others. 'She's always having a go at someone. I sometimes feel like I'm back in the navy, listening to her giving her orders. I swear, that woman puts some of my captains to shame!'

Peggy gave him a watery smile. 'I don't think

149

she likes me.'

'I don't think she likes anyone.' As she turned to go, Bill said, 'Just a minute, you forgot something.'

'Did I? I can't see–' Peggy turned to look round, as Bill Brigham reached behind her ear and produced another halfpenny.

'For the bus,' he said, pressing it into her hand.

Peggy put the Christmas show out of her mind, until a few days later when Bill Brigham came up to the ward to take the tonsillitis patients down to theatre.

'Are you coming to the rehearsal tonight?' he asked.

She shook her head. 'I don't see the point.'

'But you've got to come! They're trying out the acts tonight. It'll be a laugh.'

Peggy hesitated. 'I should get home and cook my old man's tea,' she said. Eric always liked it on the table promptly after he'd closed up the shop.

'You don't have to stay long,' Bill coaxed her. 'Come on, Peggy, please? Tell you what, I'll bring some peanuts, and we can chuck them at the acts we don't like!'

'I'll be chucking all mine at Miss Davis, I reckon!' Peggy smiled ruefully. 'Oh, go on, then. I s'pose I can spare half an hour. Eric usually does the stocktaking on a Wednesday anyway, so he won't need his tea too early.'

It was lucky Bill hadn't brought any peanuts, or they might have ended up throwing them all. The first rehearsal was a shambles.

'I suppose they're nervous, poor things,' Peggy sympathised. 'I can't say I'd like to stand up there

150

in front of everyone. Especially Miss Davis.'

'Miss Davis doesn't scare me,' Bill said. 'When you've been chased across the North Sea by U-boats for six years, you learn not to be afraid of anything.'

Peggy said nothing. She knew she shouldn't feel embarrassed that Eric hadn't served like Bill. He couldn't help having a weak chest, after all. And he had done his bit in the ARP.

But she felt a sting of shame, thinking about her husband's black-market activities. All those deals done, the mysterious packages that arrived and were kept under the counter for special customers who were willing to pay for them. Meanwhile, their regular customers had to go without. Seeing their disappointed faces after they had queued for so long broke Peggy's heart, but Eric had been unrepentant.

'You've got to make hay while the sun shines, Peg,' he had said. 'We ain't running a charity.'

The acts went on being terrible, but at least they had a good laugh.

'We shouldn't laugh,' Peggy said. 'I know I wouldn't have the nerve to stand up and do it. The last time I stood up in public was at Sunday School, and I wet my knickers!'

Bill laughed, earning himself another angry scowl from the Assistant Matron.

Next on stage was Dr Armstrong, performing a magic act. Beside her, Bill leaned forward in his seat, watching intently.

The young doctor didn't get off to a good start, tripping over his own feet as he stepped up on to the platform.

151

'Poor man,' Peggy said. 'Look at his hands shaking. He must be so nervous.'

'I hope he ain't training to be a surgeon, in that case, or God help his patients!'

Peggy laughed again, and Miss Davis shot her another dirty look.

Dr Armstrong did not get any better. Peggy cringed when the string of colourful handkerchiefs he was pulling from his pocket ended up in a hopeless knot. Then he tried to produce a bunch of flowers from inside his jacket pocket for Miss Davis but they got stuck and he ended up showering her with tattered petals.

'Poor Dr Armstrong!' Peggy sighed, as he limped off stage, his head hung in shame. 'You know, you could do better than that, Bill.'

'I couldn't do a lot worse!'

She turned to him. 'Why don't you?' she urged.

'I couldn't–'

But Peggy was already on her feet and making her way to the front where Miss Davis was sitting.

'Peggy, what are you doing?' Bill hissed as he followed her.

The Assistant Matron's stony expression nearly put her off. 'Name?' she snapped.

Peggy nudged him until he spoke up. 'Brigham, Miss. Bill Brigham.'

Miss Davis consulted the paper in front of her. 'Your name doesn't appear to be on my list.'

Peggy grinned at Bill.

'No, Miss, it won't be.' He sent Peggy a sideways glance. 'It was a bit of a last-minute decision, you might say.' Poor man, he looked so

152

shocked, it was all Peggy could do not to giggle.

Miss Davis sighed and put down her pen. 'And what do you do?' she asked.

'Magic tricks, Miss.'

'Not again!' Miss Davis rolled her eyes. 'Well, I do hope you're better than the last one.'

'Oh, he is, Miss,' Peggy said. 'He's very good.'

'We'll have to see, won't we? You have two minutes, Mr Brigham.'

Peggy was about to go back to her seat, but Bill caught hold of her arm. 'Oh no, you don't,' he said in a low voice. 'I'm going to need an assistant.'

Peggy realised what he meant and shook her head. 'I couldn't!'

'You can, and you will,' he grinned. 'Come on, girl. If I'm going to make a fool of myself then you can blooming well join me.'

Peggy understood how poor Dr Armstrong had felt. Her legs almost gave way as she took her place on the makeshift platform, facing the rows of doctors and nurses. The only thing that kept her there was knowing that she would look an even bigger fool if she fled.

'I don't know what to do,' she hissed at Bill out of the corner of her mouth, her terrified gaze still fixed on the rows of faces in front of her.

'Just follow me,' he whispered back. 'And twirl around a bit when you get the chance, try to distract them.'

Peggy sent him a panicked glance. Twirl around a bit? He was having a laugh, wasn't he? Her feet were rooted to the stage.

But her nerves seemed to melt away as Bill

153

started doing his tricks and she realised how much the audience was enjoying it. They were watching Bill avidly. Even Miss Davis had stopped frowning for a moment and was leaning forward in her seat, looking fascinated.

The time passed in a flash, and when it was over they stood side by side on the platform, making awkward bows and grinning sheepishly at each other as the audience applauded them.

'Thank you,' Miss Davis said. 'That was quite – acceptable.'

'Talk about damned with faint praise!' Peggy said, as they stepped off the stage.

'Faint or not, I'm just glad it's over,' Bill said. 'I'm telling you, Peggy, I thought I was going to pass out on that stage!'

'I thought you didn't scare easily, Bill Brigham?'

His mouth twisted. 'Looks like I was wrong about that. Still, at least it's over now.'

'I'm not so sure.' Peggy glanced back over her shoulder at Miss Davis. 'I reckon you've just earned yourself a place in the show.'

Bill groaned. 'Oh Gawd, what have we got ourselves into?'

'We?' Peggy said.

'You don't think I'm going to get up on that stage on my own, do you? We're in this together, girl. Besides, you're my good luck charm.'

Peggy shook her head, marvelling at herself. 'Wait until my old man hears about this, he'll never believe it!'

She was excited to tell Eric when she got home. But when she walked in and saw his face full of thunder, she promptly forgot all about the

154

Christmas show.

Peggy's heart shot into her throat. 'What is it? What's wrong? Oh God, it's not our Alan, is it?'

The war might be over in Europe, but Alan was still out in India, and Peggy knew she would suffer that horrible, heart-pounding, dry-mouthed fear until he was home safe.

'Keep your hair on, it's nothing to do with the kids.' Eric shook his head. 'It's your sister.'

'Oh no, what's she done now?'

'It's that man of hers. He's been arrested. You know that big deal he had going on? Turns out he was playing the gigolo, fleecing some rich heiress out of her fortune. Now he's behind bars and your sister's in a right old state about it.'

Peggy sighed. 'I'd better go and make sure she's all right.'

Pearl lay on her bed in Amy's old room, sobbing like a child into the pillow. Her son Charlie sat at the end of the bed, watching her helplessly. He turned to Peggy, his own face wet with tears.

'She won't stop crying, Auntie Peg,' he whispered.

'It's all right, son.' Peggy did her best to reassure the frightened boy. 'Can you leave us alone for a minute so we can have a chat? I've got a comic in my bag for you,' she called after him as he left the room.

She waited until the door had closed, then sat down on the bed beside her sister. She reached out and stroked the platinum blonde head.

'Oh, Pearl,' she sighed. 'What a to-do, eh?'

'I suppose you're going to say, "I told you so"?' Pearl said accusingly, her voice muffled by the

155

pillow. 'Go on, then. Let's hear it!'

'I'm not going to say any such thing,' Peggy said. 'Come on, girl. Why don't you tell me all about it?'

'Oh, Peggy!' The next moment Pearl had sat up and launched herself into Peggy's arms, her face damp against her neck. 'I thought he was different, I really did.' Her slender body quivered with sobbing. 'He called me his queen, he promised me everything. He said we were going to have such a good life together. And all the time he was with her–'

It's the same every time, Peggy thought. And Pearl fell for it every time, too. She lost her head and her heart, and more often than not it always ended up the same way, with Peggy having to pick up the pieces.

But she knew nothing she could say would ever take away her sister's heartache. All she could do was hold on to Pearl and hug her until the torrent of emotions had poured out of her. First the misery and despair would come, then the fury, and finally some kind of bitter resolution never to be hurt again.

Until the next time.

She listened patiently as Peg raged about Ralph, how he was the lowest of the low and the scum of the earth for doing the dirty on her.

'Although I suppose he was only doing it for me,' she sniffed. 'He promised us we'd be rich.'

He was doing it for himself, Peggy thought. If this woman hadn't found him out he would have been well set up with her, and Pearl would have ended up his bit on the side, being strung along

156

with endless promises.

'What am I going to do?' Pearl drew back in Peggy's arms. Her face was ravaged by tears, her carefully applied mascara running in black rivulets over her rouged cheeks.

'You know you've always got a home here.'

'Tell that to your old man. He can't wait to see the back of me.'

'That ain't true. Eric cares about you as much as I do.' Peggy hoped her sister didn't hear the lie in her voice. She didn't mention that Eric's last words to her had been, 'I suppose this means we're stuck with her for now?'

'I don't want to stay here. I don't want to spend the rest of my days stuck behind a bacon slicer!' Pearl pulled a face. 'That kind of life might be all right for you, but I've always wanted something more.'

Peggy swallowed the insult. Her sister was just upset, she told herself. 'I'm sure you'll get it one day,' she tried to console her.

'Will I?' Pearl sniffed back her tears. 'Do you really think so?'

'I know you will.' Peggy smoothed her blonde curls. 'You'll see, one day you'll meet a nice man and settle down. Then you'll have everything you've ever wanted.'

'I haven't met a nice man so far. I'm beginning to think they don't exist.'

'Perhaps you're looking in the wrong place?' Peggy ventured, as tactfully as she could, wondering how far she could go.

Pearl frowned. 'What do you mean?'

Peggy chose her words carefully, aware that the

157

wrong one could send her sister into a screaming rage.

'I mean you always seem to go for the flashy types, the ones who are too fond of a good time.'

'What's wrong with that? I like a good time too.'

'That's fine, if that's all you want. But if you're looking for something more permanent, more secure–'

'I have to look for a man like your Eric?'

Peggy saw the way her sister's mouth twisted. 'You could do worse,' she snapped, offended. 'At least my Eric knows how to provide for his family.'

Pearl's face fell. 'I know, Peg. I'm sorry. You and Eric have been so good to me, I've no right to make fun.' She dried her tears with the back of her hand. 'You're right, I do need to buck my ideas up,' she agreed. 'From now on, there'll be no flash Harry types. I'll look for my own knight in shining armour.'

'You do that,' Peggy said. 'And I bet you'll find him sooner than you think.'

After she had managed to calm her sister down, Peggy went into the living room. Eric was in his usual armchair, reading the evening paper. Nellie squatted opposite in what should have been Peggy's chair, looking like a miserable toad.

Eric looked up at her over the edge of his newspaper. 'Well?'

'She's resting.'

'Resting?' Nellie snorted. 'Anyone would think she was ill!'

'She's broken-hearted,' Peggy said. But there was no point in telling that to Nellie. She didn't

158

have a heart to break.

'And I'm famished,' Nellie grumbled. 'When are you going to get the tea on?'

It wouldn't hurt you to make a start on it, Peggy thought. 'I'll do it now,' she said, slipping off her coat.

Eric followed her into the kitchen. 'So she's stopping, then?' he said, as he watched her tying on her apron.

'Looks like it.' She sent him a sideways glance. 'If that's all right?'

'I s'pose it'll have to be, won't it? Don't look like I've got much choice in the matter. Mind, she'll have to start pulling her weight in the shop a bit more. She ought to do something to earn her keep.'

'Oh, she will,' Peggy promised.

'Although I'd still rather you were there helping me,' Eric said. 'Your sister's got a sharp tongue on her, and the customers don't like it.'

'I'll have a word with her, make sure she behaves.'

'You do that. Still, at least she doesn't give away half my stock on tick like you do,' he added, shooting her a sour look. 'You're too soft-hearted, that's your trouble.'

Peggy looked away guiltily. She couldn't help it. She knew the customers who came into the shop, they were her friends and neighbours. She wasn't going to let someone's children go hungry just because they were short till their next pay day.

With everything going on at home, it was a relief to go to work. Pearl was still sunk in self-pity and

159

slow to rouse herself from her bed each morning, to Eric's seething irritation. Every day, Peggy prayed her sister would pull herself together and she wouldn't have to come home to yet another argument.

The day of the next rehearsal, she arrived on the ward just before seven as usual, in time to help the night staff give the children their breakfasts. Then she did a quick bedpan round, and set about getting the children washed and brushed up. By the time Sister Parry arrived on the ward, they were all sitting up in their clean beds, their faces freshly scrubbed and hair combed.

Sister Parry smiled with approval. 'You've done a good job as usual, Peggy.' She looked around at the children. 'And if you're all good, I might have a nice surprise for you later,' she announced.

'And what could that be, Sister?' Peggy asked, as if she couldn't already guess. 'Not a Christmas tree by any chance?'

Sister Parry winked at her. 'You'll have to wait and see, won't you?'

Peggy's suspicions proved right later that morning, when Bill Brigham arrived, bringing a Christmas tree. It was enormous, taller than a man and heavy with it, but Bill carried it over his broad shoulder as if it weighed nothing.

'Where do you want this?' he asked with a grin.

Peggy directed him to the other end of the ward, where she had cleared a space for it. She watched as Bill shifted the weighty tree easily into place.

'What a beauty,' she said admiringly. 'Better than the sorry specimens we've had over the past few years.'

'You'll have fun decorating it, that's for sure.'

Peggy smiled at Bill. 'I don't suppose you want to stay and help me? We'll need someone tall to put the fairy on top!'

'Sorry, I can't oblige. I'm needed back down in outpatients. But I'm sure you'll have plenty of helpers.' He beamed round at the children, who were watching them eagerly.

'You're right there.'

He smiled shyly. 'Will you be at the rehearsal tonight?'

She nodded. 'If I can get away on time.'

'That's good.' He looked relieved. 'I thought you might decide to back out on me.'

'Never! We're a team, ain't we?'

'We are,' he grinned.

He was leaving the ward just as Sister Parry returned.

'Hello, Mr Brigham. You've brought our surprise, I see?'

'Yes, Sister.' He was about to leave when Sister said, 'While I've got you here, I wondered if I could ask another favour.'

'What's that, Sister?'

'I wondered if you'd dress up as Father Christmas and hand out presents to the kids on Christmas Day?'

Peggy took a deep breath and her gaze flew to Bill's. Sister Parry couldn't have known what she was asking, or she would never have said anything.

Bill stood stock-still, his face expressionless.

'We used to do it every year before the war

161

started,' Sister Parry was still talking, oblivious. 'Mr Hopkins, the head porter, used to do the honours, but he always ended up barking at the kids like a sergeant major and scaring them. I could just see you done up in a white beard and red coat.'

'No. I'm sorry, I couldn't.'

Peggy saw the dismay in his face and tried to step in. 'I'm sure we could ask someone else,' she said. 'One of the other porters, or even Dr Granger–'

'But Mr Brigham would be perfect! Honestly, you wouldn't have to do much, just dress up and hand out the presents–'

'I said no!'

His voice boomed down the ward, shocking Sister Parry into silence. One of the children burst into tears, while another started whimpering.

Bill turned on his heel and strode out, letting the double doors crash shut behind him.

'Well!' Sister Parry stared after him, confusion written all over her face. 'What was that all about, I wonder? I thought he'd be happy to do it. He's always such a jolly character.'

Peggy looked at her. 'You don't know, do you, Sister?'

'Know what?'

'Bill – Mr Brigham – lost his wife and daughter two years ago. They were caught up in that accident at Bethnal Green tube.'

'How awful.' Sister Parry looked pained. 'I'm sorry to hear it. But I don't understand what that's got to do with–'

162

'Maisie's birthday was Christmas Day. Bill always used to dress up as Father Christmas to give her her presents.'

She remembered Alice Brigham telling her about it in the shop. How her Bill would don his red coat and cotton-wool beard every year without fail.

'One day she'll be old enough to know it's him, and then where will he be?' she had laughed.

But that day had never come for little Maisie Brigham. She had gone to her grave believing that it truly was Father Christmas who brought her birthday presents.

'Poor man,' Sister said. 'I feel awful now. I wish I hadn't said anything.'

'You weren't to know, were you?'

'All the same, I should speak to him, to apologise–'

'I'll have a word with him tonight. I'm seeing him at the rehearsal.'

'You will tell him I'm sorry, won't you? Make sure he knows I didn't mean any offence?'

'I'm sure he knows that, Sister. It was probably just the shock that upset him, that's all.'

It was Bill who sought her out to apologise at the rehearsal.

'I feel such a fool,' he said. 'I should never have flown off the handle like that. And to upset those kids, too. Heaven knows what Sister must think of me.'

'She understands,' Peggy assured him. 'She was more worried that she'd upset you.'

'I daresay she thinks I'm soft.' He sighed. 'I know I should be getting over it by now, but it still catches me out sometimes. Especially at this time of year.'

'I'm not surprised,' Peggy said. 'Anyway, time has nothing to do with it. I lost my little boy ten years ago, and not a day goes by when I don't think about him.'

He looked at her sharply. 'You lost a son?'

Peggy nodded. 'John. He died of diphtheria when he was four years old.'

'I didn't know.'

'I try not to talk about it. My Eric doesn't like it.'

'I expect he finds it too hard, like me?'

Peggy was silent. The truth was, she didn't know how her husband felt about their son's death. From the day John died, he had retreated into silence. He wouldn't even talk about his son, or visit his grave. She remembered his impatience with her on the days when she would sit and cry. She told herself he was grieving in his own way, but sometimes she wondered if he hadn't forgotten his son completely.

But then, Eric had never really been a family man. For all he was a good provider, he had little warmth for any of his children. If anything, he seemed to resent them for taking Peggy's attention away from him.

'Anyway, will you tell Sister how sorry I am?' Bill's voice broke into her thoughts. 'I don't like to let anyone down, especially kids. But I can't–'

'You haven't let anyone down,' Peggy said. 'Don't even think that.'

The shop was closed by the time Peggy got home, but she was surprised to see a light on in

164

the window. As she approached, she was even more surprised to see the lanky silhouette of her husband up a ladder. He was pinning paper chains up in the shop window.

She let herself in the side entrance and through the connecting door to the shop.

'What's all this?' she asked.

Eric looked down at her from the top of the ladder, a paper chain draped across his hands. Pearl was holding on to the foot of the ladder. She had curled her hair and put on some lipstick, Peggy was glad to see.

'It was Pearl's idea. She thought we might get more customers in if we decorated the place, made it look a bit more festive.' Eric climbed down the ladder and stepped back to survey his handiwork. 'What do you think?'

'It looks lovely.' *Just as I knew it would when I suggested it last Christmas*, Peggy added silently. But Eric looked so pleased with himself, she didn't want to spoil the moment. 'Good idea, Pearl.'

'Thank you.' Pearl looked pleased with herself.

'I'll go and take off my coat then I'll give you a hand,' she offered.

'No need, we've nearly finished,' Pearl beamed at her. 'Why don't you go and make a start on the tea? Nellie's been grumbling for the past hour that she's famished. As usual!' She pulled a face.

Peggy went upstairs, where Nellie met her on the landing.

'I s'pose you've seen what's going on downstairs?' were her first sharp words.

'Yes, I think it looks lovely.'

'Waste of time if you ask me,' Nellie snorted.

165

'You don't need fancy paper chains. We never had them when my husband was alive, and that didn't stop us doing a decent trade.'

She followed Peggy into the kitchen. 'And what time do you call this?' she demanded.

'I told you I'd be late tonight. There was a rehearsal.'

'Rehearsal! You've no business gadding about and leaving your home and your family.'

'Eric didn't seem to mind. And I left food out for you, all you needed to do was put it in the oven–'

'That ain't the point!' Nellie snapped. 'The point is you should be here, looking after your family. This is where you belong, my girl.' Her eyes bulged.

'It's only for another couple of weeks and then I'll be back home,' Peggy reminded her.

'And not a moment too soon, if you ask me,' Nellie muttered.

The last rehearsal had been so much fun with Miss Tanner in charge, Peggy was looking forward to the next one. Her heart sank when she saw the Assistant Matron back in her usual place behind the table.

'Happy days are here again,' Bill whispered to her. 'Bit different from last week, ain't it?'

'Miss Tanner doesn't look much happier herself,' Peggy said. The ward sister usually had a smile for everyone, but this time she sat straight-backed at the piano, staring into space.

They weren't the only ones to feel the tension. Everyone seemed to be nervous, and no one

166

seemed to be able to get anything right. Lines were fluffed, songs were off-key, and words were forgotten. Meanwhile, Miss Davis was like an angry dog, snapping at them all.

By the time it was their turn to take to the stage, Peggy was a trembling wreck.

'Calm down, girl.' Bill smiled at her, but even his gentle encouragement didn't help. Suddenly Peggy couldn't seem to remember a single thing. She missed cues, ruined several of Bill's best tricks and ended up scattering a whole pack of cards across the stage.

'I'm sorry, Bill, I really am. I dunno what's come over me,' she whispered as she bent to gather them up.

'It's all right, Peg. No harm done.' Bill dropped to his knees at her side to help her.

'Good Lord, can't you do anything right?' Miss Davis barked at them from the front row.

'It doesn't matter.' Bill spoke up, looking the Assistant Matron in the eye.

'Of course it matters! It needs to be perfect. If you can't understand that then you shouldn't be here!'

A stunned silence followed her words. Peggy held her breath.

Bill took Peggy's arm and slowly straightened up, pulling her to her feet with him. 'Come on,' he said. 'We don't have to stand here just to be shouted at by the likes of her. This is supposed to be a daft show, not a Royal Command Performance!'

Outside, Bill gave vent to his anger. 'Did you hear the way she spoke to us? I'm not having that. Who does she think she is?'

'It was my fault. I shouldn't have dropped those cards—'

'It was an accident. Nothing to worry about,' Bill said firmly.

'But what if she throws you out of the show because of me?'

'Let her. I ain't even sure I want to be in her rotten show, if that's the way she treats people.'

A moment later the doors flew open and Miss Tanner stalked out, clutching her sheet music.

'Blimey, what's happened now?' Peggy said.

Bill opened the door a fraction and peered through. 'Looks like everyone's packing up to walk out. I reckon Miss Davis has got her comeuppance good and proper.'

He turned to her. 'Don't look so down in the dumps about it, girl. Tell you what, why don't we go down to the café and have a cup of tea, cheer ourselves up?'

Peggy hesitated. 'I should be getting home...'

'They won't be expecting you back yet, will they?'

'I suppose not.' She smiled at him. 'All right, I could do with a cuppa to steady my nerves after all that!'

They went to the café on the corner. They each had a cup of tea and Bill treated her to a bun.

'I'm not sure I deserve it, after my performance,' Peggy said ruefully.

Bill shook his head. 'Will you be quiet about that? I told you, it weren't anyone's fault.' He stirred three sugars into his tea. 'Anyway, talking of performances, I've got something to tell you.'

168

'Oh yes? What's that?'

He lowered his gaze. 'I've been thinking,' he said. 'And I've decided, if Sister still needs someone to dress up as Father Christmas – I'll do it.'

Peggy stared at him. 'You will? What changed your mind?'

'If you really want to know, it was you.'

'Me?'

'I thought about what you said. You lost your little lad, but that doesn't stop you nursing those kids, even though it must be hard for you to do it.'

'It was hard at first,' Peggy admitted. 'But knowing I'm doing something to help them ... well, it sort of helps me, too.'

'That's what I thought,' Bill nodded. 'I know my Alice wouldn't want me to shut myself away on Christmas Day feeling sorry for myself, and neither would Maisie. Christmas used to be such a happy time for us, and that's how I'd like it to be now. So, if you still want me to do it–' He lifted his broad shoulders in a shrug.

'That would be grand, Bill. And I'm sure you'll enjoy it, too.' Without thinking, she put her hand over his.

'We'll have to see, won't we? I just hope I can be as big-hearted as you are.'

Peggy felt herself blushing. 'I'm nothing special.'

'Oh, you are. You're a very special woman, Peggy Atkins.'

Suddenly his hand was covering hers and she was looking up into his face, with his flattened boxer's nose and kind, warm eyes the colour of honey...

169

She pulled away from him sharply, and the moment was gone.

'I'm sorry,' Bill muttered, sliding his hand away.

'No, it's my fault.' She stumbled to her feet, gathering up her bag. 'I should be going.'

'Peggy–'

'My Eric will be wondering where I am... He likes his tea on the table...' She was gabbling, and she knew it, but she was too flustered to do anything else.

'Peggy, wait. Please–'

She rushed out of the café.

She hurried home in a state of shock. What was she thinking of, doing such a thing? She had been so lost in the moment, it was as if she was in a dream. What if one of the customers from the shop had walked past and seen her there, sitting at a window table holding hands with another man?

Shame washed over her, even more because she could still feel the warmth of his fingers wrapped around hers.

You've no business gadding about and leaving your home and your family. Nellie's harsh words resonated in her brain. Perhaps the old woman had seen something in her, recognised what was going on, even if she hadn't seen it herself.

Eric was cashing up in the shop when Peggy got home. Nellie was with him, behind the counter.

'Where's Pearl?' Peggy asked.

'You might well ask,' Nellie said darkly.

'Gone off to the hairdresser. She's been working so hard, I gave her the time off,' Eric said.

Nellie snorted. 'Working hard! Is that what you

170

call it?'

Eric turned to his mother. 'She worked late every night last week, and she helped out with the stocktaking on our half-day.'

Peggy stared at him. It wasn't like her husband to stand up to his mother. Or to defend her sister, for that matter.

To her even greater surprise, Eric came round the counter and planted a kiss on her cheek. 'You feel like ice,' he said.

'It's freezing out.' Peggy shivered inside her coat. 'I'll soon warm up after a hot cup of tea.'

'I'll put the kettle on. You go up and get warm by the fire.'

Peggy's mouth fell open. Was this really her husband speaking? She had never in their whole married life known Eric to do anything for her.

She glanced at her mother-in-law. Nellie stood behind them, her arms folded across her chest, a belligerent expression on her face. No wonder she looked so sour, Peggy thought. She had brought her son up to believe he was a little prince, used to women waiting on him hand and foot. She wouldn't take kindly to the idea of him fetching and carrying for anyone else, let alone his wife.

'Did you have a nice time?' Eric asked, as he followed her up the stairs.

Peggy started guiltily. 'What? Oh, you mean the rehearsal?'

He laughed. 'What else did you think I meant? You haven't been getting up to anything, have you? Carrying on with another man?'

'Of course not!' Peggy snapped.

Eric looked taken aback. 'Steady on, Peg, I was

171

only having a laugh. You'd never do anything like that. You're not the type.'

No, she thought as she put another log on the fire. *I'm not the type.* And she didn't want to be, either. She was a married woman, with a nice home and a loving family. She had everything she wanted.

Nellie was right, she had no business gadding about.

It was a relief to hear that the next rehearsal would not be happening as everyone had decided to boycott it. She had managed to avoid Bill all week by hiding out in the kitchen or the sluice whenever he was due up on the ward.

But there was no avoiding him when Sister asked her to go with a young boy down to theatre. As luck would have it, Bill was due to take him.

'Haven't seen you in a while,' he said as he pushed the lift door back with a clatter.

'No.' She couldn't meet his eye.

'You'll have heard no one's going to the rehearsal?'

She nodded. 'Doesn't look like there's going to be a Christmas show after all.'

'Oh, I'm sure it will all get sorted out in the end. Lot of fuss over nothing, if you ask me.'

Peggy stared straight ahead of her as the lift jerked and rattled downwards.

'Peggy–'

'I'm not sure if I can be in the show with you,' she blurted out.

'Oh.' He sounded disappointed but not surprised. 'I see.'

172

'It's the shop, you see... Christmas is coming, and it's our busy time, and Eric needs an extra pair of hands, and–'

'It's all right, you don't have to explain. I understand.'

His voice was gentle. Peggy fought the urge to look at him, knowing she might weaken if she did.

'I'm sure you can find someone else to help you with your act.'

He sighed. 'My heart ain't really in it any more.'

The lift jolted to a halt, and Bill stepped forward to push back the metal grille. Peggy hurried through it, relieved to escape.

They walked in silence down the passageway to theatre, where they delivered their patient.

'Not taking the lift back up?' Bill asked.

She shook her head. 'I'll take the stairs.'

He nodded, quietly understanding. 'I'll be seeing you, then.'

'Yes.'

As she walked away, Bill called after her, 'Peggy?'

She stopped in her tracks. 'Yes?'

'It was fun while it lasted, wasn't it?'

Peggy allowed herself to look over her shoulder, meeting his gaze one last time. There was no need to ask what he meant; it was written there on his face.

'Yes,' she smiled. 'Yes, it was.'

173

Miriam

3rd December 1945

A sandstorm howled outside. Lavinia listened fearfully to the hot desert wind whipping at the silken folds of the tent.

'I must go,' she whispered.

'You cannot. The storm is coming closer now. You must stay. You will be safe here.'

Lavinia gazed around her. The gilded tent was lavishly decorated as befitted a prince's quarters, hung with draperies of exquisite jewel-coloured silk, the floor strewn with richly embroidered cushions. The musky scent of incense hung heavy in the air, intoxicating her.

How did she, a virginal vicar's daughter, ever come to find herself in such a place? And with such a man...

The sheikh smiled sardonically. 'There are worse places to be trapped, I think?'

Lavinia stared up at him helplessly. Trapped she was indeed, and with the most disturbing man she had ever met in her sheltered life. The sheikh was dark, mysterious and forbidden, with his burning, coal-black eyes, sharply drawn cheekbones and cruel but sensuous lips. He seemed to draw her to him like a moth to a flame.

And those hands, the fingers long and sensitive. She knew one touch could send her senses spinning into

174

realms she had never experienced before.

You will be safe here.

She felt anything but safe. She had escaped the storm, only to find herself in much worse danger. A danger to her very honour.

She wanted to resist him, but her limbs felt weak as he took her in his arms, his face lowering towards hers. She knew he was going to kiss her and even though she knew it was wrong and sinful, she was powerless as his eyes met hers and he whispered in a voice deep and dark and full of mystery–

'Sister, I think Mrs Jefferson's in labour.'

Miriam Trott stuffed her novel under a cushion and looked up at the student nurse who stood in her sitting-room doorway.

'What have I told you about coming in here without knocking?' she snapped.

'Sorry, Sister.' The young nurse lingered in the doorway, staring down at her stout black shoes.

Miriam stood up with a sigh, brushing crumbs off her uniform. How typical of wretched Mrs Jefferson to go into labour while she was enjoying her afternoon tea. These women thought of no one but themselves.

She followed the student nurse back down the passageway that led to the maternity ward. 'Have her waters broken?' she asked.

'I – I don't know, Sister.'

'What do you mean, you don't know? Didn't you think to look?'

'No, Sister. Sorry, Sister.'

'Then how do you know she's in labour, girl?'

'She ... she said so, Sister.'

Miriam stared at her. 'And you're supposed to

175

be in your third year? Good gracious, don't they teach you girls anything these days?'

'Sorry, Sister.' The young woman bit her lip. Daisy Baker might have been a decent nurse if she had spent as much time on her studies as she did flirting with the junior doctors. As it was, she was quite one of the laziest students Miriam had ever had to suffer.

'Sorry, indeed. You will be sorry, my girl, if you've disturbed me for nothing!'

As it turned out, Mrs Jefferson *was* in labour, and her copious waters had not only broken, they had soaked through the bed sheets. Mrs Jefferson was now pacing round the bed groaning and crying in pain, her slippers leaving damp imprints on the newly polished floor, while another student, Rose Trent, stood watching her helplessly.

'What is this woman doing out of bed?' Miriam demanded. 'You know I don't allow it.'

Nurse Trent looked wide-eyed. 'I tried to stop her, Sister, but she says it helps the pain.'

'I don't care about that! Matron will be doing her rounds in a minute; we can't have patients wandering about as they please.' She turned to Nurse Baker. 'Get this bed changed immediately, and clean the floor. And do stop making such a fuss!' She turned on Mrs Jefferson. 'You're giving me a headache.'

'But it hurts!' Mrs Jefferson moaned.

'Of course it hurts! You're having a baby, it's supposed to hurt. Good gracious, I would have thought you of all people would know that by now!'

Mrs Jefferson was a regular on the ward, and

176

exactly the type of patient Miriam disliked. Her family were as poor as church mice, and yet she and her ghastly husband insisted on producing more children. Six at the last count, all of them in rags and probably infested with God knows what.

And now she had the perfectly ordered ward in uproar, as the other women fretted and fussed over her. Miriam eyed the double doors. It was all very annoying; she had been hoping to finish the next chapter of *Desert Heat* before Matron came round.

Fortunately, she had managed to restore some kind of order by the time Miss Fox arrived. The bed had been changed, the floor cleaned and polished again, and the other women had been ordered back into their beds. Mrs Jefferson, meanwhile, had been ushered off to the labour room with strict instructions not to scream too loudly while Matron was on the ward.

'Good morning, Sister,' Miss Fox greeted her with a warm smile. Miss Davis was by her side, stony-faced as usual.

'Good morning, Matron. Assistant Matron.' Miriam nodded coldly to her. She still hadn't forgiven Miss Davis for the way she had spoken to her at the meeting the previous evening.

Miriam still burned with humiliation, thinking about it. How dare Miss Davis try to tell her she couldn't sing the song she wanted at the Christmas show? And in front of everyone, too. Who did she think she was?

Of course, Miriam had gone straight to Matron to let her know exactly what she thought of Miss

177

Davis and the way she was going about matters. It was not the way things were done at the Nightingale. And Miriam should know; she had been there for twenty-five years.

She wondered if Matron had reprimanded her yet. She hoped she had. Although the Assistant Matron's face gave nothing away, as usual. She really was a cold fish, with those pale blue, expressionless eyes.

Miriam led the way around the ward, and waited as Matron spoke to all the patients in turn. They had had a new admission during the night, a young woman who had given birth to her first baby in the early hours. Now she sat up in bed, looking around her with a shocked expression on her face, as if surprised to find herself there. As well she might, Miriam thought. She had her suspicions about that one.

But as usual, Miss Fox was far too kind, holding the girl's hand and speaking gently to her. Miriam caught Miss Davis rolling her eyes impatiently, and thought they had something in common at least.

When Matron had at last finished trying to coax a smile out of the girl, they moved on to Mrs Goodwood. Miriam tensed, waiting for the Assistant Matron to pass comment on her due dates again. But to her satisfaction, this time she stayed silent.

But just as she had started to think that perhaps the Assistant Matron had finally learned her place, Miss Davis suddenly turned on Nurse Baker.

'Are those cuffs clean?' she said in a sharp voice.

178

'I–' Daisy Baker, foolish girl that she was, could only stand there, opening and closing her mouth like a stupefied goldfish.

Miriam glanced down at the girl's wrists. Sure enough, the white linen was distinctly grubby.

'Go and change at once!' she hissed. She could barely suppress her rage and it was all she could do not to grab the girl by her blonde hair and drag her out of the ward herself.

She didn't know which made her more furious, the fact that the girl had had the temerity to turn up for Matron's ward round with dirty cuffs, or that it was Miss Davis who had noticed it.

She saw the quirk of Miss Davis's eyebrow as Nurse Baker hurried away If the Assistant Matron's face had been capable of expression, she would have been wearing a self-satisfied smile by now, Miriam was sure of it.

Finally, Matron and Miss Davis left the ward, and Miriam went over to vent to her friend Mrs Goodwood, who was doing *The Times* crossword.

'You seem to have had quite an eventful morning, Sister,' she observed.

'Honestly, these young girls, I swear they get more slapdash every year,' Miriam fumed. 'They don't seem to understand that pride in their appearance is fundamental to good nursing. If they are sloppy with themselves, they will be sloppy with the patients, too.'

'How right you are, Sister,' Mrs Goodwood sympathised. 'I had exactly the same trouble with the women in the WVS. And how unfortunate that it was that woman who spotted it,' she added.

Miriam gritted her teeth. 'Quite.'

179

That was the worst of it for her, that Miss Davis now thought she had got one over on her.

Mrs Goodwood changed the subject and asked about the new admission, the young girl who had arrived during the night.

'Oh, her.' Miriam rolled her eyes. 'Mrs Jones, as she calls herself. Although if that's her name, mine's the Queen of Sheba! And as for that ring she's wearing...'

Mrs Goodwood's eyes widened, scandalised. 'You don't think she's married?'

'My dear, when you've been on this ward as long as I have, you learn to spot them a mile off.' Miriam shook her head. 'I daresay she's no better than she ought to be, that one. You mark my words, there won't be any husband visiting on Sunday. I wouldn't be surprised if the father was a GI, or one of those Free French. Or a sailor from the docks. At any rate, I daresay he'll be long gone by now.'

'Shocking,' Mrs Goodwood said faintly.

'Oh, you see all sorts in here. Present company excepted, of course.' She smiled at the woman in the bed.

She paused briefly to admire the flowers in the vase at her bedside, another gift from Mrs Goodwood's devoted husband Harold.

'Anyway, I must be getting on,' she said. She could hear the sheikh summoning her from his Bedouin tent. With any luck she could finish her chapter before they had to start serving lunch to the patients.

'Before you go,' Mrs Goodwood lowered her voice, 'I wondered if you'd had any luck securing

180

me a private room, as you promised?'

Miriam shook her head. 'I'm afraid we may have to give it to Mrs Jefferson instead. She has been taken down to Theatre. It seems she needs a caesarean.' She frowned. Really, there was no end to the inconvenience the wretched woman was causing. 'We usually have to give the private rooms to patients needing post-operative care.'

'Oh.' Mrs Goodwood looked disappointed. 'That's rather unfortunate. I must admit I had rather hoped to have some peace and quiet. You know I'm a terribly light sleeper...'

'I know.' Miriam hated to disappoint her friend. Mrs Goodwood was a person of quality. Of course she should not be expected to mix with these rowdy women, with their rough and ready manners and their coarse sense of humour. Miriam was used to it, but even she found it hard to take sometimes. A woman of Mrs Goodwood's sensibilities must find it quite unbearable.

She patted her hand. 'Let me see what I can do,' she said. 'Perhaps I can have Mrs Jefferson moved back to the ward a little sooner. I'm sure she'd prefer to be back here, among her friends, anyway.' Her mouth curled. Lily Jefferson was the loudest of the women on the ward, always larking about.

'Would you? I'd be so grateful. I know I'm supposed to be resting, but it's so difficult.' Mrs Goodwood sighed, her hand going to her swollen belly.

'You leave it with me, my dear.'

She stood up to go. As she did, she noticed the newspaper lying on the bedside locker.

181

'I wonder,' she said. 'Might I have a look at this, if you've finished with it?'

'Yes, of course.' Mrs Goodwood smiled knowingly at her. 'I daresay you'll be wanting to finish off the crossword? I'm warning you, it's beastly this morning. If you can finish it, you're a better woman than I am!'

But Miriam had no interest in the crossword as she hurried back to her sitting room with the newspaper tucked under her arm. She closed the door and carefully spread the paper out on her table. She flicked past the news and the half-finished crossword, turning straight away to the only page in the newspaper that ever interested her.

The personal column.

She had been reading the lonely hearts column for as long as she could remember. Every morning she went through it, noting down any advertisements that caught her eye.

There were more than there used to be, at least. During the war there were hardly any men left to advertise, but now there were whole lists of them. Widowers, ex-servicemen whose wives had abandoned them while they were away serving their country. All looking for a woman to share their lives with.

But even as she read them, Miriam could almost hear her mother and her sisters laughing at her.

'Oh Minnie, what's to become of you?' She pictured them, shaking their heads in mock sadness. 'Can it really be so difficult for you to find a man? We all managed it.'

It was a fact that rankled with Miriam. She was

182

the eldest and yet somehow all three of her sisters had managed to get married before her. Even the youngest, Freda, had found herself a husband and she was as plain as a pikestaff.

But Miriam remained firmly on the shelf. It simply wasn't fair.

It wasn't for the want of trying, either. One of the main reasons Miriam had chosen to train as a nurse was because she intended to find a handsome doctor to marry before she had finished her training. But here she was, a ward sister for more than twenty years, and still she hadn't caught anyone's eye.

And now she felt as if she had missed her chance. She was the wrong side of forty-five, and all the doctors were far too young. And anyone remotely eligible was quickly snapped up by the likes of Nurse Baker and her silly friends.

So far, Miriam's sole experience of romance came from the torrid novels she loved to read, especially by Agatha Pendlebury. Now there was someone who understood what stirred a woman's soul! But when it came to real life, it felt as if love had passed her by.

Or so she had thought, until two days ago when Frank Tillery came into her life.

Miriam hadn't met him yet, but the woman at the discreet introductions agency spoke glowingly of him.

'He's in his forties, ex-RAF and now a bank manager. Six foot tall, dark hair, blue eyes. Very charming.'

'He sounds too good to be true,' Miriam said sourly.

183

'Oh no, he's true all right. I've met him and interviewed him personally. Utterly charming man. I'm sure he's just your type.'

'I'll be the judge of that, thank you very much!' Miriam snapped. The woman was far too chummy for her liking. Miriam wanted a man, not a best friend.

The woman had turned a bit funny at that. 'I'll make the necessary arrangements, shall I?' she said stiffly.

'You do that,' Miriam sniffed. 'Although you can be sure I will be lodging a complaint if it turns out you've wasted my time.'

The woman's mouth curled. 'I don't doubt that for a moment, Miss Trott.'

Miriam refused to feel optimistic as she arrived at the Waldorf Hotel for her first meeting with Frank Tillery. She had been here before, after all, and she had always been disappointed. She had been let down too often to pin her hopes on any man.

In the flesh, Frank Tillery was bound to be short, squat, balding and broke. If he even bothered to turn up at all.

She arrived early, even though she told herself she should be late. She was so convinced she was going to be let down, she hadn't even bothered to dress up for the occasion. She was wearing her old utility suit in a dull brown worsted that did nothing for her sallow complexion. The only splash of colour was the red carnation on her lapel that the woman at the introduction agency had insisted she wore so that she and Frank Tillery could recognise each other.

184

Although if the woman's effusive description was to be believed, such things would not be necessary. All Miriam would have to do was look for a man who bore a striking resemblance to Clark Gable.

Or probably more like Peter Lorre, she thought.

She had arranged to meet Frank outside the hotel. She didn't want to waste money on an expensive afternoon tea if Frank stood her up and she had to sit and eat it all by herself with everyone watching her.

It looked as if she was right to be cautious when ten minutes went by and there was no sign of him.

Typical, Miriam thought. Another afternoon wasted. She was just about to leave when a deep voice behind her said, 'Miss Trott?'

She turned around, and found herself staring up into the most beautiful eyes she had ever seen. She had never visited the Mediterranean, but she felt sure that the sun sparkling off the blue-green sea must be the same colour.

'I'm Frank Tillery,' he said. 'I think you're expecting me?'

He was wrong, Miriam thought. She had certainly not been expecting anything like the tall, well-dressed man who stood before her. It was as if he had stepped straight from the pages of an Agatha Pendlebury novel, with his darkly handsome looks and winning smile. She would have said there must have been a mistake but for the bright red carnation in the lapel of his jacket.

Miriam was so shocked she could scarcely speak.

185

'I'm so sorry to keep you waiting,' he said. Even his voice was thrilling, deep with a hint of upper class about it. 'The traffic was terrible, I had to get out of the taxi and walk from Holborn. Am I terribly late?'

'No, no, not at all,' Miriam instantly forgot her irritation. 'I was early.'

'Had I known such a charming lady was waiting for me, I would have run all the way down Kingsway.' He smiled disarmingly at her, and offered her his arm. 'Shall we go in? That is, assuming you aren't so horrified by my tardiness that you wish to have nothing more to do with me?'

Miriam opened and closed her mouth, but all that emerged was a weak smile.

Frank's manners were as charming as his looks. But as she stared across the table at him, Miriam felt uneasy. Surely there must be something wrong with him? No man could be so handsome and so charming, and not have been claimed already.

She was never that lucky. This sort of thing simply did not happen to her. He would be boorish, she decided. Conceited, full of himself. He would spend the whole time talking about himself, telling her how wonderful he was...

But he didn't. Instead, he was delightful company. He was funny, intelligent and talked more about Miriam than he did about himself. He was wealthy, too, judging by the expensive cut of his suit.

But still she couldn't stop looking for a fault. Perhaps it was the way he ate? Perhaps he would have no table manners, or slurp his tea? But everything about him was utterly perfect. It was as if she had conjured the ideal man from her imagination and made him real.

Even Miriam, with her uncanny ability to find fault, was utterly mesmerised.

So then, of course, she became convinced that if there was nothing wrong with him, there must be something wrong with her.

She would never be good enough for him, she decided. Although to her surprise, Frank seemed to be quite enjoying her company. He listened avidly to what she had to say, and even paid her a few compliments.

Halfway through the date, she excused herself and hurried off to the powder room, where she quickly teased her brown curls and put on some lipstick. Looking at herself in the mirror, she was quite surprised that she liked what she saw. Even her old brown suit couldn't dim the sparkle in her eyes, or the rosy flush in her cheeks.

'And do you work, Miss Trott?' Frank asked when she returned to the table.

'No. I have – independent means.'

She didn't know what possessed her to say it. All she knew was that she desperately wanted to appear interesting, and not as she was, a dull little middle-aged spinster.

'I see. So you're an heiress?'

Miriam gave a slight shrug of her shoulders. 'That would be telling,' she replied evasively.

'A woman of mystery, eh? How intriguing.' He leaned across the table, his interest kindling. 'Do tell me more, Miss Trott.'

187

Miriam thought desperately for a moment. 'Actually, my father made a fortune in the colonies,' she said. 'Before he died, that is. He contracted malaria while he was overseeing our new tea plantation in India.'

In fact, her father was an accountant and had never been further than Frinton-on-Sea. But Portia, the raven-haired heroine of *Sins of the Father*, had been left in such a precarious position. It wasn't an Agatha Pendlebury, but it was still one of her favourites.

'How extraordinary,' Frank said.

'Indeed. My uncle tried to cheat me out of my fortune, but thankfully I was able to prevail.'

'I'm glad to hear it.' He frowned, and for a moment Miriam wondered if she had embellished her story a little too much. 'And where do you live now?' he asked.

'Kensington. I live all alone, except for a couple of faithful family retainers.'

'I see.' Frank looked thoughtful. 'You have quite a story to tell, Miss Trott.'

Miriam smiled back at him. Unfortunately this part wasn't her story, but that of naïve ingénue Julianna in Agatha Pendlebury's *Innocent Passion*, but it didn't matter. She wouldn't be seeing Frank again for him to find out the truth.

Because for all her intriguing stories, she knew their first date would also be their last.

As they left the Waldorf and the doorman hailed them a taxi, Miriam was already steeling herself for the usual polite goodbye. Frank would tell her how much he enjoyed meeting her, hint at some vague rendezvous in the future – and

188

then he would go off in his cab and she would never see him again.

By the time the taxi arrived, she was ready, her brittle smile in place.

'Well, it's been delightful–' she started to say. Frank frowned.

'Aren't you getting in?' he asked.

It was only then that she noticed he was holding the taxi door open for her. 'But–'

She was about to say she would catch the bus, then remembered she was supposed to be a wealthy heiress.

'I'll take another cab,' she said.

'There's no need, I have to pass Kensington on my way home. I can drop you off. Unless you really can't bear another moment of my company?' Frank looked rueful.

Miriam smiled. 'Put like that, how can I refuse?'

This was not the way it usually happened, she thought as they drove off. Most of the time men couldn't wait to get away from her. Yet here was Frank, wanting to hold on to her company for longer. It was a strange and unnerving feeling.

She watched the streets going past, taking her further and further away from Bethnal Green. If they went much further, she would be quite lost.

Finally, she recognised the Albert Memorial and asked Frank to let her out.

'Are you sure? I don't mind taking you to your door, if you tell me your address–'

'No, it's quite all right,' Miriam assured him hastily. 'It's such a nice evening for a walk.'

Frank glanced out at the sky, threatening snow.

189

'Well, if you're certain...' He signalled to the driver to stop, then turned back to her. 'I wonder,' he said. 'May I see you again, Miss Trott?'

The question took her by surprise. 'Why?' she blurted out.

He smiled. 'Why not?'

She could think of many reasons. But all that came out of her mouth was, 'Yes. Yes, I'd like that very much.'

It had started to snow. Miriam shivered in her thin jacket as the first flakes began to fall. It was a long way back to Bethnal Green, and she didn't have the money for another taxi. All she had was her bus fare, but she did not have the faintest idea where to catch the bus back to the East End.

But she was so happy she could have burst into song.

It was late when she arrived back at the Nightingale, cold, weary and bedraggled. Sister Hyde was on her way to bed when Miriam let herself in to the sisters' house.

'Why, Miss Trott, where have you been until this hour? You look like a drowned rat.'

So would you, if you'd just walked halfway from Kensington, Miriam wanted to snap back at her but her teeth were chattering too much to speak.

Sister Hyde took charge. 'Come in and get warmed up, before you catch your death of cold. Take those wet things off and get into bed while I fetch the maid to make you a warm drink and a hot-water bottle.'

Safe in her room, Miriam looked at herself in her full-length mirror. No wonder Sister Hyde had been so dismayed. Her hat was a sodden

190

mess dripping down her neck, and there was an alarming blue tinge around her lips.

Her gaze fell to the bright red carnation in her buttonhole. Miriam plucked it off and held it to her face, feeling the softness of its damp petals against her wet cheek.

She would press it, she decided, inside the pages of her favourite novel. She still couldn't quite believe she would see ever Frank Tillery again, but at least she would be left with a lovely memory.

But she did see Frank again. And again. Over the next two weeks, they met frequently for tea, or trips to the cinema, and on Sunday they walked together in the park, holding hands like proper sweethearts. Miriam was wary at first, convinced it was too good to be true. But gradually Frank managed to charm his way past her defences. In spite of everything, he seemed genuinely interested in her.

Miriam floated through life on a blissful cloud of happiness. She felt like a different person. She chatted to the patients and admired their babies, even though most of them were ugly, grizzling little scraps. And when she caught Nurse Baker flirting with Dr Armstrong she simply smiled and thought how wonderful it was to be young and in love.

She was even able to tolerate Miss Davis at the next show rehearsal, and didn't comment once on the utter shambles the Assistant Matron was making of the whole thing.

Even so, every time Miriam saw Frank she was convinced it would be the last. Sooner or later

191

she knew he would grow tired of her, or he would see her for the dull spinster she really was.

But if anything, he seemed even more fascinated by her every time they met. Miriam had stopped telling him stories about her life as a wealthy heiress or her childhood on the tea plantation in India, but she was careful not to allude to her real life at the Nightingale, either. From time to time she wondered if she should come clean, but then she decided against it. She couldn't let herself believe that their romance was going to continue anyway, so why not simply enjoy it while it lasted?

She was so absorbed in her real-life romance, she barely had time to keep up with the fictional kind. Agatha Pendlebury lay forgotten in her bag, until one day when she and Frank were at the Ritz for tea and her handbag fell off the table, spilling its contents over the floor.

As he knelt to retrieve them, Frank picked up the novel. He looked at the cover, his dark brows rising. 'Desert Heat, eh? Sounds rather racy.'

'It's not mine.' Miriam snatched it from him. 'Someone lent it to me. I only took it to be polite.'

'So you haven't read it?'

'Good heavens, no! As if I'd read that nonsense.'

He laughed. 'I thought all women liked a bit of romance?'

'There's romance and there's rubbish,' Miriam said firmly, stuffing the book back into her bag.

'Rubbish, is it? You mean to tell me you're not looking for a handsome sheikh to sweep you off your feet?'

'Of course not! What an absurd notion. That

192

sort of thing never happens in real life.'

'Doesn't it?'

She looked down at him, on one knee at her feet. His eyes met hers so intently, for a fleeting moment she thought he was going to propose to her.

Then he was back on his feet again, and the moment had passed. But Miriam's heart still fluttered against her ribs.

'I'll believe it the day I see a camel lolloping down Piccadilly,' she said.

'Not all ardent lovers ride camels, you know.'

No, she was going to say. The duke in *Passion's Surrender* rode an enormous black stallion called Lucifer. But she stopped herself just in time.

'You seem very well informed?' she said, her brows rising. 'Don't tell me you read this rubbish?'

He smiled knowingly. 'You've discovered my dreadful secret!'

'I do hope not!'

'Then perhaps I'm just a born romantic?'

'Are you really?' She smiled at him.

His gaze held hers. 'I'm not sure I was,' he said. 'Until I met you.'

Miriam felt herself blushing. This could not be real, she told herself; it was far too wonderful. Frank even talked like a hero from an Agatha Pendlebury novel.

The bill arrived, and Frank reached into his inside pocket for his wallet. A strange, panicked look came over his face and he started frantically patting all his pockets.

'Oh no,' he murmured.

'What is it, Frank?' Miriam asked.

'This is frightfully embarrassing, but I appear to have left my wallet at home. Oh, how could I have been so stupid?'

'Don't worry, I'll pay,' she said, reaching for her handbag.

Frank shook his head. 'Oh no, I couldn't let you do that. It wouldn't be right to ask a lady to pay—'

'You're not asking, I'm offering. Besides, it's the only sensible solution. Unless you suggest we try to leave without paying?' she smiled.

Frank looked troubled as she counted notes and coins from her purse. 'I'm terribly sorry,' he kept saying. 'I can't tell you how dreadful I feel about this... I'll pay you back, I promise.'

'It's quite all right.' Miriam covered his hand with hers across the table.

He lifted her hand to his lips, his eyes holding hers across the table. 'You're a wonderful woman, Miriam Trott,' he said.

'Oh, Frank.' Miriam looked away. If only her mother and sisters could see her now, she thought, having tea at the Ritz with her very own Prince Charming.

Except Frank Tillery was not an imaginary hero from one of her novels. He was a real-life, flesh-and blood man, and he liked her. He really liked her. Perhaps even more than liked...

For the first time, Miriam began to allow herself to trust what her heart was telling her. This time, she thought, nothing could go wrong.

And then it did.

It happened on a wet Thursday morning. Matron had just finished her rounds, and Miriam

194

had stopped for her usual chat with Mrs Goodwood, who was reading *The Times.*

'Have you seen this, Sister?' She pointed to a story in the newspaper. 'They've arrested a man for conning a wealthy widow out of her fortune. Isn't that scandalous?'

'Awful,' Miriam agreed, straightening her bedclothes. 'Would you like me to plump up your pillows for you, my dear?'

'Yes, please.' Mrs Goodwood eased herself forward, still reading the newspaper. 'Apparently he's done it before to another woman. It says here both women were wealthy heiresses, and both nearly fifty. And I'm willing to bet neither of them is any Lana Turner, wouldn't you say?'

'Age and looks are no barrier to love, Mrs Goodwood,' Miriam replied testily.

'Well, no. But you'd think at their age they'd have more sense, wouldn't you? I mean, if a handsome man starts paying court, they can be sure he's only after their money.'

'Not necessarily.' Miriam punched the pillows into shape with great force. 'Perhaps his feelings were genuine?'

'And he got so carried away by those feelings that he forgot he already had a wife?' Mrs Goodwood sent her a patronising look over the edge of her newspaper. 'Oh, Sister, I never had you down as such a hopeless romantic!' She laughed. 'But I'm sure even you would never allow yourself to get carried away by a professional charmer. Good heavens, you'd have to be pretty dense to allow yourself to be taken in by such a con man. I'm sure the likes of you and I would see through this

195

character in a moment!'

'Indeed.' Miriam had a sudden picture of Frank patting down his pockets, the look of despair on his face when he realised he had forgotten his wallet.

I can't tell you how dreadful I feel about this... I'll pay you back, I promise...

'I can imagine him now, can't you? All good looks and smooth charm, making this poor lonely woman feel as if she was the most desirable and fascinating creature in the world. I suppose it's easy enough to fall for someone like that, if you were quite desperate,' Mrs Goodwood went on, folding up her newspaper. 'Women like that are to be pitied, aren't they? They're so hungry for love they'd fall for anything they were told. I say, you couldn't fill up my water jug, could you? I do so hate to be a nuisance...'

'Certainly, Mrs Goodwood.' Miriam snatched the jug from the bedside locker and headed off with it. Halfway up the ward, she found Nurse Baker deep in conversation with Nurse Trent.

'You there!' she roared at them. 'Don't just stand there gossiping. Fill this up for Mrs Goodwood. And if you've got nothing better to do, you can scrub out the bathrooms. Well, don't just stand there!' she snapped, as they gawped at her. 'Get on with it, before I give you another job to do.'

The two nurses scuttled off, looking over their shoulders at her. Miriam knew they must have got used to her being all smiles around them, but the last thing she felt like doing now was smiling.

She should have known. All her instincts had

196

told her there was something about Frank that was too good to be true, and now she knew she should have listened to them.

But even then, a small part of her refused to believe it. Frank was not the man in the story. His name was Ralph and he had been locked away behind bars for his crime. Just because one man fleeced rich women out of their life savings, it did not mean that every man would do the same. Even if they did happen to be good-looking and charming.

Frank had forgotten his wallet, it was as simple as that. Was she really going to condemn him for one mistake?

Even so, she was on her guard when she met him again that night.

Frank noticed it straight away. 'Are you all right, my love?' he asked her, all tender concern.

'Of course.' She forced herself to smile back, even though her heart felt like lead in her chest.

'Are you sure? You don't seem like your sprightly self.'

'I'm quite well, thank you.'

Thank goodness they were going to the cinema that evening. Usually Miriam enjoyed talking to Frank, but tonight she was so on edge she wasn't sure she could have spoken more than three words to him.

'Are you sure you have your wallet with you this time?' she joked feebly, as they lined up at the box office for their tickets.

'Yes, of course.' He looked embarrassed. 'I do apologise for that, I was utterly mortified. Thank goodness you were there to help me out.' He reached into his pocket for his wallet. 'In fact, thank you for reminding me, I must pay you back...'

'Thank you.' Miriam took the money, feeling relieved. Frank was no con man, after all, she told herself, otherwise surely he would have found an excuse not to repay her?

Then he ruined it all by saying, 'Of course, I suppose that's one advantage of stepping out with a wealthy heiress, isn't it?'

He laughed, and Miriam tried to laugh with him, but her face muscles were too taut to manage anything but the slightest of smiles.

'True,' she said. 'Although isn't it rather embarrassing for a bank manager to find himself short of funds?'

His smile dropped a fraction. 'Yes,' he said. 'Yes, I suppose it is.'

'Remind me again, which bank did you say you worked at?'

Frank hesitated. 'Hardcastle's,' he said at last.

'And which branch?'

He gave her a quizzical half-smile. 'Goodness me, what is this? Some kind of interrogation?'

'I was just curious, that's all.'

'If you must know, I work in High Holborn. Does that satisfy your curiosity?'

Was it her imagination, or did he seem rather ill at ease?

Miriam smiled. 'Yes, thank you,' she said, then added, 'I hope you didn't mind me asking?'

'No,' he said, irritably. 'Why should I?'

Why indeed, Miriam thought.

Frank paid for their tickets and they went into

198

the darkened auditorium, where the usherette showed them to their seats. But try as she might, Miriam could not keep her mind on the film.

And neither could Frank. She could feel him shifting restlessly beside her. And when she sent him a sidelong glance, even in the gloom of the cinema she could see the dark frown on his face.

There was definitely something on his mind, she thought. Was it his guilty conscience playing him up? Or had he realised she was on to him?

She tried to put her worries to the back of her mind when she went along to the rehearsal. Last time Miss Tanner had been in charge, and it had been such a jolly affair, ending up with them all having a festive sing-song around the piano. So when she walked into the dining room Miriam was disappointed to see Miss Davis back in her usual place in front of the stage.

She said as much to Violet Tanner. But her fellow ward sister barely seemed to respond. She sat at the piano staring blankly at her sheet music, as if she had never seen it before in her life.

It was going to be an interesting rehearsal, Miriam decided.

And it was. No one was happy to see Miss Davis back in charge, and it wasn't long before she began to get under everyone's skin.

Miriam knew her performance wasn't her best. She couldn't stop thinking about Frank so she forgot her words and sang slightly off-key. There were only a couple of tiny mistakes, but it didn't help that Miss Davis sat wincing in the front row.

By the end of the song she knew the Assistant Matron would have something to say to her, and

199

she was ready for her. But to her surprise, Miss Davis dismissed her from the stage without a word. Not even a thank you, she noticed as she swept past her table. As she passed, she tried to glance over the Assistant Matron's shoulder at the notes she was making, but her spidery scrawl was so tiny Miriam could not make head nor tail of them.

After her came a burly porter, who was doing a magic act. Miriam had been rather impressed by his tricks at previous rehearsals, but for some reason this time nerves seemed to get the better of him – or his assistant, at any rate – and it all went to pot. It ended with the assistant flapping around, trying to pick up a pack of playing cards she had somehow managed to scatter all over the stage.

Miriam actually found it quite amusing, and wondered if it might be good to add a bit of a comedy twist to their act. But Miss Davis didn't see the funny side. She really let fly at the poor woman, who just stood there and took it. But then the porter jumped to her defence and Miss Davis let him have it too, virtually ordering him off the stage.

Then Miss Tanner tried to step in and sort it out, and the feathers really flew. It ended up with the porter and his assistant walking out, and Miss Tanner following them.

Everyone was rather stunned by their departure, and there was a lot of awkwardness as they all looked round at each other, wondering what to do next. Miriam waited for a moment to see if Miss Davis would ask her to step in and play the piano, just so she could have the pleasure of refusing her. But so many other people started to leave by then, Miriam decided to join them.

Which was how she managed to find herself with an hour to spare in the middle of a snowy Friday afternoon. Just enough time to make a quick trip to Holborn...

At least there was a branch of Hardcastle's bank to be found on High Holborn. Miriam's heart had been in her mouth as she made her way down the busy street, half expecting that the whole of Frank's story might turn out to be a sham.

But there it was, a very solid, respectable-looking building. She only hoped her suitor would turn out to be just as solid and respectable.

As she pushed open the heavy wooden doors, Miriam began to feel rather foolish. Now she was here, her nerve deserted her and she didn't quite know what to do.

What should she say when she came face-to-face with Frank? She had prepared what she thought was a good story on the bus from Bethnal Green, something about needing advice with an important investment. But it all seemed rather flimsy now she was standing here in the marble-tiled hall, with customers passing to and fro around her. She felt certain that Frank would see straight through her. He would realise she didn't trust him, and then their romance would be over.

But then she knew that if she didn't get the reassurance she needed, it would probably be over anyway. A tiny seed of mistrust had been planted in her heart, and she knew it would only

201

go on growing unless she uprooted it quickly.

She went up to the wooden counter with fresh determination. The bespectacled young man peered at her from behind the panel of glass.

'Yes? Can I help you, Miss?'

Miriam cleared her throat. 'I'm here to see Mr Tillery.'

Straight away she saw the flash of doubt behind his spectacles. 'Who, Miss?'

'Mr Tillery. Frank Tillery? He's the manager at this branch.'

The young man looked confused.

'I'm sorry, Miss, but I think you must be mistaken. Our manager is Mr Abbott. As far as I know we don't have a Mr Tillery working here.' He must have seen the disappointment on Miriam's face because he added, 'But I could ask one of the other clerks? They might know someone of that name...'

'No,' Miriam shook her head. 'No, there's no need. You're right, I must be mistaken.'

'I'm sorry I couldn't help you, Miss. Perhaps if you try Barclays across the road...' The young man's voice followed Miriam as she left the bank.

Miriam stood outside on the pavement, at a loss. The snow that had fallen earlier had turned to dirty slush and the icy wetness seeped through her good shoes.

Don't you dare cry, Miriam Trott, she warned herself. *You're a fool and you only have yourself to blame.*

After all, what did she really expect? Happy endings were strictly for novels, not for the likes of her.

202

She tried to put it to the back of her mind, but over the following days her anger grew, consuming her. She snapped at the patients and berated the nurses at the slightest excuse. And when she saw a copy of the new Agatha Pendlebury novel lying on a patient's bedside table, it was all she could do not to fling it on the ward fire.

'Have you read it, Sister?' The woman looked up at her, smilingly oblivious. 'It's ever so good.'

Miriam looked at the cover. The sight of the couple in a tender embrace made her feel sick.

'*Be Still, My Beating Heart,* indeed!' she snapped. 'What a foolish notion. You'd be in a lot of trouble if your heart did stop beating, let me tell you!'

She also determinedly ignored Frank's increasingly desperate telephone calls. Part of her wanted to confront him over his deception, but the other part was too humiliated to face him.

And yet another part of her wanted to see him because in spite of what he had done to her and all the hurt he had caused, her treacherous heart still belonged to him.

In the end her self-righteous side took over. Why should she hide herself away? She had done nothing wrong. And she had no reason to feel humiliated, either. She wasn't one of the foolish women that Mrs Goodwood had poured such scorn on when she read about them in the newspaper. Miriam was strong; she had found Frank out and outwitted him.

He should be the one slinking away in shame, not her. She decided there and then that she was going to confront Frank Tillery one more time.

203

And she would make him answer for what he had done to her.

Of course Frank had no idea of her intentions when she agreed to go for a walk with him in Hyde Park. Miriam made sure she was late, just to teach him a lesson. She had almost expected him to give up and go home after half an hour. But he was still waiting at the gates, clutching a bunch of red carnations and gazing up and down the road, an anxious expression on his face.

Miriam stiffened like a cat as she approached him. Even now, knowing what he was, she could not stop her heart lifting with happiness at the sight of him.

He saw her and smiled broadly. 'There you are! I was beginning to worry.'

'Did you think I'd jilted you?' Miriam said coldly.

His smile turned to a frown. 'Not at all. I was concerned that something might have happened to you, that's all.' He proffered the bunch of red carnations. 'These are for you,' he said. 'To remind you of the day we first met. Do you remember, at the Palm Court? We both wore them in our buttonholes?'

Of course she remembered. She still had the flower pressed carefully between the pages of one of her novels. She hardened her heart to the memory. He would not charm her again, he wouldn't.

'Thank you.' She took the flowers from him reluctantly, as if they might bite her.

'Shall we go?' Frank offered her his arm. 'Although I'm not sure it's a good day for walking,' he added, looking up into the ashen sky. 'I believe it

204

might snow again later. Are you sure you wouldn't prefer to find somewhere warm? I wouldn't want you to catch a cold.'

Of course, Miriam thought bitterly. *You wouldn't want me to sicken and die, would you? Not until you've managed to secure yourself as heir to my fortune.* The same thing had happened to Morwenna, the innocent heroine of *Rake's Revenge*. She was just about to have her inheritance stolen from under her nose by a swindling suitor when Black Jack Craven, the incorrigible rake with a heart of gold, arrived to save the day.

'I'd prefer to walk, if you don't mind,' she said shortly. She anticipated there would be a scene, and she had no desire to make a spectacle of herself in a public place. Besides, it would be easier to walk away from him in a park.

That was what her mind told her, but her heart knew better. Walking away from Frank was never going to be easy.

They walked for a while. Frank did his best to keep up the conversation, but Miriam barely answered him. She was too tense and angry, thinking about what was to come.

How should she approach it? Should she blurt out what she knew? Should she be angry, hurt? She searched her mind, trying to find the right words. But nothing came into her mind. Even her romantic novels failed to offer any inspiration. Morwenna hadn't ever had to confront her conniving suitor, because Black Jack Craven had shot him in a duel before she had the chance.

Finally, Frank said, 'Have I done something to offend you, Miriam?'

205

'I don't know. Have you?' she replied shortly.

He was instantly all concern. 'I have, haven't I? I thought I must have when you stopped answering my calls. Oh, my dear, what is it? What have I done?'

Miriam felt her anger building inside her, like a kettle coming to the boil. 'You tell me.'

He frowned. 'I don't understand. You're speaking in riddles...'

'You're the one who speaks in riddles, Frank Tillery. If that is indeed your name!'

She had him, she could tell. His face paled, giving him away. 'What?'

'It's all right, you can spare me the act.' Miriam turned on him. 'I've been doing some detective work, and I know who you really are – or rather, what you are.' She looked at him in contempt.

She wanted him to deny it. Even now, she hoped that he might say something, anything, to make her believe it was all a silly misunderstanding. She so desperately wanted it not to be true.

But his shoulders slumped and his face took on a resigned look. 'I see.'

Miriam's heart plunged. 'Is that all you're going to say?'

'What else is there to say? You've found out my secret.' He sighed. 'I might have known you'd work it out sooner or later. You're too clever to deceive for long.'

She stared at him. Even now, he was trying to flatter her, to wheedle himself out of trouble. He really was utterly sickening.

'And you're not as clever as you think you are,' she retorted. 'Bank manager, indeed! You don't

206

even look like a bank manager.'

He smiled. 'Oh, I don't know, I think I can look quite respectable when I try.' He straightened his tie. 'But I suppose you're right, it's time I found myself a new identity. Something that might be a little harder to discover next time, I think. What do you think of fisherman? Or Arctic explorer? I've always rather fancied myself as a pioneer...'

He looked so pleased with himself, Miriam wanted to slap the smile off his face. He could have tried harder to convince her, instead of treating it all as a big joke. 'I'm glad you find it so amusing,' she snapped.

His mouth curved. 'Well, you have to admit it is rather funny when you think about it.'

'I'm sure all those poor women you've deceived don't see it that way.'

Frank's brows drew together in a frown. 'That's a rather strong way of putting it, don't you think? I don't think I've deceived anyone. More ... misled, I suppose. They never find out who I really am, anyway. And if they did, I imagine they'd find it quite ... intriguing.'

'Intriguing?' Miriam echoed coldly.

'Anyway, why should they mind, as long as they get to enjoy a little bit of fantasy?' Frank went on. 'That's all I do, after all. I offer them a little bit of excitement, a chance to escape from their humdrum lives for a while. Where's the harm in that?'

Rage burned inside her. 'And is that what you think of me? Humdrum?'

'Oh lord, no! Of course you're different.' He looked at her strangely. 'I say, you're not seriously upset about it, are you? I mean, I understand

207

you're cross that I didn't come clean from the start–'

'That's one way of putting it,' Miriam muttered.

'I was going to tell you, honestly. I thought about it several times. But I suspected you might not approve of the other women in my life–'

'Of course I don't approve! It – it's utterly monstrous.'

'Oh, come on. It's only a bit of harmless fun. And it pays rather well, too.' He grinned sheepishly. 'How do you think I manage to afford all those afternoon teas at the Ritz? It's all courtesy of the lovely Vanessa, and the Honourable Lady Hortense and all the other ladies.' He smiled tenderly. 'But you must know you're the only one who has my heart, dear Miriam...'

He reached for her, but Miriam squirmed from his grasp.

'Don't touch me,' she hissed. 'You're utterly despicable!'

'Miriam!'

'Don't you Miriam me! You – you think I'd want anything to do with you now I know what kind of a man you are? If you can even call yourself a man!' she spat.

He looked hurt. 'I don't understand ... I thought you cared for me?'

'How can I possibly care for you after what you've done?'

'But I told you, it's nothing to do with the way I feel about you!'

He reached for her, his hands closing on her arms with surprisingly strength as he swung her

208

round to face him.

'I love you, Miriam Trott,' he said huskily.

They were the words she had always wanted to hear, and yet she knew they meant nothing. They were all part of his smoothly rehearsed charm, just like the manly embrace he held her in, and the way he was looking at her with those intense blue-green eyes.

He was a deceiver, but a good one. Even now, Miriam could feel herself weakening.

She steeled herself.

'How can you possibly love me, when you don't know me?' she said, pulling herself from his grasp.

He frowned uncertainly. 'I don't know what you mean–'

'I mean you're not the only one who's capable of deception, Mr Tillery. I'm not the woman you think I am, either.'

'Oh?'

'I'm not a wealthy heiress. I am a nurse at the Nightingale Hospital in Bethnal Green.'

His frown deepened. 'But I don't understand. Why didn't you tell me the truth?'

Miriam laughed harshly. 'That's rich, coming from you!'

'I suppose you're right.' He looked downcast. 'So you're a nurse, you say? And I suppose there's no mansion in Kensington, either?' Miriam shook her head. 'And no wicked uncle trying to get his hands on your tea plantation?'

Even now, she could see the faintest glimmer of amusement in his sea-green eyes.

Her chin lifted. 'Disappointed, are you?'

209

'Well yes, I suppose I am. It would have been nice if you'd had a fortune stashed away, I must admit.'

'I daresay it would!' Miriam gasped. Frank Tillery had a nerve, she had to admit that. Even now he seemed completely unrepentant.

'But it doesn't really change anything, does it?' Frank went on. 'I still love you. I'll just have to carry on earning my own living, that's all.' He smiled wryly.

Miriam stared at him, stunned. Was she really hearing this? 'You can't possibly mean that? You propose to go on – doing whatever it is you do?'

'Why not?' He shrugged. 'Look, I know you don't approve, but I promise you'll get used to it in time. You might even find it rather exciting.'

Once again he tried to reach for her, but this time Miriam was too quick for him.

'You're disgusting!' she spat out the words. 'Quite the most appalling man I've ever met in my life. Do you seriously think I'd want any part in what you do?'

'Miriam–'

'Don't touch me! I don't ever want to see your face or hear from you again, do you understand?' She thrust the flowers back at him, hitting him square in the chest. 'And you can give these to someone else, too.'

'Miriam, please. Listen to me–'

'I don't want to listen to any more of your lies, thank you very much. Just go back to Vanessa and Lady Hortense and all your other women. I hope they make you very rich and very happy!'

Furious as she was, it was hard to make herself

210

walk away. She had half expected him to follow her, but he didn't. It was only when she was at a safe distance that she finally allowed herself to look back.

There was Frank, still standing there watching her, looking like a lost little boy, scarlet carnations strewn around his feet.

Daisy

1st December 1945

'Oh go on, it'll be fun,' Daisy said.

'Fun?' Her friend Rose Trent did not look up from the textbook she was studying. 'It sounds awful. I can't think of anything worse.' She flipped the page, still not looking up. 'Sorry, Baker, you can count me out this time.'

Daisy pulled a face. It wasn't like Rose not to join in when she had one of her good ideas.

'They've never had a Christmas show at the Nightingale since we've been here,' she went on, disregarding her friend's lack of interest. 'I heard two of the staff nurses talking about it earlier on. They were saying how much they used to enjoy putting on a performance for the patients. I'll bet everyone else is doing it,' she added, looking round the common room. Usually there would be music playing on the gramophone and girls chatting and gossiping, but today the other half a dozen students all sat with their noses in their

211

books. The State Finals were coming up and no one wanted to fail.

Rose had also taken to her books, much to Daisy's frustration.

'We could sing a song,' Daisy said.

'Neither of us is remotely musical, in case you hadn't noticed.'

'Then how about a comedy skit of some kind? We could poke fun at Sister Wren. That would be a scream, wouldn't it? Our chance to get revenge on her for the awful way she treats us.' Daisy gazed down at her hands. Once they had been her pride and joy, but now they were red raw where Sister had them scrubbing floors and bathrooms day in and day out.

'Are you mad?' Rose said. 'We have another two months on Wren ward. Imagine how she'd make us suffer if we upset her. She's hard enough on us as it is.'

'We'll think of something else then,' Daisy said.

'I told you, I'm having nothing to do with it. You can jolly well do it on your own, if you're that keen.'

Daisy was horrified. 'Oh no, it wouldn't be nearly so much fun by myself. Besides, you know I can't do anything without my terrible twin!'

Rose smiled reluctantly. 'That's true.'

Since the day they had arrived for training three years earlier and been assigned to share a room, they had been the best of friends. They went through Preliminary Training together, studied together, worked together on the wards and even spent their rare days off together. They were more like sisters than friends, hence the nickname they

212

had earned from the other girls in their set.

They might have passed for twins, too. They both had the same thick brown hair and hazel eyes, although Daisy liked to think hers were more green. But that was where the similarity ended. Daisy was the more outgoing of the pair. She loved boys, and dressing up, and excitement, and she was always the one surrounded by friends. Rose was the clever one, quieter and more thoughtful. But somehow they brought out the best in each other. Rose had dragged Daisy through her studies, and Daisy liked to think she brought out a fun side in her friend.

But for once it looked as if her friend was not going to get involved in her wild scheme.

'I'm sorry, Baker,' Rose shook her head. 'The exams are coming up and we'll need all our time to revise.'

'There's plenty of time for that,' Daisy said airily. 'Besides, you already know it all anyway.'

Rose's mouth curved. 'I wish I had your confidence.'

'She'll need more than confidence to get her through the State Finals!' Betty Philips said from the other side of the room.

Daisy glared at her. Betty Philips fancied herself as the leader of their set, and was jealous of Daisy's popularity. She had also never forgiven Daisy for stealing her boyfriend in their first year.

Daisy hadn't set out to do it. It was hardly her fault that the medical student had decided he preferred her to Betty. She certainly hadn't encouraged him, apart from the slightest hint of flirting while they were both on night duty. And

213

once he had abandoned Betty, Daisy had made it perfectly clear that she wanted nothing to do with him. But for some reason that made Betty resent her even more.

'Of course, you know why she really wants to be in this show, don't you?' Betty said to Rose.

'Shut up, Philips,' Daisy snapped. 'I was having a private conversation with my friend, if you don't mind.'

'It's because of Tom Armstrong,' Betty went on, ignoring her. 'She's heard he's going to be taking part, and she thinks this will give her a chance to get closer to him.'

'Take no notice of her,' Daisy said to Rose. 'She thinks she knows everything.'

'I know you're always running after him like a puppy!' Betty said, and the other girls laughed.

'Oh, and you play so hard to get with men, don't you?' Daisy shot back.

'For heaven's sake!' Rose closed her book with a loud bang, silencing them both. 'I'm going to our room to revise in peace and quiet. You may think we'll breeze through our exams, but I still need to get to grips with the bones of the human foot.'

'I'll come with you–' Daisy started to her feet, but Rose stopped her.

'No,' she said. 'You'll only distract me, going on and on about this wretched show of yours.'

'I wouldn't have to go on and on if you'd just say yes,' Daisy called after her as the common door closed.

Betty Philips turned on her. 'Why don't you leave the poor girl alone, Baker? Surely you must

214

understand why she doesn't want to get involved with this show?'

Daisy stared at her blankly. 'I don't know what you mean.'

'You mean you don't remember?' Betty looked incredulous. 'It'll be a year at Christmas since her fiancé died.'

'Oh!'

'You really didn't remember, did you?' Betty shook her head, a nasty smile on her lips. 'And you're supposed to be her best friend!'

Daisy looked at the other girls' reproachful faces. For once Betty was right; she should have remembered.

Rose had been engaged to be married to her childhood sweetheart, Laurence, but he was killed in a bombing raid over Germany just before last Christmas. Rose was devastated, and Daisy had spent months trying to pull her friend out of her deep despair.

Slowly but surely Rose had started to get better, and Daisy had hoped she was on the mend at last. But it simply hadn't occurred to her that poor Rose might be dreading the anniversary coming up.

Her friend was sitting cross-legged on her bed when Daisy walked in. She looked up at her over the edge of her textbook, her expression wary.

'I do hope you're not going to start again–' she began, but Daisy shook her head.

'I won't utter another word about it, I promise. I – I just wanted to say I'm sorry.'

'What for?' Rose looked surprised.

'I should have thought before I opened my

215

mouth. I know it's coming up to a year since Laurence died–' She saw the shadow pass over Rose's face, her smile fading. 'I should have realised the last thing you'd probably feel like doing is cavorting about on stage...'

Rose looked down at the textbook in her hands. 'You're right,' she said. 'I am worried about how I'll cope, with the anniversary coming up. That's partly why I've been throwing myself into work, to try to push it to the back of my mind. And when you first mentioned this show, I really couldn't imagine anything worse. But I've been thinking about it, and – I reckon it might be good for me.'

'You do?' Daisy stared at her in surprise. 'What made you change your mind?'

'I've been dreading Christmas.' Rose's face was forlorn, and it upset Daisy to realise how little she had noticed her friend's sadness. 'But it won't make it any easier if I sit around feeling sorry for myself, will it? It might actually help if I try to keep busy.' She smiled ruefully. 'This show will certainly be a distraction, if nothing else.'

'Are you sure? You know you don't have to do it for my sake...'

'I know,' Rose said. 'But I also know you probably won't shut up about it unless I do. Besides, I can't be the one to stand in the way of true love, can I?'

Daisy blushed. 'Take no notice of Betty Philips. She's a cat.'

'She's right, though, isn't she? I know you like Tom Armstrong.'

Like wasn't the right word, Daisy thought. She

216

had already made up her mind that she was in love with the junior registrar. She had fallen for him from the first moment she saw him striding into the ward, his white coat flapping behind him. Now every time she saw him her heart did a little dance against her ribs.

And the fact that he barely seemed to notice her only piqued her interest even more. Without being too vain about it, Daisy knew that she could have almost any man she wanted at the Nightingale. But Tom Armstrong was a challenge, and she could never resist one of those.

'Thank you,' she said.

Rose smiled. 'I only hope he's worth us making fools of ourselves over!' She put down her book. 'But promise me we can find some time to study too?'

'Yes, yes, of course,' Daisy said. But her mind was already miles away from her books, wondering how she could impress Tom Armstrong.

As it turned out, they had very little chance to impress anyone at the first meeting. Daisy was still struggling to catch Tom's eye across the room when Sister Wren got into an argument with the Assistant Matron. Before she knew what was happening the meeting had ended and they were all filing out of the dining room.

'Well, that was a waste of time!' Rose said. But Daisy was hardly listening.

'Look,' she hissed, 'Tom Armstrong's leaving. Let's try to catch him at the door.'

Dragging a protesting Rose behind her, she made a dash for the door, elbowing her way through the crowd to get to him.

217

They arrived at the door just in time for her to accidentally on purpose brush shoulders with him.

'Oh, hello, there.' Daisy smiled at him, trying to look casual as she fought for breath. 'I didn't know you were here.'

'Didn't you?' Tom Armstrong eyed her uneasily. He wasn't her usual type by any means. She preferred her men dark and mysterious and well built. Dr Armstrong was tall and lean to the point of lankiness, and his hair was the colour of dirty straw. But he had a wonderful smile, and behind his spectacles his eyes were the colour of emeralds. 'I could have sworn you were looking straight at me for most of the meeting.'

'Was I? I must have been miles away,' Daisy lied. She followed him out of the door and down the passageway, still dragging Rose behind her.

'Are you taking part in the Christmas show?' Tom asked.

'Well, I wasn't sure about it, but Rose talked me into coming.' Daisy ignored Rose's glare which she knew would be fixed on the back of her head. 'How about you?'

'I thought I might try out my magic act.'

'You're a magician?'

He looked embarrassed. 'I'm not that good, I've only just started doing a few tricks. Now I'm not sure I'll even bother to audition–'

'Oh, but you must!' Daisy burst out, then regretted it when she saw his startled expression. 'I mean – where's the harm in trying?' she blathered on to hide her embarrassment. 'Rose and I are definitely going to do something, aren't we?'

218

'Do you have an act prepared?'

'We're going to do a song together.' Once again, she ignored her friend's stunned expression.

'So you're musical, then?'

'No,' Rose said stonily.

'Take no notice of her,' Daisy said. 'She's just being modest.'

'In that case I look forward to hearing you.' He smiled at Rose.

'And I look forward to seeing what tricks you have up your sleeve!' Daisy flirted back.

As he walked off, Rose turned on her. 'Why did you tell him we were singing? You know we're both tone deaf!'

Daisy smiled, her gaze still following Tom Armstrong. 'We'll just have to think of something, won't we?'

But finding a song that suited their voices was more difficult than she had imagined. It didn't help that Rose refused to help her, and spent most of the week before the first rehearsal with her nose buried in an anatomy textbook.

'We'll fail the audition if we don't practise!' Daisy complained.

'I'd rather fail an audition than my State Finals,' Rose replied.

Without Rose to push her along, Daisy soon got distracted and gave up on finding a song. By the time they arrived at the first audition they were woefully unprepared.

It didn't help when Betty Philips took to the stage and played the most perfect violin solo.

'She's awfully good, isn't she?' Rose whispered, awestruck.

'Worse luck!' Daisy groaned. 'Why did they have to put her on before us? Now she'll make us look even worse!'

All too soon it was their turn, and they took to the stage.

'Well, this is it!' Rose grimaced, as they stood side by side on the makeshift platform. Looking out over the rows of expectant faces, Daisy felt her throat dry up in panic. Right at the front sat Miss Davis the Assistant Matron, her pen poised, wearing her usual sour expression.

It did not go well. Neither of them knew the words, and halfway through the song Rose forgot the tune as well. Daisy could feel her whole body engulfed in heat, as if she was blushing from her toes upwards. She tried not to look into the audience, but when she did the first face she saw was Betty Philips, laughing her head off with some of the other girls from their set.

At least Tom Armstrong didn't seem to be paying any attention to them. He was too busy rehearsing his own tricks at the side of the stage.

After what seemed like an eternity, the song finished and they could escape at last.

'I'm glad that's over.' Rose breathed a sigh of relief as they hurried from the stage to a smattering of sarcastic applause from Betty Philips and her cronies, and a cold glare from the Assistant Matron. 'At least we won't have to do that again.'

'No,' Daisy agreed sadly. All she could see were her dreams of getting to know Tom Armstrong fading into nothing.

Rose must have noticed her disappointment. 'Cheer up,' she said. 'I'm sure you made an impression on him.'

'Oh, I'm sure I have,' Daisy said gloomily. 'Now he thinks I'm a complete fool. I daresay he'll want nothing more to do with me.'

'Shall we stay and watch his act?' Rose asked.

'No,' Daisy said. 'Let's go. I can't stand the way Betty Philips is smirking at me.'

The following day, Daisy was emptying out bedpans in the sluice when to her surprise Tom Armstrong appeared in the doorway.

'Can I have a word?' he asked.

Daisy was so shocked she dropped the pan she was emptying. It landed in the sink with a dreadful clatter that she was sure would bring Sister Wren running.

She froze for a moment, steeling herself for the sound of footsteps. But no one came.

When she was sure it must be safe, she turned to Tom. 'Yes, Doctor?' she said politely.

'Why don't you call me Tom, since it's just the two of us?'

A small thrill ran through her. 'And you can call me Daisy,' she said.

'Daisy.' She liked the way he said it, in that deep voice of his. She only wished she wasn't standing in the sluice, surrounded by stinking bedpans. It was hardly the most romantic spot in the hospital.

'I suppose you heard I made a complete fool of myself at the rehearsal yesterday?' he said.

Daisy knew all about it from listening to Betty Philips and the other students giggling about it in the common room. It sounded utterly excruciating. 'I'm sure you can't have been any worse than Rose and me,' she replied tactfully.

221

'Has Miss Davis crossed you two off her list as well?'

Daisy pulled a face. 'She put such a thick cross through our names I think she broke her pen nib!'

'That's a shame. I thought you were rather funny.'

'Thank you.' It didn't bother her that their act was supposed to be serious. The fact that he'd even noticed her was enough.

'Anyway, I've been thinking,' Tom said. 'Perhaps we should join forces?'

'What do you mean?'

'I mean, since we both seem to have obvious comedic talents, albeit unintentional, perhaps we should turn them to something else, something that might win favour with Miss Davis. A comic sketch, perhaps, or another song?'

'What a good idea!' Daisy was so thrilled, she completely forgot her promise to Rose that they would never have to set foot on a stage again. She was already thinking of all the private rehearsals she could have with Tom Armstrong. 'Count us in.'

Tom frowned. 'Shouldn't you talk to Nurse Trent about it first? She might not want to do it.'

'Oh, there's no need. I know Rose will be as keen as I am,' Daisy lied. 'She was so disappointed when she found out we weren't included. She's desperate to be involved.'

Before Tom had time to reply, they heard the sound of footsteps echoing up the passageway outside, approaching the sluice. Daisy froze at the sound. If Sister Wren found them together, all hell would break loose. She would be hauled

222

up before Matron in a moment, probably by her hair if Sister had anything to do with it.

At least Tom Armstrong had the presence of mind to duck behind the door as it swung open and Miss Trott stuck her head inside.

'Have you finished with those bedpans yet, Baker?' she asked.

'Nearly finished, Sister.'

'Well, hurry along. There are other jobs to be done, once you've finished.'

'Yes, Sister.'

She started to close the door but just as Daisy was about to breathe again, Sister Wren added, 'And should you not be on the consultant's rounds, Dr Armstrong? I'm sure Mr Powell will be looking for you, too.'

The door closed and Daisy and Tom stared at each other.

'Did you hear that?' Dr Armstrong said.

'I did, but I don't believe it.' Daisy shook her head. For a young student nurse to be found alone with a doctor was an offence that carried the severest of punishments. Daisy could easily have been on her way home by the end of the day.

Some ward sisters turned a blind eye occasionally, but not Miss Trott. She never, ever missed an opportunity to punish a student.

Until now.

'She's been in a strange mood for a few days now,' Daisy said. 'I broke a thermometer yesterday and she didn't even send me to Matron. She just smiled and said accidents will happen.'

Tom shook his head. 'That doesn't sound like her. What do you think could have happened?'

223

'I don't know. Rose thought she might have been at the medicinal brandy.'

'Perhaps she's in love?'

Daisy laughed. 'Sister Wren? I doubt it.'

'At any rate, let's not chance our luck. I'd best go. Have a word with Nurse Trent and let me know, won't you?'

'I will,' Daisy promised. 'But she'll love the idea, I know she will.'

As it turned out, Rose did not love the idea. Daisy broke the news to her later as they were cleaning the bathrooms together.

'He sought me out especially to ask me,' she said excitedly. 'Which means he must be interested, don't you think?'

She had expected her friend to be as excited as she was about her romantic conquest, but Rose sat back on her heels, scrubbing brush in her hand.

'You could have asked me first,' she said.

'There wasn't time.' Besides, Daisy added silently, you would only have said no. 'You will do it, won't you?' she pleaded. 'Oh, Trent, please don't be a wet blanket. You know how much it means to me.'

Rose sighed. 'It doesn't look as if I have much choice, does it? Even if I say no you'll probably just go on and on about it until I change my mind.'

'Probably!' Daisy laughed, pleased with herself.

Daisy made sure she was properly done up for the next rehearsal. Even though she was still in uniform she curled her hair artfully around the edge of her cap, and even risked putting on a bit

224

of make-up.

'You know Miss Davis will have a fit if she sees you,' Rose warned her as she watched Daisy applying her lipstick.

'She'll never notice.'

'You must be joking! Her eagle eye never misses anything.'

'Oh well, it's worth the risk,' Daisy shrugged. 'It's about time Tom got a look at me in my finery.'

'Well, I shall look as dowdy as ever and remain quietly in the background,' Rose said. 'That way you can have all the limelight for yourself.'

Daisy smiled. She wasn't too worried about that. She had every intention of dazzling Tom Armstrong so much he wouldn't notice anyone else.

When they got to the dining hall they found out that it was the delightful Sister Jarvis in charge of the rehearsal, and not crabby Miss Davis. Daisy and Rose had both worked with Miss Tanner down in the sector hospital when they were training, and she had been positively angelic to them. Unlike most of the other ward sisters, she did not treat her students like slaves, or believe that they had to suffer in order to learn anything.

As they came in she raised her eyebrows at Daisy's lipstick, but passed no comment.

'You see?' She smiled at Rose. 'I told you there was nothing to worry about.'

Rose sent her a shrewd look. 'You have the luck of the devil, Daisy Baker!'

Daisy's grin widened. 'I do, don't I?'

She certainly felt as if her luck was holding

225

when Tom Armstrong sought them out.

'I've been working on our song,' he said. 'I've come up with some words I think you'll like.'

'I'm sure we will,' Daisy beamed.

'Shall we find somewhere quiet to practise?'

'Lead the way.'

Daisy smiled over her shoulder at Rose as they followed him to the far end of the dining hall. This was working out even better than she had imagined.

As it turned out, Tom Armstrong was better at writing songs than he was at performing magic tricks. He had made up some very amusing words to the tune of 'In an English Country Garden'.

'What kind of people will you hope to find in the Nightingale Hospital?' he hummed the chorus for them. 'There are patients there of every kind in the Nightingale Hospital...'

Daisy laughed loudly, interrupting him. 'That's so funny!' she cried.

'I haven't really started yet,' Tom Armstrong said, slightly apologetic.

'It's still very clever. Isn't he clever, Rose?'

Rose sent her an odd look. 'That second line doesn't scan properly,' she said to Tom. 'Wouldn't it be better if it was slightly longer?'

'It sounds fine to me the way it is,' Daisy said firmly, seeing Tom's frown.

'No, you're right.' Tom turned to Rose. 'I did think that myself, but I couldn't think of anything else to say.'

Rose thought for a moment. 'How about if instead of "patients" you said something like, "wounds and diseases of every kind"?'

226

'Wounds and diseases?' Tom hummed it under his breath. 'Yes, I suppose that does sound better,' he said.

'What's the next line?' Daisy urged, flashing a warning look at Rose. 'Do tell us, I'm dying to hear it.'

'All right.' Tom cleared his throat and sang, 'What kind of people will you hope to find at the Nightingale Hospital? There are wounds and diseases of every kind at the Nightingale Hospital. Jaundice, mumps and adenoids, Hernias and haemorrhoids ... and I'm afraid I rather ran out of inspiration at that point.' He looked apologetic.

Once again, Rose thought for a moment. 'What about "Fractures of the carpal scaphoid"?' she suggested.

Daisy stared at her. What happened to keeping quiet in the background?

Tom nodded. 'Yes. Yes, that's perfect. And for the next line we could have, "There are gallstones and sores..."'

'"...and infections galore"?' Rose finished for him.

'Yes!' Tom laughed as he scribbled down the words 'That was a stroke of genius, Nurse Trent. You're like Gilbert to my Sullivan.'

Rose smiled. 'I used to enjoy poetry at school.'

As they carried on rehearsing, Daisy started to feel a bit frustrated. Up until this moment, it hadn't actually occurred to her that they would be doing any work. She had half thought they would just be larking about and flirting.

But Tom and Rose seemed to be getting stuck in, poring over his piece of paper. Every so often

227

Rose would take the pencil from him and write something. He would read it, then say, 'Yes. Yes, that's even better. Well done, Nurse Trent!'

Daisy had always been useless at English at school, so she could only sit there, twisting one of her artful curls around her finger and hoping that he might notice her at last.

Finally, the rehearsal ended, and Miss Tanner gathered them all around the piano for a jolly sing-song.

As they took their places, Daisy was aware of Betty Philips sidling up to her.

'Isn't it nice to see her so happy?' she sighed.

Daisy frowned over her shoulder at her. 'Who?'

'Your friend Trent, of course. The poor girl's had such a miserable time of it lately, it's good to see her smiling again. And I suppose she has you to thank for it,' she went on. 'I must say, Baker, it's awfully good of you to step aside for your friend. I would never have imagined you making such a sacrifice.'

Daisy glared at her. There was something about the knowing smile on Philips' face that she did not trust. 'What are you talking about?'

'Oh, you mean you haven't noticed?' Betty's face was the picture of innocence. 'Dr Armstrong seems to be taking rather an interest in her. Look at them, laughing together. If you ask me, he's smitten.' She smiled sweetly. 'And there was me, thinking you wanted him for yourself. You're a real pal, Baker.'

Miss Tanner struck up the opening bars of 'We Wish You a Merry Christmas', but Daisy found she had suddenly lost her voice. All she could do

228

was stare across the piano to where Rose and Tom Armstrong were standing together, singing away. They weren't looking at each other, but there was something about the way they stood with their shoulders brushing that sent a warning prickle up her spine.

Betty Philips was just being a cat as usual, she told herself. Tom Armstrong wasn't interested in Rose, and she definitely wasn't interested in him.

As they headed back to the nurses' home later, Rose said, 'You know, Baker, I'm glad you talked me into doing this. I had fun tonight.'

'I'm glad someone did,' Daisy muttered.

Rose looked sideways at her. 'Didn't you enjoy yourself?'

'To be honest, I was rather bored. And Tom hardly looked at me. He was too busy composing his silly song with you!'

'I know. I'm sorry. But it's only the first proper rehearsal,' Rose consoled her. 'There's still plenty of time for him to notice you.'

Daisy looked at her friend closely, but Rose's smiling face gave nothing away.

'You're not interested in Tom Armstrong yourself, are you?' she blurted out.

Rose stared at her, astonished. 'No, of course not. Why would you even ask such a thing?'

'I don't know,' she shrugged. 'It was just something Philips said...'

'I wouldn't take any notice of what Philips says,' Rose dismissed. 'You know she'd say anything to stir up trouble and upset you.'

'I know, but he seemed to be paying you a lot of attention this evening...' She felt wretched even

229

saying it.

'He was only being friendly,' Rose said. 'Honestly, Baker, you should know I'd never do anything like that.'

Daisy looked at her friend's face. Behind Rose's smile, she could still see the lingering sadness of her loss. She knew it would be a long time before Rose felt anything for another man.

But even so, when Tom Armstrong sent Daisy a note the following day asking if the three of them could meet up to practise by themselves before the next rehearsal, Rose excused herself.

'You go by yourself,' she said. 'I have a ton of revision to get through.'

Daisy felt a stab of guilt. 'I don't mind you coming, honestly,' she said. 'I hope you're not staying away because of what I said last night...'

'No,' Rose said, 'but I do want to study. Besides, this will give you a chance to be alone with him so you can make him succumb to your womanly wiles!' Her eyes gleamed with mischief.

Daisy grinned. 'I'll do my best!'

Not that Tom seemed remotely interested in any of her wiles, womanly or otherwise.

'Where's Rose?' were his first words when Daisy arrived.

'She's studying.'

Tom looked put out. 'Perhaps we should postpone our practice till another day if she can't join us?'

'I'm sure we can manage without her just this once,' Daisy replied through gritted teeth. 'Besides, we need to practise, don't we?'

'I suppose so,' Tom agreed. He seemed very

230

grudging about it, much to Daisy's annoyance. She couldn't help feeling a stab of annoyance towards Rose, too, even though she had done nothing wrong.

But Daisy was determined to make him forget her friend. For the next hour she flirted with grim determination. She played with her hair, brushed her hand against his, batted her eyelashes until she was seeing double, but to no avail.

'How about if we dance cheek to cheek at this point?' she suggested desperately.

Tom frowned. 'I'm not sure...'

'Let's try it, shall we?' Before he had a chance to protest, Daisy launched herself into his arms, pressing her cheek to his so he could feel the softness of her hair against his face and breathe in her new perfume.

'I really don't think that works,' Tom said, carefully extricating himself from her grasp. 'We're singing about hernias and haemorrhoids, I don't think it's necessary to start dancing.'

Daisy stared at him in frustration. A lesser man might have been brought to his knees by her flirting, but Tom barely noticed. If anything, he seemed rather irritated by her.

He was simply preoccupied with getting the song right, Daisy decided. She could not allow herself to consider the possibility that he wasn't interested. There was not a red-blooded young man in London who could resist Daisy Baker once she turned on the charm.

She knew she should give up on him. But perverse as she was, his lack of interest only increased hers. The more he resisted her, the more

231

she wanted him.

After the rehearsal, he offered to walk her back to the nurses' home.

'It's a shame Rose couldn't join us,' he said, as they headed across the courtyard.

'Yes, well, she isn't really interested in the show at all,' Daisy replied. 'I had to force her to do it in the first place.'

'Oh.' There was no mistaking the disappointment in Tom's voice. 'I thought you said she was dead keen?'

'Not really. To be honest, I think she finds the whole thing very tedious.'

'I see.' Tom paused for a moment, then said, 'Does she have a boyfriend?'

Daisy shot a sideways look at him. He was trying to sound casual, but there was no mistaking his interest.

'No,' she said, then added, 'she was engaged to be married, but her fiancé was killed in a bombing raid last Christmas.'

'Ah.' Tom's face fell. 'I'm sorry to hear that.'

'Yes,' Daisy said, warming to her theme. 'She's still completely distraught, as you can imagine. Utterly heartbroken. She hasn't looked at another man since, and I don't think she ever will.'

'Right. I see.'

Daisy looked at Tom's crestfallen expression and felt a jab of satisfaction. She might not be able to pique his interest herself, but at least she could stop him being interested in anyone else.

It was the truth, anyway, she told herself. Rose had said that she wasn't remotely interested in Tom Armstrong. All she had done was save her

232

friend the embarrassment of having to give him the brush-off.

Rose was sitting on her bed, surrounded by open textbooks. She was busy making notes, but she put down her pen when Daisy walked in.

'How did it go with the dashing doctor?' she asked.

'Very well,' Daisy said, turning away to take off her coat so Rose wouldn't see her expression.

'Oh, come on! You must give me more details than that. I've been wrestling with the digestive system all evening, I need cheering up.' She leaned forward, her expression avid. 'Did you flirt with him madly?'

Daisy forced a smile. 'He flirted with me,' she said. 'And we danced cheek to cheek, too. I practically had to fight him off.'

'You see?' Rose said, delighted. 'I told you he likes you.'

'Yes,' Daisy said, with no conviction at all. 'Yes, I think he does.'

She thought she had managed to warn Tom Armstrong off, so she was surprised to see him talking to Rose after his rounds the following morning. Luckily for them, Sister had retreated to her sitting room with her morning tea; her good mood of the previous two weeks seemed to have evaporated, and she was back to her sour, sniping old self again.

She didn't see her friend again until they were doing the beds and backs round later. Daisy waited for Rose to tell her all about her meeting with Tom. Surely she would be keen to mention it, knowing Daisy's interest in the man? But Rose

233

was very quiet as they went about their work.

Finally, the anticipation got too much for Daisy.

'Was that Tom I saw you talking to this morning?' she said, as casually as she could manage as they changed a bed together.

'Oh yes.' Rose sounded vague.

'What did he want to speak to you about?'

'Nothing.'

Daisy looked at her friend across the bed. Rose's expression was evasive as she smoothed down the drawsheet.

'I hope you put in a good word for me?' she teased.

Rose hesitated, then said, 'Actually, we were talking about Laurence.'

Daisy looked up at her sharply. 'What about him?'

'Tom was telling me his brother was in the RAF. He was killed during the Battle of Britain.' She straightened up and reached for the top sheet which was draped between two chairs at the end of the bed. 'He offered to go with me to Laurence's grave,' she said quietly.

Daisy was surprised. Rose had never visited the place where her fiancé was buried; she always said it was too painful for her. 'And will you go?'

Rose paused for a moment. 'I told him I'd think about it. But yes, I think it might be the right time.'

Daisy felt a stab of jealousy. 'What changed your mind?'

'It was something Tom said. He didn't think he would ever be able to bring himself to visit his brother's grave either, but when he did finally go

234

he said it actually made him feel a lot better.'

'Well, I must say I'm surprised,' Daisy said. 'Whenever I've offered to go with you, you've always refused.'

'This is different,' Rose said. 'I think it might help to have Tom there, as he knows what I'm going through.'

'And I wouldn't?'

Rose sighed irritably. 'I told you, I'm only thinking about it,' she said. 'I haven't made up my mind yet.'

But in the end, Rose decided she would go with Tom. Daisy tried to hint that she could join them, but Rose refused.

'This is going to be difficult enough for me, without you there trying to flirt with Tom,' she said.

'As if I would!' Daisy said crossly. 'I'm not that insensitive.'

Besides, it wasn't about her flirting with Tom. She was more worried about what he and Rose might get up to without her there to keep an eye on them.

All day, she seethed with jealousy. She tried to keep her mind on her work, but she was haunted by visions of them at Laurence's graveside. Rose would be upset and vulnerable, and Tom would draw her into his manly embrace to comfort her. Then Rose would look up at him, her eyes shimmering with tears, and before they knew it they would be consumed with passion...

'Nurse, are you going to gawp out of that window all day?' Sister Wren's snapping voice startled her out of her reverie. 'The patient in bed eleven

235

needs shaving and an enema. And then when you've finished that you can start on the tea round.'

Rose and Tom still hadn't returned by the time the students gathered for their evening meal in the dining room. As Daisy's luck would have it, she found herself eating at the same end of the table as Betty Philips.

'Is Trent not back yet?' she took great delight in asking. 'Goodness, they've been gone hours, haven't they? They must be having a good time.'

'Hardly, since they're visiting her fiance's grave!' Daisy snapped back.

'I suppose you're right,' Betty said, then added, 'but then again, I daresay emotions will be running high. And you know what happens then, don't you?'

Of course Daisy knew. She had been picturing the same scene all day.

Betty's lips drew back in a smile, exposing her horsey teeth. 'Look at you, you're lost without your terrible twin!' Then she added nastily, 'Still, I daresay you'll have to get used to spending more time on your own, the way things are going.'

Rose finally returned just before lights out. Daisy watched her approaching up the drive towards the nurses' home and rushed to get out her books, so her friend wouldn't guess she had been standing at the window for most of the evening.

Rose walked in, brushing the snow from her hair. She looked pretty, Daisy thought. The cold had brought a glow to her cheeks, and her eyes had a sparkle about them that Daisy hadn't seen for a long time.

236

Rose smiled when she saw the books laid out on Daisy's bed.

'Hard at work? That's not like you!' she joked.

'You're not the only one who studies, you know!' Daisy snapped back. She closed the book without even looking at it. 'Where have you been, anyway? Surely you haven't been at the cemetery all this time?'

Rose shook her head. 'We missed the last bus and had to walk all the way back to Bethnal Green.' She shivered. 'I'm so c-cold. I do wish the Home Sister would let us have a fire in this room.' She looked gloomily at the empty grate.

'I was worried about you,' Daisy said.

'That's so sweet of you, but there was really no need. Tom took good care of me.'

I'll bet he did, Daisy thought furiously. Another image of Tom with his arm protectively around Rose's shoulders came into her mind, and she batted it away furiously.

'How did it go?' she asked.

Rose's face grew sombre. 'It was hard,' she murmured. 'When we first walked up there and I saw the stone with Laurence's name on it...' She closed her eyes briefly. 'But I'm glad I did it. And having Tom there definitely helped.'

Daisy tasted bitter jealousy in the back of her throat. 'Well, I'm very happy for you,' she managed to choke out.

As she settled down to sleep, Daisy felt horribly mean. Her friend had been through a hard day, and she should be pleased that she had had someone there to help her.

She went to sleep vowing to be kinder, and not

237

to allow that wretch Betty Philips to get into her head and make her see things that were not there.

Daisy was late getting to the next rehearsal, thanks to Sister Wren's ever darkening mood. She had decided that Daisy had not made a good enough job of cleaning the kitchen, and had to do it all again.

She knew better than to protest. Sister was in such a temper that one wrong word from Daisy would have meant she'd be scrubbing the whole ward from top to bottom.

'I'll stay and help you, if you like?' Rose offered. 'Sister's off to the rehearsal herself soon, so she'll never know.'

Daisy was sorely tempted to take her up on her offer and hand her a scrubbing brush, but instead she smiled bravely and said, 'No, you go. I won't take long.' The kitchen was spotless, anyway; Sister Wren had only ordered her to do it because she was feeling vindictive.

'We'll wait for you,' Rose promised.

Daisy watched her go. There might have been a time when Rose would have insisted on helping her, but now she looked as if she couldn't wait to get out of the door.

Sister Wren went off to rehearsals shortly afterwards, and Daisy hoped the staff nurse would take pity on her and let her go. But Staff Nurse Giles was just as strict as Miss Trott, and insisted that she cleaned every inch. Then she took an agonisingly long time to check her work. Daisy waited tensely, her hands balling into fists inside the folds of her apron as the staff nurse carefully ran her finger along the tops of the cupboards

238

and inspected the crack where the floor met the skirting board.

Finally, she pronounced herself satisfied, and told Daisy she could leave. She hurried down to the dining hall, out of breath and desperately trying to straighten her cap and make herself presentable. But as she approached, she saw everyone coming out of the dining room, looking most disgruntled.

'What happened?' she asked June Phipps, one of the girls from her set.

'There was another row,' June said. 'Miss Davis tore a strip off Miss Tanner, and we've all walked out in protest.'

'Where's Rose?' Daisy looked around the throng of people.

'I don't know. She went off with Dr Armstrong, but I don't know where they went.'

Daisy finally found Rose and Tom in the courtyard. They were sitting together on the bench, studying a piece of paper, oblivious to the snow falling around them. But it was the way they were sitting, their heads so close together, that stopped Daisy in her tracks. She could feel the chemistry between them. Rose had Tom's coat draped around her shoulders, she noticed.

The next moment Rose looked up, saw her and beckoned her over.

'You found us,' she smiled. 'We were going to wait for you, but I wasn't sure how long Staff Nurse Giles would keep you cleaning.'

'Isn't it a bit cold to rehearse out here?' Daisy said.

'Is it? I hadn't really noticed.'

239

No, Daisy thought. You wouldn't. She probably wouldn't notice the cold either, if Tom Armstrong was sitting so close to her.

Rose handed her the piece of paper. 'Tom's written another verse. What do you think?'

Does it matter what I think? Daisy wanted to snap back. There was only one person Tom was interested in, and it certainly wasn't her.

'Very clever, I'm sure.' She handed the paper back without looking at it. 'Anyway, it's too cold for me to stay out here,' she announced. 'I'm going back to the nurses' home.'

'I'll come with you.' Rose was on her feet straight away, but Daisy shook her head.

'No, you stay here. I'm sure you'll have a better time without me, anyway.' She glared at Tom as she said it, but he didn't meet her eye.

'Don't be like that … Baker?' She heard Rose's voice following her as she stomped off. She half expected her friend to follow her anyway, but as she left the courtyard she realised that Rose was not at her heels. Glancing back, she saw her friend was still sitting on the bench, Tom beside her. They were pressed against each other, their sides touching. Daisy couldn't tell from a distance, but she had a feeling he might have been holding her hand.

Daisy had washed and changed into her flannel nightgown by the time Rose finally returned. Daisy had already made up her mind that Rose would be very apologetic, so she was taken aback when Rose barely acknowledged her as she walked into the room.

'You took your time,' Daisy said accusingly.

240

'We were talking.' Rose sat on the bed with her back to her, taking off her shoes.

Daisy waited for her to say more, but she was silent.

'Did you enjoy your rehearsal?' she asked finally.

'Yes, thank you. You should have stayed.'

'Oh no, I know when I'm not wanted. You know what they say. Three's a crowd.'

Rose twisted round to look at her for the first time. 'I don't know why you're being like this,' she said.

'Don't you?'

Rose sighed. 'If you've got something to say, then say it.'

Daisy stared at her friend. She had expected Rose to plead for her forgiveness, but she was unnervingly calm.

'Surely you're the one who should have something to say to me?'

They looked at each other for a moment. Rose was the first to lower her gaze.

'I'm going to bed,' she said.

She gathered up her wash things and went off to the bathroom. Daisy lay under the covers, shivering with the cold and with pent-up anger.

Rose was hiding something, she knew it.

This was all wrong; it wasn't the way it was supposed to be. Usually it was Rose who would be sitting up in bed when Daisy tripped in late from a night out. Daisy would tell her all about her night out, and they would giggle over everything that had happened, and then they would settle down to sleep.

But tonight, Daisy could feel the tension in the air. There was something unspoken between them, and she knew she wouldn't be able to sleep until she had had it out with, her friend.

When Rose returned from the bathroom, Daisy was ready for her.

'So are you and Tom courting now?' She lay on her back, staring up at the ceiling. She was afraid if she looked at her friend she would see something in her face that confirmed her worst suspicions.

'No!' Rose sounded shocked.

'Come off it! I saw you together on that bench. Talk about love's young dream!'

She felt her bed sink as Rose sat down on the end of it. Daisy held her breath, waiting for her to deny it, to tell her she was being silly. Even now, she desperately wanted to believe it was all a mistake, a silly misunderstanding.

'You're right,' she murmured. 'Tonight, when we were talking – Tom told me he had feelings for me.'

Daisy sat upright. 'I knew it! How could you do this to me? You knew I liked him–'

'I haven't done anything,' Rose protested.

'Of course you haven't! I suppose you haven't been encouraging him all this time, pretending to be so sweet and innocent, when all the time you've been scheming about how to take him away from me–'

'I didn't! We're not all like you, you know.'

'And what's that supposed to mean?'

Rose faced her boldly. 'How many boyfriends have you stolen from the other girls?'

242

Daisy felt guilty heat rising in her face. 'That's different,' she mumbled. 'I'd never do it to my best friend.'

'Neither would I,' Rose shot back. 'Anyway, it's not as if you and Tom were even together–'

'We might have been, if you hadn't come along and stuck your nose in!'

'You wouldn't,' Rose cut her off. 'Tom was never interested in you.'

'And how do you know that?'

'Because I asked him.'

Daisy jerked back as if she had been slapped. 'You did what?'

'I was worried,' Rose said. 'I'd started to have feelings for him too, and I didn't want to do anything to hurt you. So I talked to Tom about it, and he said he had never thought of you in that way. And you weren't that interested in him, either,' she went on. 'I know you, Baker. You love the chase, but once you've got a man you don't want him any more.'

Daisy stared at her, too shocked and humiliated to speak. She didn't know which was worse, that Tom had no feelings for her, or that Rose had asked him the question.

'I know you're hurt,' Rose was saying, 'but I can't help the way I feel, truly I can't. You must believe me, I never set out to fall for him like that. But that day we went to visit Laurence's grave, he was so kind and understanding, I couldn't help it...'

'Oh, I can just imagine it!' Daisy lashed out bitterly. 'What kind of girl sobs over her dead fiance's grave while making eyes at another man?'

243

It was a vicious thing to say, but Daisy was so full of burning venom she had to let it out.

Rose stared at her, appalled. 'Do you really think that's what happened?' she said in a hushed voice.

'Who knows? You're devious enough to try anything, I reckon.'

The colour drained from Rose's face. 'If you feel that way, it's a wonder you're my friend.'

'Who says we're friends?'

The words hung in the air between them.

The bedsprings creaked as Rose got to her feet.

'I loved Laurence with all my heart,' she said in a small, choked voice. 'But I know he wouldn't have wanted me to spend the rest of my life mourning him. He would have wanted me to be happy. I thought you of all people might feel the same.'

Daisy remained stiff and still under the covers. She knew she should apologise, but pride and anger were stopping her from doing it.

From then on, the atmosphere was icy between them. When Daisy went into their room, Rose would leave. If they did have to be in the same room together for any length of time, they didn't speak a word to each other. They ignored each other on the ward wherever they could.

As word spread of their argument, the other girls in their set all took Rose's side. When Daisy went into the common room, they all turned their backs on her. Daisy burned with humiliation, but she refused to be intimidated. She sat in the corner with her textbook, listening to the others all giggling together as they studied.

244

Daisy could barely see the words on the page for the mist of anger. It wasn't fair. Rose was the one in the wrong, not her. It was Daisy who should have had the other girls around her, comforting her over what Rose had done.

It was all Betty Philips' fault, she decided. She had been waiting for the chance to get back at Daisy over that business with the medical student, and now it had finally come. How she must be enjoying watching Daisy get her comeuppance!

But if she was honest, Daisy knew there was a small part of her that deserved it. Betty wasn't the only girl Daisy had wronged in the past. She might have had more allies if she hadn't been so selfish and thoughtless.

And now she had lost the only real friend she had ever had.

Daisy knew she couldn't take part in the show. She couldn't bear to see Rose and Tom together, especially as she and Rose were not speaking.

'Not you too?' Tom said when she told him.

'What do you mean?'

'Hasn't Rose told you? She's pulled out as well.'

'Why?'

'I thought you might be able to tell me that, since you two are such good friends.'

Daisy was silent. Obviously Tom hadn't heard about their falling out. 'She hasn't mentioned anything to me,' she said quietly.

'Nor me.' Tom looked troubled. 'She's stopped speaking to me, anyway. She won't even look at me when I'm on the ward doing my rounds. You know, I really thought–' He paused, shaking his

245

head. 'I think I must have said the wrong thing,' he sighed. He looked at Daisy. 'I suppose you must know I told her how I felt about her?'

Daisy nodded, too choked to speak.

'It was a foolish thing to do, but I couldn't help it. I knew I was taking a risk, but I really thought she felt the same...'

Daisy saw the desolate look on his face and realised with a shock that he really did have feelings for Rose. This was not just a simple flirtation, the kind she was used to, passionate and intense one minute and forgotten as soon as the chase was over. This was something deep and special.

It was deep and special for Rose, too. Unlike her, Rose didn't give her heart away easily. Now she had, and Daisy had ruined it for her.

'I'm sorry,' she said.

He smiled bracingly at her. 'It's not your fault. If anything it's mine for falling for a girl who's still in love with her dead fiancé.' He sighed. 'Anyway, it doesn't matter now. She's made it clear it's over, and that's all there is to it.'

'It's a shame about the act,' Daisy said. 'You put in so much hard work.'

Tom shrugged. 'It doesn't look as if there's going to be a show anyway. Everyone's up in arms about the last rehearsal and there's talk of boycotting the whole thing.' He looked rueful. 'But it was fun while it lasted.'

As Daisy walked away, he said, 'I know it probably won't do any good, but if you wouldn't mind putting in a good word for me with Rose? Tell her I'm sorry.'

'I will, if I get the chance.'

You're not the only one, Daisy thought as she walked away.

PART TWO

Violet

23rd December 1945

Dr Gruber was being discharged, and his cousin Gerte had come to collect him. She was fussing around him as usual, just as she always did whenever she came to visit.

Dr Gruber took it all in good part, although Violet could tell he found his cousin's ministrations quite trying.

'It's quite all right, Gerte, I can carry a few books myself,' he protested mildly, as he watched her clearing out his bedside locker.

Gerte sent him a strict look. 'Isaak, you have been very sick. We need to take care of you,' she insisted. She leaned forward, peering into his eyes. 'Are you sure he's quite well enough to go home?' she said to Violet. 'He looks rather pale...'

'The doctor saw him first thing this morning and said he was fit to be discharged,' Violet said.

Dr Gruber raised his eyebrows. 'What, you don't want me to come home now?'

'Of course we want you to come home; the whole family is looking forward to seeing you,' Gerte said. 'We're going to have a party tonight to celebrate...'

Violet caught Isaak Gruber's look of dismay and stepped in.

'It might be a good idea to keep him quiet for a

251

few days, just to give him time to get his strength back,' she said.

Dr Gruber gave her a grateful smile. 'You hear that, Gerte? I need to stay quiet. Just in a room with my books and I will be well in no time.'

'Books!' Gerte scorned. 'Some good food and good company is what you need.'

Dr Gruber turned to Violet. 'You see, she pays no attention to anyone. Perhaps I should stay here, after all?'

'*Nein*, Isaak, you're coming home where you belong,' Gerte said firmly.

Dr Gruber looked wistful, and Violet could almost tell what he was thinking. Where he belonged was back in Germany with his wife and his children and the life he used to have. But fate had given him a new life, and now she could see from his face that he was wondering how he would fit into it.

She hoped Gerte would have the good sense to give him the time and space he needed to adjust. She was a kindly soul, and she obviously adored her cousin, but there was a danger she might smother him if she wasn't careful.

'Did you bring those things I asked you to?' he asked Gerte.

'Of course. I have them somewhere...' Gerte searched through her capacious bag. 'Ah yes, here they are.'

She produced two neatly wrapped packages and handed them to her cousin.

Dr Gruber passed one of them to Violet. 'This is for you, *Schwester*,' he said. 'To thank you for taking such good care of me.'

252

'Thank you. How thoughtful of you.' Violet unfastened the narrow ribbon on the box and opened it. Inside were half a dozen pastries, dusted with a drift of sugar and smelling deliciously of cinnamon and fruit.

'*Rugelach*,' Gerte said. 'Fresh from my husband's bakery this morning.'

'I thought you might care to try them?' Isaak Gruber looked as anxious to please as a child.

'They look delicious.' Violet took an appreciative sniff. 'I'll share them with the other nurses this morning.'

Isaak nodded, satisfied. Then he handed her another package, wrapped in brown paper. 'And I wonder if you would give this to *Fraülein* Davis for me?'

'Miss Davis?'

Isaak Gruber nodded. 'I had hoped to see her myself before I left, but alas, it seems I won't have the chance...' He glanced at Gerte, who was already poised with his suitcase, ready to go.

Violet looked at the package in her hands. 'I didn't know you were that well acquainted with the Assistant Matron?' she said.

'Oh yes, we often talk together.'

'I've never seen her here.'

'Mostly she comes to see me during the night. Like me, she has trouble sleeping. So we sit up into the night together, and tell each other stories.'

'Stories?'

He nodded. 'We both have many stories to tell, *Schwester*.' He pointed to the package in her hands. 'That is why I have given her a journal, so she can write down her stories when I am not

253

here to listen to them. It may help her, I think.'

'I'll see she gets it.' Violet looked down at the package in her hands, intrigued.

The porter arrived with a wheelchair to take Dr Gruber downstairs. Violet walked beside him, with Gerte bringing up the rear, still fussing over his bags.

'What kind of stories?' she asked.

Isaak Gruber sent her a shrewd look over his spectacles. 'That is not for me to say. *Fraülein* Davis may tell you herself one day. I hope she will, for her own sake.' He gazed down at the string of blurred numbers etched down his left arm. 'But I will tell you that she and I have both seen things no human being should ever have *to* see. And those horrors can stay with you forever. You never feel the same again. From then on you are always – separate.'

They reached the doors, and Violet held them open for the porter to push the wheelchair through. Outside the air was cold and fresh, with the promise of yet more snow.

'This is where we say goodbye, I think.' Isaak rose slowly from his wheelchair, wincing at the unfamiliar movement. 'Thank you again, *Schwester*, for all you have done for me.'

'You're welcome, Dr Gruber.'

Gerte led the way to the car where her husband waited. Seeing them, he got out and opened the boot to load Dr Gruber's bags.

Isaak Gruber started towards them, then turned back to Violet.

'Be kind to her, *Schwester*,' he said. 'She deserves your respect more than you can imagine.'

254

Violet stood on the steps of the hospital and watched the car as it drove away. Through the back window, she could see Gerte leaning towards her cousin, fussing over him.

Poor Dr Gruber, she thought. Gerte would kill him with kindness if he allowed it.

She looked down at the package in her hand.

Be kind to her, Schwester. *She deserves your respect more than you can imagine.*

What did Dr Gruber mean? He seemed to be speaking in riddles.

She returned to the ward. The staff nurses and students were busy with their morning routine, but they were delighted when Violet handed out the pastries that Gerte Gruber had brought. Shortly afterwards, the porter arrived with the newspaper trolley, and Violet made sure she took a copy of *The Times.*

She retreated to her office and flicked through to the personal columns to check that her advertisement was still there, just as she did every morning.

Seeking Dorothy Eloise Tanner. Anyone with information as to her whereabouts, please contact Violet Tanner at PO Box Number 758, London.

Seeing it there every morning gave her a tiny glimmer of hope. Surely today would be the day when someone would see it? If not her mother herself, then perhaps a friend, or a neighbour...

She checked the post office box every other day, her heart sinking when she found another day had gone by with no replies. Her mother had apparently disappeared from the face of the earth.

Violet tried to stay optimistic for Oliver's sake.

255

He was very hurt by his grandmother's disappearance, and kept asking Violet why she might have done it.

'I don't understand,' he would say. 'I thought she liked us? Why would she write to me in the first place if she was just going to disappear the next minute? It doesn't make sense.'

Violet remained guiltily silent. She knew it was her own harsh words that had sent her mother away, and now she regretted them bitterly.

She had had time to reflect on what her mother had said, and now she understood that Dorothy Tanner was only looking out for her child, just as Violet looked out for Oliver. They went about things very differently, but her mother had been trying to protect her, in her own way.

Now she desperately wanted to tell her mother that she understood, that she no longer blamed her for what had happened.

But it seemed it was too late.

'I wish I could have seen her once more, just to say goodbye,' Oliver had said to her that morning.

'Me too,' Violet said.

The harsh ring of the telephone shattered the peace of the ward. It was the signal that Matron was on her way. Each ward would ring the next to warn them to be at the doors and ready by the time Miss Fox arrived.

Violet put aside the newspaper, straightened her bonnet and went out to gather her nurses.

Miss Davis was with Miss Fox as usual, but Violet barely spared the Assistant Matron a word of greeting. The two women had not spoken to

256

each other since the night of that last rehearsal, when Miss Davis had been so unforgivably rude to her.

Now, after talking to Isaak Gruber, Violet found herself watching the Assistant Matron through new eyes.

She was a thoroughly unlikeable young woman, who made no effort to make herself popular with anyone. If anything, she seemed to go out of her way to push people away.

But then Violet remembered what Dr Gruber had said.

She and I have both seen things no human being should ever have to see. And those horrors can stay with you forever... From then on you are always – separate.

What if she wasn't really the cold fish she seemed to be, but someone who had chosen to close down a part of themselves, shut off their emotions for their own protection?

She still couldn't imagine the chilly Assistant Matron forming any kind of friendship with anyone, least of all someone as genial as Isaak Gruber. But then she saw the look of shock and disappointment on Miss Davis's face when they reached what had been his bed, which now lay empty.

'Oh, has he gone?' she blurted out.

Violet nodded. 'He was discharged this morning. His cousin arrived first thing to take him home.'

'What a shame,' Miss Fox said. 'I would have liked to say goodbye to him. He was quite a character, wasn't he?'

257

'Yes, he was.' Violet looked at the Assistant Matron as she spoke. Miss Davis had carefully composed her face into her usual chilly mask, giving nothing away.

'He left you a present, Miss Davis,' Violet said.

Miss Davis looked up, dismay in her pale blue eyes. 'A present? For me?'

'I'll fetch it for you.' Violet went to retrieve the package from her desk drawer.

Miss Davis looked at it guardedly. 'What is it?'

'A journal, I believe. He said he hoped it would help you.'

'What else did he say?' Miss Davis's voice was an urgent whisper.

'Nothing. Except that he wished you well, and he wanted you to go on telling your stories.'

'Goodness, you must have made quite an impression on him, Miss Davis,' Miss Fox commented. She looked at Violet, her brows rising sceptically.

Miss Davis did not reply. She went on looking down at the package in her hands. Violet thought she could see the faintest tinge of colour in her cheek.

The next minute she was all business again. Tucking the package under her arm, she said briskly, 'With your permission, Matron, I will inspect under the beds. The springs were really quite dusty yesterday.'

'Of course, Miss Davis.'

As the Assistant Matron walked away, Kathleen whispered, 'How extraordinary. I wouldn't have thought of her as a writer, would you? What sort of stories do you think he meant?'

258

'I don't know,' Violet said. But she was beginning to have her suspicions.

As Dr Gruber had said, perhaps there was more to Charlotte Davis than met the eye.

Charlotte

23rd December 1945

The whole camp was so quiet. There was no sound at all and yet there were people everywhere. They were like ghosts. You didn't know whether they were living or dead. Most of them were dead. Some were trying to walk, some were stumbling, some on hands and knees. There was an oppressive haze over the whole camp. The sun was shining, but everything seemed to be lifeless...

Charlotte wrote without thinking, letting all the words spill out on to the page as they came to her, worried that if she allowed herself to consider them for too long she would not dare write them down.

As she wrote, she could feel some of the tension flowing out of her. Dr Gruber was right: writing down her story did bring her some kind of release. Not as much as talking to him, but it still helped.

The doctor had only been gone a few hours, and already she missed him. Night after night they would sit together in the darkened ward, and Charlotte would spill out her thoughts to him,

259

things she had never expected to share with anyone. And Isaak Gruber would listen, and nod thoughtfully, and gently urge her to go on when the words became too much for her.

At first Charlotte had worried that dredging up her old memories would open old wounds, but as Dr Gruber had explained to her, the opposite was true. Hidden away, her fears and memories festered and grew, poisoning her from the inside. By bringing them out into the open, exposing them to the light, they seemed to lose their power and turn to dust.

She couldn't remember the last time she had been woken by one of her nightmares.

She finished writing and closed the journal, then put it away in her bedside drawer. Outside, the snow had started to fall again, eddies of swirling flakes in the light from the street lamps.

Tomorrow was Christmas Eve. In two days' time, the patients would be gathering in the dining hall, expecting to see a Christmas show.

Only Charlotte knew there wasn't going to be one.

Sooner or later she knew she would have to tell Matron. She should have told her days ago, after no one turned up to the last rehearsal. But somehow Charlotte had been praying that a miracle might happen.

Miss Fox had asked her about it earlier, when they were in the office.

'Well, Miss Davis,' she had smiled at her. 'Are there any more rehearsals before the big performance on Christmas Day?'

Caught off guard, Charlotte had replied, 'There

is a final dress rehearsal tomorrow, Matron.'

'Splendid. If you don't mind, I'd like to come and see it?'

Lost for words, Charlotte could only stutter, 'Of course, Matron.'

'I shall look forward to it.'

As Miss Fox closed the door to her office, Charlotte allowed her head to sink into her hands. Now she had done it. If she wasn't in trouble before, she certainly was now.

What had possessed her to say that? It was her chance to come clean to Matron, to confess what had happened. She had to do it sooner or later.

But the thought of uttering the words, of admitting she had failed in the one simple task Miss Fox had given her, was beyond her.

At first she had blamed everyone else. They had let her down badly, every single one of them. And they had let the hospital and the patients down, too. How dare they walk out on her?

But the more she thought about it, the more she realised Miss Tanner had been right. She only had herself to blame. If she had gone about things differently, treated people with respect instead of barking out orders, then things might have turned out better.

Perhaps it wasn't too late to put things right, she thought. She might just catch Miss Tanner before the end of her shift. It would be difficult for her to swallow her pride, but she knew she had to do the right thing, for everyone's sake.

Miss Tanner was supervising a first-year student who was giving her first injection. Charlotte saw

261

the flash of dislike on the ward sister's face when she pulled aside the screens and saw her standing there.

'Miss Davis.' She quickly masked her dismay behind a smile. 'What can I do for you?'

'I would like a word with you in private, if that's possible?'

Miss Tanner hesitated for a moment. 'Wait in my office while I finish off this injection, then I'll be with you.'

Miss Tanner's office was off the main ward. It was small and the tiny window made it dark, but a pot of bright red poinsettias on the desk gave a splash of colour to the gloom.

Charlotte fought the urge to tidy the scattered paperwork on the desk. She was supposed to be here to build bridges, not to destroy even more. But even so, she couldn't stop herself from carefully folding the copy of *The Times* that lay open at the personal columns.

She seated herself, only to stand up again a few minutes later and pace the room. She had just decided to sit down again when the door opened and Miss Tanner entered.

'Well?' she said. 'What can I do for you, Miss Davis?'

Her voice was brisk, sparing her no pleasantries. Charlotte winced at her tone. It was no more than she deserved.

She took a deep breath. 'It's about the Christmas show,' she said.

Miss Tanner's brows rose. 'What about it?'

Charlotte looked into the ward sister's dark brown eyes. Miss Tanner's face was carefully

262

composed, giving nothing away.

'I wanted to apologise. For the way I behaved.'

'Oh.' That took her by surprise, Charlotte could tell.

'You were right, I went about it in entirely the wrong way, and I upset everyone in the process.' She looked down at her fingers, lacing and unlacing in her lap. 'I should never have agreed to do it in the first place. I was completely out of my depth from the moment I started. I knew it, too, which was why I was so ... heavy-handed.'

There was a time when she might have been able to take it all in good part, to laugh and joke and not take any of it too seriously. But those days were gone, and she wasn't sure if she would ever be that young woman again.

She looked up at Miss Tanner. 'I intend to go to Matron and take full responsibility for what's happened. But I wondered if you might agree to speak to everyone, get them to agree to perform? I won't be involved, obviously. The patients are all looking forward to a show, and I don't like to let them down.'

Miss Tanner was silent for a moment. Then she said, 'Perhaps if you spoke to them yourself—'

'No, I couldn't do that.' Charlotte shook her head. 'They wouldn't listen to me anyway, and I don't blame them for it. I'm afraid I don't inspire the same loyalty as they have for you. They like you.'

'They'd like you too, if you gave them a chance.'

Charlotte managed a smile. 'I doubt it, Miss Tanner. I know what they all think of me, and they're right. I'll admit, I'm hopeless with people.'

263

As Charlotte stood up, Miss Tanner said, 'I spoke to Dr Gruber before he left.'

Charlotte tensed, instantly wary. 'What did he tell you?'

'Not much,' Miss Tanner said. 'But enough that I could work it out for myself.' She gazed at Charlotte across the desk. 'You were there, weren't you? When they liberated the camps?'

Once upon a time Charlotte might have retreated, denied it and told her to mind her own business. But this time she took a deep breath and nodded.

'I was one of the first nurses they allowed in.'

She steeled herself. If Miss Tanner asked, then she would answer her, no matter how difficult it might be.

But the ward sister simply nodded and said, 'I see.' There was something about the way she said it, as if Charlotte had somehow answered all her questions without really saying anything.

Charlotte stood up. 'So you'll talk to everyone?' she said.

'I'll do my best.'

She had reached the door when Miss Tanner said, 'You know, Miss Davis, you don't have to shut people out all the time. They will help you, if you'll only ask.'

There's no harm in leaning on others occasionally. You don't have to be strong all the time.

Charlotte heard Major Hugh's words inside her head, as clear as if he were there, saying them to her himself.

If only she could believe them.

Charlotte spent most of the night rehearsing what she was going to tell Matron the following morning. But to her dismay, Miss Fox was in meetings all day, so she didn't get the chance to see her.

All afternoon, Charlotte kept looking at the clock on the wall, watching the hands creeping slowly towards six o'clock, when the dress rehearsal was due to start. As it turned past five, she began to hope that perhaps Miss Fox had been so busy she had forgotten all about it.

She was forcing herself to concentrate on the following week's staff rosters when the door opened and Matron strode in, just before six o'clock.

She seemed surprised to see her. 'Why, Miss Davis, I didn't expect to see you here. Surely you should be in the dining hall? The rehearsal is due to start at six, isn't it?'

Charlotte stared down in confusion at the ink blot her pen had made on the rosters.

'I–'

'Or were you waiting for me?' Miss Fox said, unfastening her cloak and slipping it from her shoulders 'I won't keep you a moment. We'll walk down together, shall we?'

Charlotte could feel hot blood scalding her cheeks.

'Matron, I have to tell you something...' Her voice emerged, barely above a whisper.

'Tell me what, Miss Davis?'

Charlotte looked up at her. Miss Fox was staring back at her, a quizzical half-smile on her face. 'It's about the show,' she said. 'You see, I–'

Suddenly there was a knock on the door. Miss

265

Fox held up her hand to silence Charlotte for a moment.

'Enter,' she called out.

A student nurse stuck her head around the door.

'Yes?' said Miss Fox. 'What do you want, Nurse Philips?'

'Please, Matron, Sister Jarvis sent me to tell Miss Davis we're all ready for her in the dining hall when she wants to join us.'

Charlotte stared at the girl, perplexed.

'Thank you, Philips.' Miss Fox turned to Charlotte. 'Shall we go?' she smiled. 'We don't want to keep everyone waiting, do we?'

Charlotte felt as if she was in a state of unreality as she walked beside Miss Fox down the staircase. She had no idea what was going to be waiting for her in the dining hall. Part of her still feared it was all a horrible practical joke, and they would walk into an empty room.

But when Miss Fox swung open the doors, there they were. Two porters were busy hanging up a curtain around the makeshift stage, while a couple of ward maids made last-minute adjustments to a medical student's costume. All around the dining hall, people were humming tunes, trilling up and down their scales and pacing about, silently trying to memorise their lines.

Charlotte stared around her, unable to believe her eyes. There were fewer performers than there had been originally, but still more than enough to put on a good show.

Miss Tanner sat at the piano, arranging her music in front of her. She looked up at Charlotte

266

and smiled.

'Are you ready to begin, Miss Davis?' she said brightly.

'Yes. Yes, of course.' Charlotte went to her usual seat, still feeling dazed. Miss Fox sat beside her.

'I must say, I'm rather looking forward to this,' she whispered to Charlotte as the first of the performers took to the stage.

Somehow, for once they all seemed word perfect and in tune. Not that Charlotte would have noticed anyway. She was too stunned to speak for most of the rehearsal. All she could do was sit and watch as act after act took to the stage.

Afterwards, Miss Fox turned to her and said, 'Thank you, Miss Davis. That was very entertaining. I'm sure the patients will appreciate all your efforts. I must confess, when I first gave you the task I wasn't sure what kind of job you would make of it. But it seems I was wrong.'

Charlotte blushed guiltily, aware of Miss Tanner listening close by. 'Matron, there's something you should know—'

'Miss Davis?' Miss Tanner interrupted her. 'Do you think you could spare a minute to look at the opening music with me? I have a few new ideas, but I need your approval.'

'Yes, of course. But—' Before she had a chance to say any more, Miss Tanner's hand closed on her arm, guiding her firmly away.

'I don't think Matron needs to know about our ... difficulties with the show, do you?' the ward sister whispered in Charlotte's ear. 'Especially as they're all in the past now, anyway.'

'Yes, but surely I should tell her it was you who

267

saved the show?' Charlotte replied.

'Why?'

'Well, because – because it's only fair.' Charlotte was troubled. 'Don't you want to take the credit for your efforts? You deserve it.'

Miss Tanner shook her head. 'I'm not interested in taking the credit for anything,' she said. 'Besides, I didn't save the show. Everyone is here because of you.'

Charlotte stared at her, bewildered. 'Me? Why?'

'Because we're a family here,' Miss Tanner said. 'We may have our squabbles and our fallings out, but in the end we all care about each other.'

Charlotte looked away, humbled. 'I owe you an apology,' she murmured. 'The way I spoke to you at the last rehearsal... I know you were only trying to give me advice, but I was too pig-headed to accept I needed it.'

'Oh, it's all forgotten.' Miss Tanner brushed her apology away. 'Besides, it wasn't all your fault. I could have been more patient with you, but you caught me at the wrong moment, I'm afraid.'

Charlotte looked at Miss Tanner's profile as she bent over her sheet music. She hadn't noticed before how troubled she looked. Her brown eyes were ringed with deep purple shadows.

Once she might have told herself not to get involved, but this time she took a deep breath and said, 'Is it to do with your missing relative, Miss Tanner?'

Miss Tanner flashed a look at her. 'How did you know?'

'I couldn't help noticing the newspaper in your office. You'd circled a particular advertisement...'

Miss Tanner was silent for a long time, and Charlotte feared she might have overstepped the mark. But then she said, 'It's my mother. She disappeared a couple of weeks ago. She left her lodgings with no forwarding address, and no one seems to know where to find her.'

'How strange. Might there be a reason for her to leave so suddenly?'

Miss Tanner's mouth twisted. 'Me, I think. We haven't spoken to each other in fourteen years, then she suddenly came back into our lives, and I'm afraid I wasn't as warm or welcoming as I might have been.' A faraway look came into her eyes. 'I just hope nothing has happened to her.'

Charlotte looked at her, seeing the worry etched on her face. She found it quite hard to believe that someone as calm and composed as Violet Tanner might have heartaches she didn't share with anyone.

And she had thought she was the only one with secrets.

'I hope you get some good news about your mother soon,' she said.

'I'm sure I will.' Miss Tanner summoned a brave smile. 'You never know, perhaps a Christmas miracle will happen and she'll appear on our doorstep to have dinner with us.'

But even as she said it, Charlotte could see the tremble in her lips and the lack of hope in her eyes.

They walked together down to the hospital entrance. As they emerged into the cold, snowy night, the bells started to chime at St Peter's on the Green, calling people to the Christmas Eve service.

269

'Listen to that,' Miss Tanner said. 'It's not that long ago we weren't allowed to have church bells ringing. It makes you appreciate it all the more, doesn't it?'

'Indeed,' Charlotte said.

'Well, I go this way.' Miss Tanner pointed towards the gates. 'I'll see you tomorrow. Good night, Miss Davis.'

'Good night, Miss Tanner. And thank you,' Charlotte called after her.

She watched the ward sister's tall, elegant figure picking her way down the long drive towards the porters' lodge.

Poor Miss Tanner, hoping for her Christmas miracle.

Charlotte had given up believing in miracles the day she walked into Bergen-Belsen, just as she had given up on believing in the goodness of humanity. But being at the Nightingale had convinced her that there were still good people in the world.

And as for miracles ... well, she had already witnessed one of those today when she walked into the dining hall, thanks to Miss Tanner.

Surely it might be possible for her to arrange a miracle of her own in return?

Daisy

24th December 1945

Wren ward was busy on Christmas Eve, with several mothers already in labour, determined to have their Christmas babies. On top of that, there were two cases of mastitis, a cracked nipple, a pyelitis and a cystitis to deal with, and a new caesarean in the private room.

Daisy spent all day dashing around, fetching bedpans and fomentations, checking samples and cajoling the urinary infections to drink more fluids.

On top of it all, Mrs Goodwood was making her usual fuss. As if the nurses weren't all busy enough, she had decided to complain of backache. So as well as all her other tasks, Daisy found herself constantly plumping the woman's pillows and listening to her complaints.

'If you ask me, she's just annoyed that she's not getting all the attention for once,' Daisy said to Rose as they changed the post-op's dressings together. 'And to think we've got to put up with her for the next month!'

It wasn't until she saw her friend's stony face that Daisy remembered they were still not speaking to each other. Rose said nothing as she pretended to concentrate on cleaning the wound with antiseptic.

271

This had gone on far too long, Daisy thought. Over a week had passed since they had spoken to each other, and the silence was killing her. She desperately missed her friend, and she had almost forgotten why she was so angry with her in the first place. But now their argument had taken on a life of its own, and both of them were too proud to make the first move.

They finished changing the dressing and Daisy cleared everything away. As luck would have it, just as they were leaving the room they bumped into Dr Armstrong.

'Oh, hello.' He looked straight at Rose as he spoke. 'Sister Wren has asked me to come up and look at a patient. She thinks there might be a possible thrombosis.'

'That'll be the patient in bed seven, Doctor,' Rose replied, her tone formal.

'Right. Thank you.' Tom Armstrong gave them a quick nod, then hurried off down the ward.

Daisy saw the way Rose kept her gaze deliberately averted. She also noticed how Tom Armstrong looked back over his shoulder at her, stealing one final quick glance before Staff Nurse Giles claimed him and ushered him away to where the patient was waiting behind the screens.

They were as wretched as each other, she thought. And it was all her fault.

She opened her mouth to speak but Rose was already gone, pushing the trolley into the sluice to dispose of the dressings.

'What have you done now?'

Daisy turned round to see Marjorie Carroll,

272

another girl from their set, standing behind her. 'What?'

'Trent looked upset just now. I hope it wasn't something you said?'

Daisy glared at the girl. Marjorie Carroll wasn't even a particular friend of Rose's, but like the other girls she had decided to become very protective of her lately.

She was about to tell her to mind her own business, then thought better of it. 'What do you want, Carroll?' she snapped. 'Because if you've nothing better to do there's a mastitis patient in bed two needing another fomentation. Or you could massage Mrs Goodwood's bad back?'

'I don't take orders from you, thank you very much!' Marjorie Carroll's chin lifted. 'Sister wants you to fetch two drip stands from the basement.'

Daisy frowned. 'Why doesn't she ask me herself?'

'She's gone to the dress rehearsal, hasn't she?' Marjorie looked huffy. 'You can ask Staff Nurse Giles if you don't believe me, but I'm sure she won't thank you for interrupting her while she's with a patient.'

Daisy glanced over at the screens around bed seven. Behind them, Staff Nurse Giles was in consultation with Dr Armstrong.

'Surely there must be some drip stands in the equipment cupboard?' she said to Marjorie.

'Sister wouldn't ask you to go down to the basement if there were, would she?' Marjorie sounded impatient. 'For heaven's sake, Baker, why are you making such a fuss about it? Surely you don't

273

believe the basement's haunted?'

'No!' Daisy said quickly. 'I just didn't want a wasted journey, that's all.'

'Well, if I were you I'd hurry up about it, before Staff Nurse Giles comes back and finds out you've disobeyed Sister's orders. And watch out for those ghosts, won't you?' Marjorie called after her.

Daisy ignored her, but her heart was racing as she made her way down to the basement. In spite of what she had said to Marjorie Carroll, she was nervous.

She had heard all the stories about the haunted basement, passed down among the nurses. There was a tale of a tragic young nurse who had given birth in secret down there and then hanged herself in shame. Some claimed to have heard the faint sounds of a baby crying, while others reckoned they had seen a ghostly shape swinging gently from the beams. Other people said they had seen a senior nurse called Miss Hanley, who had been killed at the hospital during the Blitz.

Either way, the basement was not a place any nurse willingly ventured alone, and especially not after dark.

Daisy tried to push all these thoughts from her mind as she made her way down the narrow flight of stone steps to the heavy wooden door. She pushed it open gingerly and stepped inside.

Almost immediately she was enveloped by inky blackness. The air felt damp and icy against her skin, and there was a reek of damp.

Daisy fumbled for the light, her hand scraping rough brickwork before it found the switch. A bare bulb flickered into life above her head, its dim light barely piercing the gloom. Before her, the basement was divided into long, narrow rows by high cupboards and shelves, each piled with boxes and equipment that cast long, eerie shadows in the light from the open doorway.

Daisy stayed close to the door as she looked around, trying to adjust to the darkness. Now, where to start looking for drip stands?

It was no use, she decided. She would have to venture deeper into the basement and search for them. The quicker she found them, the quicker she could get out of this dreadful place.

She took a deep breath and plunged into the gloom, quietly cursing Sister Wren and Staff Nurse Giles and anyone else she could think of.

She hurried down the narrow spaces between the rows of shelves, searching them frantically. The shelves towered over her, closing her in. She felt as if she was in some horrible maze, with no way of escape.

She turned the corner, and stopped dead. At the far end of the row, a shadowy figure swung gently from the beams, its head lolling, arms dangling by its sides. Daisy screamed, just as the light bulb above her head fizzled, then went out with a pop.

She swung round, blundering in the darkness, trying to get back to the door. The open doorway still cast a dim rectangle of light, showing her the way. She had nearly reached it when she heard the scutter of footsteps behind her. A second later a hand came out of the darkness, closing on her shoulder.

'Baker?'

Rose's calm, clear voice was the last thing she had expected to hear.

'Trent?' she whispered. 'What are you doing here?'

'Carroll told me what she'd done. I thought I'd come and find you.'

Daisy was confused. 'I don't understand... She told me Sister wanted me to fetch a drip stand...'

'She was playing a trick on you. I daresay Philips egged her on to do it.'

'A trick?' Daisy could hardly believe it.

'A very cruel trick,' Rose said. 'I know how scared you are of the dark.' She took her arm gently. 'Come on, let's get out of here.'

Just at that moment there was a crash, and they were plunged into darkness.

'Someone's shut the door!' Daisy whimpered. 'We'll never find our way out now!'

'Of course we will.' Rose released Daisy's arm and fumbled in her pocket. A moment later there was a click and a narrow beam of light illuminated her friend's face.

'You brought a torch!' Daisy cried. 'I didn't think of that.'

'No,' Rose said. 'I didn't think you would. Come on, I think the door's this way...'

They trailed up and down the narrow aisles, Rose leading the way with her torch. Even with its beam to light the way, they kept blundering into cupboards in the darkness. Once a pile of boxes toppled over and Daisy cried out in fear.

Rose sighed. 'For heaven's sake, it's only a cardboard box!'

276

'You don't understand,' Daisy whimpered. 'I – saw something.'

'What? What did you see?'

'It was back there.' Daisy pointed a shaking finger. 'A body, hanging from the beams.'

'Let me see–' Rose started towards it, but Daisy held her back.

'Are you mad?' she said. 'Don't go near it.'

But Rose had already extricated herself and was making her way towards the far end of the basement. 'This way, did you say?'

'Let's get out of here, please...' Daisy begged.

'Just a minute, I want to see–' Rose stopped in her tracks and pointed her torch upwards. 'Oh!'

'What? What is it? Can you see her?'

'Come and see for yourself.'

'No, I don't want to, it's too terrifying–' Daisy said, but Rose reached for her sleeve, yanking her back to her side.

'Look,' she said.

Slowly, gingerly, Daisy forced her gaze upwards. There, dangling from the beams, its head lolling limply on its bony shoulders, was a skeleton similar to the one that graced the corner of their classroom for anatomy lessons.

Rose laughed. 'Oh Baker, imagine you being scared of that!'

'I didn't know, did I?' Daisy turned on her furiously. 'It's all right for you, you've got no imagination!'

'And you've got no common sense!' Rose snapped back.

They stared at each other, hostile in the darkness. Daisy couldn't see Rose's face, but she

277

knew she was struggling to keep her temper.

'Let's get out of here,' she muttered.

'That's the first sensible idea you've had,' Rose replied.

They finally made their way to the door. But when they tried it, they realised it was stuck fast.

'It's locked.' Panic assailed Daisy. 'Someone must have locked us in.'

'Don't be silly, I expect it's just a bit stuck. Here, let me try...' Rose shouldered her to one side and tried the door. Daisy was half pleased that it wouldn't budge for her.

'You see?' she said. 'It's locked.'

'Perhaps it was one of the porters,' Rose said.

'Or perhaps it was one of your friends?'

Rose turned on her. 'I hope you're not suggesting I had anything to do with this?'

'I'm not suggesting anything,' Daisy shrugged.

'Yes, you are. You're making out this was all a big plan on my part to trap you down here.'

'Isn't it?'

'Come off it, Baker. Why on earth would I want to be locked down here with you, of all people?' Rose turned and started hammering on the door. 'Hello?' she called out. 'Hello, can anyone hear me?'

Daisy ignored her, too stung by her friend's comment to reply.

'They can't hear me,' Rose gave up in defeat. 'The door's too thick.'

'What do we do now?' Daisy asked.

'I don't know, do I? I suppose we'll just have to sit here and wait until someone comes down here

278

and finds us.'

'That could take hours. Or days!' Panic rose in her throat. 'Oh God, imagine if we're stuck down here all Christmas Day. Imagine if we're never, ever found!'

'Now you're being overdramatic.' Rose upturned a box and sat down on it. As Daisy watched, she calmly took out a bar of chocolate and started eating it.

From above them came the sound of voices and shuffling footsteps. Daisy looked up at the ceiling. 'What's that noise?'

Rose glanced up. 'The dining hall must be up there. It sounds as if they're getting ready for the dress rehearsal.'

'If we can hear them, they must be able to hear us. Let's find something to make some noise...' Daisy started searching around. She found an old broom handle and started pounding on the brickwork above their heads. 'Hello?' she called out. 'Hello up there!'

'They'll never hear you,' Rose said through a mouthful of chocolate. 'Once the music starts it'll be far too noisy to hear anyone.'

No sooner had she said it than they heard the sound of the piano, as Miss Tanner moved her hands swiftly over the keys.

'Hello!' Daisy called out more desperately. She pounded the ceiling with the broom handle again. She dislodged a chunk of brickwork, bringing down a shower of powder brick and distemper over her face and shoulders.

'You see?' Rose said, as Daisy wiped her face with her apron. 'You're just doing more harm

279

than good.'

'At least I'm doing something!' Daisy snapped. 'That's typical of you, sitting around doing nothing while you wait for someone to rescue you!'

'It's better than running around like a headless chicken, getting nowhere!' Rose sighed and pushed a box towards her. 'For goodness' sake, sit down.'

Daisy dragged the box a few feet away from her friend and plonked herself down on it, glaring balefully at the door. Rose offered her some chocolate but she refused out of sheer stubbornness.

'This is all your fault,' she muttered.

'How do you work that out?'

'If you hadn't turned everyone against me, they wouldn't be playing stupid tricks on me.'

'I didn't turn anyone against you. You did that all by yourself.'

Daisy hugged herself. 'I'm cold,' she complained.

'There are some blankets on one of the shelves. I saw them earlier–'

'Listen!' Daisy held up her hand. 'Can you hear that?'

'Hear what?'

'A sort of ... scurrying.'

'It's probably rats,' Rose said calmly.

Daisy shot to her feet. 'Rats!'

'Don't worry, they won't come near you. Not unless you fall asleep, that is.' Rose smiled wickedly.

'I'm glad you find this funny!' Daisy felt herself growing dangerously near to tears. 'We could be

280

trapped down here forever. We could die down here...'

'Don't be ridiculous!'

Daisy slumped back down on her box and turned her back on Rose. For a long time they sat in silence, punctuated only by the scurrying of rats, the sound of Rose unwrapping her chocolate and the faint music coming from upstairs.

Then, out of nowhere, came the sound of Sister Wren's high, warbling voice.

'Here she goes,' Rose sighed. 'We can't ever escape from that screeching, can we?'

'Imagine if that was the last sound we ever heard?' Daisy replied.

They looked at each other in the gloom, and suddenly they were both laughing.

'Are you sure you wouldn't like some chocolate?' Rose said, holding it out to her. 'It's Fry's Five Boys – your favourite.'

Daisy took a piece and they sat in silence for a while.

'I'm sorry the other girls turned against you,' Rose said at last. 'I didn't want it to happen, honestly.'

'I daresay I deserved it,' Daisy sighed. 'I haven't been very kind to any of them in the past.' She looked across at Rose. 'I'm sorry for the horrible things I said. I suppose I just wasn't used to playing second fiddle to anyone, and it came as a shock.'

'It doesn't matter now, anyway,' Rose said. 'I've told Tom I'm not interested.'

'But why? I thought you liked him?'

'I did.' She smiled sadly. 'But I'm not sure I'm

281

ready to fall in love with anyone again, not after Laurence. And besides, I didn't want to lose you as a friend.' She looked up at her. 'It's been awful, not speaking all this time.'

'You're right,' Daisy said. 'I've missed you, Rose.'

'I've missed you too. Promise we'll never fall out over a man again?'

'Never!'

The door flew open with such force it crashed back on its hinges, flooding them with light from the passageway beyond.

Daisy jumped to her feet. 'Did you see that?'

'I couldn't miss it, could I? Someone must have come down and unlocked it.' Rose stood up and ventured a few steps to the doorway. 'Hello? Is anyone there?'

Daisy stood rooted to the spot with fear. 'Why did it open so suddenly like that?'

'I don't know ... perhaps the wind blew it?' They both looked at each other. Beyond the door, the air was completely still.

'Or perhaps there really is a ghost?' Daisy whispered. She bolted for the door, Rose hot on her heels.

They didn't stop running until they had reached the end of the passageway. Then they both collapsed against the wall, holding their sides and laughing at their own terror.

'I thought you didn't believe in ghosts?' Daisy teased her.

'I didn't. But now I'm not so sure.'

'Well, if it was a ghost, I reckon it must have been a friendly one,' Daisy said. 'It locked us in

282

the basement together until we both came to our senses!'

'True,' Rose said. They smiled at each other. Daisy knew her friend was as pleased as she was that their friendship was back on track.

As they walked back to the ward, Daisy said, 'You know, I really think you should give Tom Armstrong a chance. No, I do,' she insisted, as Rose sighed. 'I know you say you're not ready, but you've got to take the plunge sometime. Besides, I've seen the way you look at him. You're smitten with him, and he is with you.'

'I don't know.' Rose brushed the cobwebs off her apron. 'What about you?'

'Oh, don't worry about me,' Daisy said. 'I've given up on Tom Armstrong. Besides, there's a rather handsome new anaesthetist I've got my eye on...'

'Typical!' Rose grinned at her.

They turned the corner, just as Tom was coming in the opposite direction. He had his head down, consulting some notes he carried in his hand, and he didn't notice them until they had practically bumped into him.

'Do excuse me, I'm – oh!' He stopped short when he came face-to-face with Rose. His notes fell from his hand, scattering over the floor.

'Let me help you.' Rose knelt beside him, gathering up the papers. Daisy looked from one to the other. It was hard to say which of them was blushing the deeper shade of red.

'I'm glad we bumped into you,' she spoke up. 'Rose was just saying how much she would like to perform your song in the Christmas show.'

'Oh?' Tom glanced at Rose. 'Really? Because I'm game, if you are?'

'Well–'

'She'd love to,' Daisy said, ignoring her friend's hard stare. 'Honestly, she's talked about nothing else.'

'Well, in that case–' Tom remembered his manners and looked at Daisy. 'Will you be joining us?'

'Oh no,' Daisy said. 'I think it's better as a duet than a trio, don't you think?'

'Yes,' Tom said, smiling shyly at Rose. 'Yes, I think it is. I'll have a word with Miss Davis then, shall I? I'm sure with a bit of judicious begging she'd let us back in.'

'You do that.'

As he hurried off, his notes tucked under his arm, Rose turned to her. 'Why did you do that?' she hissed.

Daisy grinned at her. 'Because that's what friends are for,' she said.

Miriam

25th December 1945

'Merry Christmas, Miriam!'

The first thing Miriam Trott saw when she stepped out of her room at the sisters' home on that Christmas morning was Sister Hyde's smiling face. She very nearly slammed the door on her.

284

'Merry Christmas,' she mumbled, even though the last thing she felt was merry. She had spent another night crying into her pillow over Frank.

'And it's snowed again overnight, too. It was such a beautiful scene when I looked out of my window this morning.'

Miriam glared at her. Sister Hyde had taken over the Female Chronics ward a year ago. She was young, fresh-faced and so resolutely positive, it was all Miriam could do not to slap her.

'Yes, I can imagine the snow-capped roof of the local glue factory is a sight worthy of a Christmas card,' she said.

She set off, Sister Hyde trotting behind her determinedly, in spite of Miriam's best efforts to shake her off.

'It must be so lovely for you, being on the maternity ward on a day such as this,' Sister Hyde trilled. 'I wonder if any Christmas babies will have arrived overnight?'

'Oh, I daresay they will.' Miriam grimaced at the thought. 'The nursery will be full of them, all screaming at the top of their lungs while their mothers sleep peacefully. And then their besotted fools of husbands will arrive, and we'll spend the next hour finding vases for all their wretched flowers!'

Sister Hyde looked startled. 'Oh! Well, I suppose I'd never thought of it like that.'

'Yes, well, you should count yourself lucky that your ward is full of dotty old dears who never get any visitors,' Miriam said. 'Believe me, they're more trouble than they're worth.'

'We still like to make things nice and festive for

285

our patients,' Sister Hyde huffed. 'We'll have a proper Christmas dinner, and a lovely little party–'

'I don't know why you bother, since most of them don't even know what day it is!'

They reached the doors to the hospital, and Miriam barged ahead of Sister Hyde, allowing them to swing back in her face.

'Season's greetings to you, too!' she heard the ward sister's muffled voice through the glass.

Miriam was right; there had been several Christmas babies born overnight, two of them caesareans, which meant dressings to be changed and all kinds of extra work. But no one else seemed to mind; the nurses were all in a frivolous mood, chattering and laughing excitedly among themselves. Even Baker and Trent, who had been keeping their distance from each other for over a week, seemed to have made up their differences. They were giggling together like a pair of silly schoolgirls as they changed the beds.

In the middle of the morning, Miriam gathered the nurses together in her sitting room for coffee, as was customary every Christmas. She knew they were expecting her to get out the medicinal brandy as most of the other ward sisters did, and she briefly enjoyed the look of disappointment on their faces when she left it locked in the cupboard. They were even more disappointed when they realised she had not bought them any Christmas gifts.

Miriam did feel rather mean when they presented her with the tin of lily of the valley talc they had clubbed together to buy. And she could

286

tell the other nurses were thinking the same.

'It wouldn't hurt her to get us something,' she heard Nurse Baker complaining to Nurse Trent. 'We deserve it, after what we have to put up with.'

'And to think a month ago she was positively angelic,' Trent agreed. 'It hardly seems possible, does it?'

'I still think there was a man involved,' Baker said. 'Believe me, I know a broken heart when I see one.'

It was all Miriam could do not to turn round and lash out at her. If she said anything, they would guess the truth and realise what a fool she had been.

Except she hadn't been a fool, not really. Frank hadn't managed to dupe her. Oh no, she was far too clever for him, not like those other foolish women who had fallen for his charm. No one pulled the wool over Miriam Trott's eyes.

She had spent the last week telling herself what a lucky escape she'd had. But she didn't feel very lucky. In fact, part of her wished she had allowed herself to go on believing him, just for a little while longer. At least then perhaps she wouldn't be feeling so wretched and empty inside.

Since it was Christmas Day, Matron in her infinite wisdom had declared that there should be a special visiting time that afternoon. She had also lifted the ban on more than two visitors per patient, which meant endless amounts of children running about, getting under everyone's feet. All the noise and chaos gave Miriam a headache. The only pleasure she had was standing at the door, banning the children from taking their toys

287

on to the ward.

'Toys carry germs,' she declared, holding a teddy bear at arm's length by its ear.

'Have a heart, Nurse. It's brand new!' the child's father pointed out. 'He's ever so excited to give it to his new baby brother.'

'He'll have to wait until he goes home, won't he?'

She was similarly upset when one of the new fathers turned up with an armful of red carnations.

Just seeing them nearly brought tears to Miriam's eyes.

'Take these away.' She snatched them from the man's grasp and thrust them at Nurse Baker.

'What shall I do with them, Sister?'

'I don't know, do I? I don't really care, as long as I don't have to look at them. I will not have carnations on my ward!' She stomped off, ignoring the astonished looks Nurse Baker and the new father were giving her.

After Christmas dinner had been served and cleared away, it was nearly time for the concert. Miriam still hadn't made up her mind whether she was going to take part, even as she joined the other performers in the dining hall. How could she sing about love when her heart was so heavy with misery?

'But you must,' Miss Tanner encouraged her. 'What would the Christmas show be without "Lo, How a Rose E'er Blooming"? Your public will be expecting it.'

Miriam glanced at the ward sister suspiciously. It was always difficult to tell whether Violet

288

Tanner was joking or not.

But then she saw Miss Davis in the background, with a definite smirk on her face. Since when had the Assistant Matron cracked a smile at anything?

But sarcastic or not, she had to admit Miss Tanner had a point. 'Perhaps I will sing, after all,' she sighed. If nothing else, she would bring a touch of finesse to the proceedings that they would otherwise lack. 'But don't expect me to wear a costume,' she added. 'I'm not in the mood.'

'I wouldn't dream of it, Miss Trott,' Violet Tanner replied, with a quick look at Miss Davis. Now they were both smiling. Since when did she and Miss Tanner become so thick together? Miriam had always been under the impression they couldn't abide each other. It was all most peculiar.

She took to the stage, surveying the rows of audience in front of her. At the front she could see her great friend Mrs Goodwood, her pregnant bulk concealed by a vast flannel dressing gown, smiling encouragingly up at her. Miriam nodded to Miss Tanner, who struck up the opening bars on the piano. She looked up, surveyed her audience and opened her mouth to sing, when a bright flash of scarlet at the back of the dining hall caught her gaze. Miriam turned her head to see Frank Tillery standing at the back of the room, clutching an enormous bunch of red carnations.

At first she thought she must be seeing things. But no, there he was, large as life. When he caught her eye, he lifted his hand and gave her a little wave.

289

'Get on with it, love!'

Miriam hadn't realised she had forgotten to sing until she heard the laughter coming from the audience. Startled, she gazed across at all the amused faces, then down at Miss Tanner. Violet was still tinkling away determinedly on the piano, playing the opening bars over and over again, a puzzled frown on her face.

Miriam opened her mouth to sing, but her throat was dry and her mind so blank she couldn't remember a single word. Humiliated, she did the only thing she could, and fled off stage.

She pushed her way through the crowd of performers waiting to go on stage, ignoring their murmurs of concern, and hurried outside, desperate to escape the scene.

'Miriam?' She heard Frank's voice behind her in the passageway, but she didn't stop. 'Miriam, please! Wait!'

She stopped, whirling round to face him, spitting with fury. 'What are you doing here?'

He looked taken aback. 'I – I had to see you,' he stammered. 'I couldn't leave it like this. I wanted to talk to you, to explain–'

'There is nothing to explain,' she cut him off. 'We've said all we had to say to each other.'

She started to turn away from him but he took hold of her arm, swinging her back round to face him.

'Miriam, please, listen to me–'

'You're wasting your time, Frank. I told you, I'm not a rich heiress. So why don't you leave me alone and go off and chase some rich woman instead?'

290

He stared at her blankly. 'What are you talking about?'

'You know very well, Frank Tillery.' She pulled herself from his grasp and started to walk away.

'I'll give it up,' he called after her.

She turned round. 'What?'

'I'll give it up, if that's what you want. I'll talk to my publishers, tell them I'm not doing it any more. If that's what it takes to win you back–'

Miriam interrupted, 'Publishers? What publishers?'

Frank frowned. 'That's what all this is about, isn't it? My writing?'

Miriam stared at him. 'You're a writer?'

Frank looked offended. 'There's no need to be unkind. I know you've already made it clear what you think of my novels–'

'Your novels?'

'Agatha Pendlebury's novels, I should say. What did you say about them?' He paused for a moment, searching for the words. '"There's romance and there's rubbish," I believe were your words.' He smiled self depracatingly. 'I suppose you're right, they're hardly works of great literature. And it's not really a job for a man, is it? I only started doing it when I came out of the RAF, for a bit of fun more than anything. But then I realised I had rather a knack for it, and it paid well, so–' He shrugged.

'Agatha Pendlebury?' Miriam echoed faintly.

'My mother's maiden name. She's rather pleased with her famous name, I must say.' He looked rueful. 'But you're more important to me than any old books, so if you don't approve–'

291

'I had no idea,' Miriam whispered.

'But we talked about it.' Frank tilted his head to one side. 'You made it clear enough you disapproved...'

Miriam felt herself blushing. 'I thought you were a con man and a gigolo,' she admitted quietly.

'A gigolo?' His mouth dropped open. For a moment he could only stare at her, his ocean-blue eyes wide. Then he started to laugh.

'What was I supposed to think?' Miriam tried to defend herself. 'It was the only thing that made sense. You did say you offered women fantasy, an escape from their humdrum lives–'

'So you immediately assumed I must be a gigolo, trying to get my hands on your fortune?' Frank roared with laughter.

He laughed so much that Miriam felt the corners of her mouth twitching. 'It's not funny–' she protested, but in the end she couldn't help laughing too.

She was still laughing when Frank took her hands and pressed them to his lips. 'You're quite absurd, do you know that?' he said, smiling fondly into her eyes.

'At least I don't pretend to be a woman called Agatha!'

'That's true.' He sighed. 'So will you forgive me for my dark deception, my love?'

'I will,' Miriam said happily. 'On one condition.'

'What's that?'

'You must never give up being Agatha Pendlebury. Your books bring happiness to so many women. Including me,' she admitted shyly.

His brows rose. 'So you do read them?'

'I did,' she said. But she knew she would never have to read another one. Not now she had her very own romantic hero. One she didn't have to share with thousands of devoted readers.

'Oh, my darling...'

She knew he was going to kiss her as his arms closed round her. But unlike the lovely, innocent Lavinia in *Desert Heat,* she had no intention of fighting him off...

'Sister!' Daisy Baker's cry of alarm stopped them in their tracks seconds before his lips touched hers. The girl was standing at the other end of the passageway, her face full of panic. 'Sister, you must come straight away. Mrs Goodwood's gone into labour!'

Peggy

25th December 1945

'Are you sure you cooked these potatoes properly? They're like bullets.'

Peggy gazed down the length of the table to where her mother-in-law sat, stuffing her face.

'I cooked them the same as always, Mother,' she replied patiently.

'Well, they don't taste the same as always,' Nellie Atkins replied through a mouthful of food.

That hasn't stopped you eating them, Peggy thought, looking at Nellie's bulging cheeks.

She looked around the table and stifled a sigh.

293

She had so been looking forward to her first peacetime Christmas in years, but it wasn't the merry day she had been hoping for.

No one else seemed to be enjoying it either. Pearl had been in a foul mood all day. She had planted herself on the couch with a box of buttered brazils and refused to help out in the kitchen. Now she sat, her arms folded, staring at her untouched plate with a sour expression.

Peggy wished her sister would make more effort. Eric was already fed up with her. He had been nagging Peggy to convince her to move out ever since she gave up her job at the hospital a week earlier.

'We don't need her now you're back in the shop,' he had said. 'And she never pulled her weight anyway.'

'I thought you two were getting on like a house on fire?' Peggy had said.

'That ain't the point,' Eric mumbled. 'The point is this is our home, and I'm sick and tired of having her hanging around. Tell her she's got to go, Peg.'

Peggy had tried, but Pearl had refused point blank to move.

'So your old man wants me out, does he?' she had said. 'Well, we'll see about that. Let him tell me himself, if he wants me to go. And I'll have a few things to say to him, too!'

Since then, neither of them had spoken to each other. They all sat in tense silence around the Christmas table. The only sounds were Charlie scraping his chair and Nellie chewing noisily on a chicken bone.

Peggy allowed her mind to drift back to the Nightingale. The children would be having their Christmas dinner soon, and even though they were away from their parents and in hospital, she knew it would be a much jollier affair than the dinner she was having. She could just imagine all the fun and laughter as they pulled their crackers and put on their party hats and dived into the pudding for the threepenny bit.

And then, of course, there was the visit from Father Christmas to look forward to. Peggy wished she could be there to see their little faces light up when he strode on to the ward with his sack of presents for them all...

Then she thought about Bill, and how nervous he would be feeling as he put on his red coat and beard. Would he be able to go through with it? If only she could have been there to give him a little pep talk...

Her mind veered away. She couldn't allow herself to think about Bill, because then she would have to think about how much she missed him.

'This meat's very dry,' Nellie commented, breaking into her reverie.

'Sorry, Mother.' Peggy sighed, waiting for Eric to defend her. But he sat at the far end of the table opposite her, chewing placidly on his vegetables.

She turned her attention to her sister, still with her untouched plate of food in front of her.

'Aren't you going to eat that?' she asked.

'I don't fancy it. I'm a bit off my food, as a matter of fact.'

'I'll have it, if she don't want it.' Nellie reached

across for her plate and scraped it on to her own. 'Waste not, want not.'

Peggy barely noticed, she was too busy staring at her sister. 'You do look a bit peaky,' she said. 'Are you sickening for something?'

'You don't catch what I've got.'

Peggy looked into her sister's wretched, angry face and the truth dawned. 'Oh Pearl, you ain't–'

Pearl stared down at her now empty plate. 'I reckon I might be,' she muttered.

'Oh, Pearl!'

'What's that?' Nellie looked up sharply. 'What's going on?'

'Pearl reckons she might be in the family way.' Suddenly it all made sense. No wonder her sister had been in such a foul mood recently.

'Oh, she is, is she?' Nellie sounded ominous.

'Is it Ralph's?' Peggy asked.

Pearl shook her head. 'I've been seeing someone else.'

'Well, that's something, I s'pose.' At least the kid wouldn't have a jailbird for a father, Peggy thought. 'Does he know you're expecting?'

'He does now,' Pearl said.

Peggy frowned in confusion. 'I don't understand–'

Pearl looked at Eric. 'Are you going to tell her, or shall I?' she said.

Peggy turned to her husband. Eric had gone very still, all the colour draining from his face. 'Eric? What do you know about this?'

'You might well ask!' Nellie retorted. 'Bleeding hell, girl, I reckon you must be the only one who don't know what's been going on around here.'

296

She pointed her fork at Pearl. 'That hussy of a sister of yours has been carrying on with my fool of a son right under your nose.'

'Never!' It was such a ridiculous idea, Peggy laughed. Eric laughed too, a little too high and a little too loud.

'Don't be ridiculous, Mother! I don't know what you're talking about, I really don't.'

'I've got eyes and ears,' Nellie snapped back. 'I know what's going on, even if your own missus is too daft and trusting to guess. You think I ain't heard what goes on in the back room of that shop? Stocktaking, indeed! I knew what the pair of you was up to. I'm surprised it ain't halfway round Bethnal Green by now. Shameless, the pair of you.' She turned her fork on Peggy. 'Although you're as much to blame as either of them. If you'd been where you should be, looking after your husband, this would never have happened.'

Peggy took no notice of her. All her attention was focused on her sister.

'Is this true?' she whispered.

Pearl looked straight back at her, unrepentant. 'Yes, it's true.'

'Why?'

'Terrible, ain't it? And after the way you took her in and looked after her, too,' Nellie chimed in. 'It's a shocking business, it really is. Mind, it was her set her cap at my son, with her lipstick and her nylons,' she went on. 'He can't be blamed for any of this. He's only a red-blooded man, after all.'

Eric shot to his feet. 'It was all a mistake,' he blurted out. 'Mother's right, she seduced me.'

297

'Seduced you!' Pearl looked scornful. 'You weren't exactly fighting me off, as I recall. You told me you loved me. You said I was the one you wanted, that you were going to leave her for me...'

'Is this true?' Peggy looked at Eric.

'Men,' Nellie dismissed. 'They'd say anything in the heat of the moment.' She shook her head, her jowls wobbling. 'No, he's been a fool, and that's all there is to it. Now it's up to him to put things right.' She glared at Eric.

'I'm trying, Mother. Give me a chance!' Eric turned back to Peggy. 'Like I said, it was a mistake. I was lonely. Mother's right, it wouldn't have happened if you'd been here.'

'Don't you blame her!' Pearl snorted. 'You should be thanking me for showing you the kind of man you married,' she said to Peggy.

Peggy felt numb. It was as if she was floating above her body, watching the scene from on high. None of it was real, it was all too far-fetched.

And yet it *was* real.

'Why?' she whispered.

Pearl lifted her chin. 'Because I could,' she said. 'And because I was sick of being beholden to you all the time. Do you know what it's like to have to listen to you day in, day out, reminding me what a saint you are to take us in and give us a home?'

'I never—'

'And all the time, you're telling me what to do, reminding me what a mess I've made of my life, just because I've made a few mistakes and I'm not as perfect as you,' Pearl went on, ignoring her. 'God, I can't even find a boyfriend without you having to stick your oar in. Find a good man, you

298

said. Someone steady and reliable, who'll look after me. So that's what I did.' She gave her a nasty smile. 'Bet you didn't expect it would be your man, did you? So now you know what it feels like to be the odd one out, the one no one wants!'

Peggy stared at her, astonished by her vehemence. She had never realised how jealous her sister was, or how much resentment she harboured.

'Take no notice of her,' Eric said. 'She means nothing to me. You're the only woman for me, Peggy. You always have been, right from that day I found you sitting on that park bench. Do you remember that day?' His eyes pleaded with her. 'I said I'd look after you, didn't I? I promised I'd give you a home, somewhere you could feel safe at last.'

'You promised me that, too,' Pearl reminded him in a hurt voice. But Eric ignored her.

'I know I've been a fool, and I'm sorry for it. But we can get through this. We can put things right. We've got to, for the sake of our family. For Alan and Amy.'

'And what about my baby?' Pearl demanded.

'We've only got your word for it that it's Eric's,' Nellie muttered.

Pearl turned on her. 'What are you saying?'

'I'm saying we all know you'd drop your drawers for anyone. Blimey, if you'd go with your own sister's husband, there's no telling what else you'd do! There might not even be a baby,' Nellie went on. 'I wouldn't put it past you to make the whole thing up, just to cause trouble.'

'There's a baby, all right. And it's his.' Pearl

299

glared across the table at Eric.

Peggy listened to them all bickering among themselves. Not once had any of them bothered to ask her what she thought, or how she felt or what she wanted. It was all about them.

But then, it always had been, she thought. Everything in her life had been done for someone else. She had given up her school to look after Pearl, married Eric to provide a home for her sister. She had worked in the shop, brought up her children, made sacrifices and done her best for all of them.

And look how they had all repaid her.

Eric was speaking again, in that lofty voice he always used when he was making one of his pronouncements. 'God knows, I'm not a man to walk away from my mistakes. If she is expecting—'

'If,' Nellie put in.

'Then we'll sort something out. Peggy will look after it. She loves kids, don't you, Peg?'

Pearl looked offended. 'I ain't having her look after my baby!'

'Why not? She looks after your other one more than you do.' Nellie glared at Charlie, who ploughed calmly through his Christmas dinner, oblivious to the storm raging around him.

'You take that back! I'm a good mum.'

'Good mum, my backside!'

'Peggy will help,' Eric's voice cut across them. 'She's always wanted another baby, ever since our John passed away...'

The mention of John's name galvanised Peggy, bringing her sharply to her senses. She brought her spoon down with a clatter, shocking them all.

300

'Don't you ever mention my boy's name,' she hissed.

Four faces turned to look up at her in surprise. It was as if they had forgotten she was even there. She stood up, untying her apron strings with shaking hands.

'Peggy?' Eric's voice wavered uncertainly. 'Peg, where are you going?'

'Out.'

'Yes, but where?'

'Never you mind.'

'Who's going to serve the Christmas pudding?' Nellie wanted to know.

'What time will you be back?' She could hear the panic in Eric's voice as he followed her into the hall and watched her put on her coat. 'You will be back, won't you? Peggy?'

'That I can't say.'

'I don't want you to go.' His voice was plaintive now, wheedling.

She looked at him, thinking how weak he looked. 'I reckon I'm past caring what you want any more, Eric Atkins.'

She went towards the front door but Eric barred her way. Peggy glared at him. 'Let me pass.'

'Not until you tell me where you're going.'

She sighed and shoved him out of the way.

'You're not to go. I'm your husband and I'm telling you I forbid it–'

Those words were the last she heard as she slammed the door.

The hospital was deserted. Everyone was in the dining hall, enjoying the Christmas show. Peggy thought about sneaking in to watch, but as she

301

approached the main hospital block she realised she couldn't face it, and headed instead for the courtyard.

The bench was covered in snow. Peggy brushed a space for herself and sat down, gathering her coat around her. If she hadn't left in such haste she would have remembered her gloves and scarf.

Sister Parry had once told her about when she worked in Casualty, and some of the horrific accidents she had treated. She had seen men with limbs hanging off, who laughed and joked with the nurses and hardly seemed aware of what had happened to them because their brains hadn't yet assimilated it.

That was how she felt. She knew she should be devastated by Eric and Pearl's betrayal, but her brain had yet to take it all in.

She couldn't even feel shock at what they had done. They had gone on and done as they pleased and never taken her feelings into account because they had never had to. It probably hadn't occurred to them that she even had feelings. Pearl, Eric, his mother ... they all just took what they wanted from her.

'Peggy?'

She looked up to see a figure approaching across the snowy courtyard. A tall, burly man dressed in a red coat with a long white beard.

Her heart leapt at the sight of him. 'Bill!'

'What are you doing here?'

She smiled sadly. 'I had nowhere else to go.'

'Do you mind if I sit with you, or would you rather be on your own?'

She gazed up into his kindly eyes, twinkling

above his beard. 'I wouldn't mind some company,' she said.

He brushed the snow from the seat and sat down beside her, carefully arranging his red coat around him.

'You've been up to the ward, then?' she said. 'How did it go?'

'It went well. I was glad I did it, in the end.'

'I bet the kids loved it.'

'They did.' He smiled at the memory.

They lapsed into silence for a moment, both of them lost in their thoughts. Then Peggy said, 'I thought you'd be in the show?'

He shook his head. 'The show's finished, on account of one of the patients going into labour.'

Peggy turned to him. 'You what?'

'A woman had a baby backstage.'

'Never!'

'It's true. Right in the middle of Mr Hopkins' monologue, too. He wasn't best pleased, I can tell you.'

Peggy laughed in spite of herself. 'Well I never. Sounds like that was the highlight of the show. You ain't going to top that with your magic act, Bill!'

'I know. Pulling a rabbit out of a top hat don't compare, does it?' He looked rueful.

They lapsed into silence again. 'Do you want to talk about it?' Bill asked.

Peggy shook her head. 'Not really.'

He nudged her. 'Well, whatever it is you're going through, Peggy, I know you'll get through it. You're a strong girl.'

'I don't feel like it at the moment.'

'I know, but you will. Things will sort them-

303

selves out for the best, you'll see.'

'I hope so, Bill.'

He got to his feet. 'I dunno about you, but I wouldn't mind going back indoors. It's a bit nippy out here. What do you say we see if they've put the show back on? Or you never know, that woman might be giving birth to twins.'

She smiled wearily. 'That might be nice. I could do with a laugh.'

'I almost forgot,' he said. 'I've got a present for you.'

He reached into his coat and produced a bunch of paper flowers with a flourish.

Peggy beamed. 'Thank you very much.'

'You're welcome. Shall we go?' He offered her his hand and after a moment's hesitation she took it.

Kathleen

25th December 1945

The Christmas show was in full swing, but Kathleen hardly paid any attention to the performers on the stage. She was too busy staring at the clock on the far wall of the dining hall.

Nearly seven o'clock. James must have gone by now, she decided. He and Simone would be on a cruise ship, heading across the Atlantic, bound for their new life.

She wondered if he had waited for her. Her

heart ached at the thought of him lingering on the dockside while everyone embarked, scanning around him, looking for her.

Or perhaps he had forgotten her already? Perhaps he had become so caught up in the excitement of preparing for his new life that he couldn't wait to board the ship, hoping all the while that she wouldn't embarrass him by turning up...

Of course he waited for you. He's been waiting for four years.

Miss Hanley's voice intruded on her thoughts, so clearly that Kathleen looked at the seat beside her, thinking the Assistant Matron might somehow be there. Major McLaren smiled quizzically back at her.

'Everything all right, Matron?' he asked.

'Fine, thank you.'

'Good show, isn't it?'

'Yes, it is.'

'Miss Davis has done an excellent job.' Pride shone in his face.

'Yes, she has.'

'Pity about that woman running off the stage just now, but still, that's hardly Miss Davis's fault, is it?'

'No indeed.' Kathleen turned her attention back to the stage.

I couldn't do it. She silently addressed the voice in her head. *I could never be the one to break up his marriage...*

His marriage was over long before you came along. You were just too afraid to take the risk and go with him.

Perhaps she was right, Kathleen thought. Either

305

way, it was too late for her and James Cooper. But there was still time for her to make a new start of her own.

Her resignation letter had been written, and was in her bag. As soon as the show was over, she was going to post it.

There was nothing for her at the Nightingale any more. Once the hospital had been like a home to her, a place where she truly felt she belonged. The staff had been her extended family. But the war had ended all that. Now when she looked around, all she could see were strangers, fractured relationships. It was no longer a place of warmth and friendship.

It was no longer a place she wanted to be, not any more.

Further along the front row, a woman let out a loud moan. Beside her, the Major leapt to his feet.

'Good lord, what was that?'

Kathleen turned round, just in time to see Mrs Goodwood fall to her hands and knees. She was making a strange grunting sound, like a wounded animal.

The rest of the audience started to gather round her, but she seemed oblivious to them as she wailed and moaned in pain.

Kathleen edged her way through the throng. 'Everybody stand back, please, give her some air.' She dropped to her knees beside Mrs Goodwood. 'What is it, my dear? What's wrong? Is the baby coming?'

'Of course the baby isn't coming!' Mrs Goodwood snapped through clenched teeth. 'It's not due for another month.'

306

'Well, something is happening, that's for sure.' Kathleen looked around. 'Where is Miss Trott?'

'I don't know, Matron,' Nurse Baker said, her astonished gaze still fixed on Mrs Goodwood. 'No one's seen her since she ran off the stage.'

'Find her, please. And ask one of the porters to fetch a wheelchair. Mrs Goodwood needs to get back to the labour ward.'

'I'm not in labour – aah!' Mrs Goodwood let out another low moan of agony.

'I think this is more than a bad case of indigestion, my dear.' Kathleen got to her feet, brushing off her uniform.

Miss Davis moved in, taking charge. 'Can the sisters please get everyone back to their wards?' she called out.

'But we haven't seen the end of the show,' Mr Donnegan complained. 'I want to watch the finale.'

'I reckon you're watching it, Percy mate!' his friend Mr Church chimed in. 'Oops, looks like the fun's over,' he nodded to Miss Davis who advanced on them. Her arms flung wide, like a sheep herder.

The porter arrived with the wheelchair at the same time as Miss Trott appeared. She looked very flushed, Kathleen noticed, as she pushed her way through the crowd.

'What's going on?' she demanded, unfastening her starched cuffs.

'I think Mrs Goodwood might be in labour,' Kathleen told her.

'But it's not due for–'

'Yes, we know!' Kathleen cut her off impatiently.

307

'We were about to take her to the labour ward.'

'I'll examine her first.' Miriam nodded to the porter. 'Get her on to the stage, please. We'll pull the curtains around her, give her some privacy.'

It took two porters to haul Mrs Goodwood's bulky body up on to the platform. Kathleen slipped inside the curtains and watched as Miss Trott examined her.

'Well?' she said.

Miss Trott looked up at her, white-faced. 'The baby is coming,' she confirmed.

Kathleen sighed. 'I think we all knew that, Miss Trott.'

'No, Matron, you don't understand. The baby is coming now, this minute!' Miss Trott paused for a moment as she continued her examination. 'I can see the head.'

Kathleen darted back through the curtains and instantly began directing the nurses to bring towels, sheets, hot water and equipment.

'Can I help, Matron?' Dr Armstrong stepped forward.

Kathleen looked him up and down. He was hardly dressed for a medical procedure, in his striped blazer, bow tie and false handlebar moustache that reached past his ears.

'Thank you, Dr Armstrong, I'll let you know if you're needed,' she said kindly.

As it happened, Mrs Goodwood didn't need any assistance. Miss Trott didn't so much deliver the baby as catch him in mid-air as he slipped into the world five minutes later.

Kathleen emerged from the curtains, dazed, as Miss Davis and Violet Tanner returned from shepherding the patients back to their beds.

'Has she gone to the delivery room?' Violet asked.

'It was too late for that,' Kathleen said.

Miss Davis stared at her. 'You mean–'

A lusty wail went up from behind the curtains. 'A boy,' Kathleen said. 'We haven't had a chance to weigh him yet, but he looks a healthy size.'

Miss Davis looked triumphant. 'What did I tell you? I knew she was big for her dates.'

'You certainly did, Miss Davis.'

'It'll be a nice Christmas surprise for Mr Goodwood, anyway,' Violet said.

'Oh yes, he's in for a surprise, all right.' Kathleen couldn't help smiling.

Miss Davis frowned quizzically. 'What is it, Matron?'

'I think you'd better go and see the baby.'

Miss Davis disappeared behind the curtain and returned a moment later. 'I see what you mean,' she said quietly.

'What's going on?' Violet looked from one to the other.

'The baby clearly has a ... different parentage from the one you might expect,' Kathleen chose her words carefully.

'He's coloured,' Miss Davis put it more bluntly.

'Ah.' Violet nodded knowingly. 'I see.'

'My guess is that his father might have been one of those American GIs we had around here during the war,' Kathleen said.

'It seems Mrs Goodwood may have offered him more than a cup of tea and a piece of cake from her WVS trolley,' Miss Davis said. 'That's taking hospitality a bit too far, I think.'

Kathleen and Violet looked at each other and roared with laughter. Miss Davis looked from one to the other.

'Is something amusing?' She looked genuinely perplexed.

'Oh, Miss Davis! You made a joke.'

'Did I?' Miss Davis considered it for a moment. 'Yes, I suppose I did, didn't I?' She looked pleased with herself, like a child who had learned to amuse the adults with a party trick.

'But I don't think even Mr Goodwood will be in as big a state of shock as Miss Trott,' Kathleen said. 'The poor woman looked utterly devastated.'

'I'm not surprised,' Violet said. 'Mrs Goodwood was her idea of the perfect woman.'

'And this American GI's, apparently,' Miss Davis murmured. Kathleen and Violet laughed again, and this time Miss Davis joined in with them.

They were still laughing when Major McLaren appeared. 'Is the coast clear?' he asked. 'I thought I'd best make myself scarce once the lady went into labour.'

'It was probably for the best, Major,' Kathleen said.

'I just wanted to say how much I enjoyed the show.' He addressed himself to Miss Davis. He seemed quite dazzled by her, Kathleen noticed.

'It wasn't quite what I had intended,' she said, lowering her gaze.

'Nevertheless, it was splendid.'

'It was a joint effort. Wasn't it, Miss Tanner?' Miss Davis smiled at Violet.

'Ah, so this is Miss Tanner?' Major McLaren turned to Violet. 'I was coming to look for you.'

'Me?' Violet looked puzzled.

'I have someone outside waiting to see you.'

'Who?'

'Your mother.'

Violet staggered back a step, as if she'd been dealt a blow. 'My mother? But I don't understand–'

'I asked the Major if he could help to find her,' Miss Davis said.

'I still have a few contacts, so it didn't take long.' Major McLaren grinned. 'It was just good luck that she had moved out to Aldershot, and had started working for a military family. But I must say she was rather wary about coming here tonight. She seemed fairly convinced you wouldn't want to see her.'

'Where is she?' Violet whispered.

'She's waiting outside. Better go quickly, before she changes her mind. I had the devil's own job to get her here.'

Violet looked at Kathleen, who nodded her assent. 'Go,' she said.

As Violet hurried off, Miss Davis turned to Major McLaren. 'Thank you,' she said quietly.

'You're most welcome. I told you, didn't I? Any time you needed anything, all you have to do is call.'

Miss Davis looked away, embarrassed. Kathleen looked from one to the other, willing one of them to say something.

Major McLaren straightened his shoulders, his hands locked behind his back. 'Anyway, I sup-

311

pose I'd best be going,' he said.

'Yes,' Miss Davis said. Neither of them moved.

Then, finally, Major McLaren seemed to galvanise himself. 'Merry Christmas, Miss Davis. Matron.'

'Merry Christmas, Major.'

Kathleen noticed how Miss Davis's gaze followed him longingly from the dining hall, as if she couldn't quite bear to let him go.

'You know he wants you to go after him, don't you?' she said.

Miss Davis frowned, uncomprehending. 'I beg your pardon, Matron?'

'He's in love with you, Miss Davis. And if I'm not mistaken, you feel the same about him.'

'I – well, that is, I couldn't – I don't–' Miss Davis stared down at her shoes, red with mortification.

Kathleen sighed impatiently. 'What are you waiting for, girl? Go after him before it's too late!'

'Yes, Matron!' Miss Davis broke into a smile, and suddenly Kathleen saw a glimpse of a happy, carefree young woman under the severe mask she wore.

She looks happy, Miss Hanley observed.

'Yes, she does. I hope we'll see her smiling more in the future.'

She looked around the dining hall. Miss Davis was right, the show hadn't been exactly what she had intended. But it had still achieved what Kathleen had hoped. It had brought everyone together, and created some memories they would all laugh about in the years to come.

You've done a good job, Matron, Miss Hanley said.

312

It's a start, Kathleen thought. But there was still so much to do, so much to put right...

'Matron?' Kathleen turned round. Sister Hyde stood in the doorway, smiling as usual.

'The other sisters and I were thinking we might partake of a small sherry, just by way of a Christmas celebration. We wondered if you'd care to join us?'

Kathleen smiled. 'I'd love to, Sister. But I have something I need to do first.'

Sister Hyde nodded. 'We'll see you in the common room of the sisters' home later.'

'Thank you.'

Outside, the full moon illuminated the snow, turning it an eerie blue. With the jagged rooftops and holes in the brickwork covered by a perfect snowy blanket, one could almost imagine the Nightingale as it once was, before all the bombs.

Kathleen's footsteps made a muffled crunch as she trudged through the snow. As she passed through the courtyard, she noticed several figures in the shadows. Miss Davis and the Major, Peggy Atkins and one of the porters, Violet and her mother, and Miss Trott– Kathleen stopped short. Was that really Miss Trott with a man? Things were strange indeed, she decided.

She paused by the post box, the letter in her hand. After a moment's hesitation, she tore it up and stuffed the pieces back in her pocket. Then she turned to head back to the warmth of the hospital, where welcoming lights blazed in the windows.

She had almost reached the sisters' home when a figure separated itself from the shadows and

313

stepped into her path.

'Hello, Kath.' James Cooper's voice came from the darkness, deep and warm as a caress.

Kathleen stopped dead.

'James?' she whispered. She put out a hand to touch him, feeling the rough wool of his heavy overcoat. But even then she couldn't quite believe it wasn't her imagination playing cruel tricks on her. 'What are you doing here? Why aren't you on board the ship?'

'Do you really think I could go without you, knowing how I feel about you?'

'But Simone—'

'Is currently enjoying herself to no end, if I know her.' There was a cynical edge to his voice. 'She'll be settling in to her first-class cabin, ordering the staff about and enjoying a glass of champagne.'

'She went without you?'

'Of course. Between you and me, I think it was the idea of going to America that was the biggest attraction for her. I was only ever a means to an end. Once she realised I was still prepared to pay for her passage and keep her in style, she was as happy as a lamb.'

Kathleen winced. 'Surely she must have been upset when you told her you weren't going with her?'

James shook his head. 'To be honest, I think she was relieved. She knows as well as I do that our marriage should have ended a long time ago. The only thing that kept us together was money and her pride.'

'I'm sorry.'

314

'Are you?' He stepped closer, so close she could feel the warmth of his breath fanning her face. 'Would you rather I'd gone with her?'

She wanted to do the right thing, to say something wise and sensible. But the pounding of her heart against her ribs was telling her otherwise.

'No,' she said.

'That's a relief.' He took her hands in his. His fingers were warm and reassuring, wrapped around hers. 'Oh God, Kath, I've missed you so much. I waited for you to come, but deep down I knew you wouldn't. So I knew I had to come back for you.'

'I'm sorry,' she murmured. 'I wanted to come, I really did. But I didn't want to ruin your new start—'

'You still don't understand, do you? The only new start I want is with you.'

She looked up at him. The dim light from the window of the sisters' home illuminated the snowflakes sparkling in his dark hair.

'So what happens now?' she said.

'Well...' He pretended to think about it. 'I could sweep you into my arms and then we could walk off into the sunset and live happily ever after?'

'That sounds wonderful.'

'So why do I hear the word "but" at the end of the sentence?'

Kathleen smiled. How well he knew her! 'I still have work to do here.'

His brows lowered in a frown. 'I seem to remember you said that the last time you left me?'

'I know,' she sighed.

'So did I do the wrong thing, coming back?'

315

'No!' Her hands gripped his, not wanting to let him go in case he disappeared forever. 'No, not at all. I love you, and I want us to be together, truly I do. But I have a duty to this hospital to try to put it back together, restore it to the way it was.' She looked up at him tentatively. 'You do understand, don't you?'

His mouth twisted. 'I wish I didn't, but – yes, of course I understand. It's one of the things I love about you.' He shook his head. 'Oh well, I suppose if you won't run away with me, I'll just have to stay here with you.'

'Really? You mean you'll come back to the Nightingale?'

'I don't have much choice, do I?' He did his best to sound long-suffering, but once again Kathleen could hear the smile in his voice. 'I walked away from you once, Kathleen Fox. I have no intention of making the same mistake twice.'

They looked at each other for a long time. 'I suppose this means we won't be walking into the sunset?' Kathleen said.

'No, but I could still sweep you into my arms, couldn't I?'

She grinned. 'I'd like that very much.'

I suppose you'll have something to say about my decision? She thought as James gathered her to him for a kiss. But Miss Hanley's voice was silent, and Kathleen had a feeling she would not be hearing it again. Her future was settled, she no longer needed the Assistant Matron's guiding hand, and now Veronica Hanley could finally rest in peace.

316

The publishers hope that this book has given you enjoyable reading. Large Print Books are especially designed to be as easy to see and hold as possible. If you wish a complete list of our books please ask at your local library or write directly to:

Magna Large Print Books
Magna House, Long Preston,
Skipton, North Yorkshire.
BD23 4ND

This Large Print Book for the partially sighted, who cannot read normal print, is published under the auspices of

THE ULVERSCROFT FOUNDATION

THE ULVERSCROFT FOUNDATION

... we hope that you have enjoyed this Large Print Book. Please think for a moment about those people who have worse eyesight problems than you ... and are unable to even read or enjoy Large Print, without great difficulty.

You can help them by sending a donation, large or small to:

The Ulverscroft Foundation, 1, The Green, Bradgate Road, Anstey, Leicestershire, LE7 7FU, England.
or request a copy of our brochure for more details.

The Foundation will use all your help to assist those people who are handicapped by various sight problems and need special attention.

Thank you very much for your help.